Hair of the Dog

Ian Walker

2nd DI Diane Rothwell novel

SPEAK EUNIQUE

ISBN 9798363486838

'Hair of the dog', short for 'hair of the dog that bit you', is a colloquial expression in the English language predominantly used to refer to alcohol that is consumed with the aim of lessening the effects of a hangover. – Wikipedia

Disclaimer

Chapter 1
Monday lunchtime, April 11th, 1971

So smile for a while and let's be jolly
Love shouldn't be so melancholy
Come along and share the good times while we can
I beg your pardon, I never promised you a rose garden
Along with the sunshine, there's gotta be a little rain sometime …

The two teenage girls on the back row of the bus were having a great time singing along to their radio.

"Can you turn that music off and quit your caterwauling?" the driver shouted at them. "Nobody appreciates your racket."

"Well said, driver," declared an old woman, who was sitting just in front of the girls.

"Bloody oxygen thief," muttered one of the two girls.

Penny Foster and Alice Barlow were in their final year at St Helena's High School in Chesterfield. They were both pretty girls, although Penny, with her long raven-black hair and turned up nose was the most striking of the two. In a little over a month's time, the girls would be taking their A levels, after which the two of them were hoping to go to university. Penny had been offered a place at the University of East Anglia studying Economics with Economic History, whereas Alice was due to study French at the University of York. That was providing they got the required grades, of course.

Both of them had been revising hard over the Easter holiday and, as a result, they were really looking forward to their five-day walking break. Not that they were going very far. They'd decided to go youth hostelling in the Peak District, which was why they were on an ancient Hulley's bus travelling between Chesterfield and Buxton on Easter Monday.

Mind you, the girls weren't intending to travel as far as the bus's final destination. Instead, they were heading for the small youth hostel in the isolated village of Bleckley.

Bleckley wasn't on any bus route, so they got off in Eyam, the nearest stop to their destination. From there it would take them about an hour and a half's walk before they finally reached their accommodation.

Penny stuck her tongue out at the driver as they left, which told him precisely what she thought of his instruction to switch her radio off. Both she and Alice struggled through the door of the bus, their progress hampered by the antiquated A-framed rucksacks on their backs. Neither of the girls possessed their own rucksacks. They'd borrowed a couple from school, ones that were normally used for the Duke of Edinburgh's award scheme.

The bus had dropped them by the Miners Arms and the girls walked through the village, past the church and Eyam Hall before turning right, onto the road towards Grindleford. Their destination was only two miles away, but it involved a climb of over 500 feet. Eyam itself was 800 feet above sea level. The youth hostel in Bleckley, where they were booked in for the next three nights, was located on a ridge high above the village. At 1,300 feet above sea level, it was the highest youth hostel in Derbyshire and one of the highest in the country.

The two girls intended to go on several walks in the area before moving on to the youth hostel in Elton, where they planned to spend their final two nights.

The climb got even steeper as they left the main road and followed the footpath that took them up and over Bleckley Edge.

"Turn the radio on again," said Alice as they took a break from the climb and sat down on a fallen tree trunk. It was half past twelve and time for a sandwich and a can of coke.

Penny obligingly searched her backpack until she found the transistor and pressed the on button. Radio One was playing 'Love grows where my Rosemary goes' by Edison Lighthouse. It was one of their favourites.

"Sharon Moore shagged one of the members of Edison Lighthouse at the Radio One roadshow in Tenby last year," commented Penny after turning the volume down so that Alice could hear her.

"I bet she didn't," replied Alice. "Sharon Moore is a liar. She wouldn't know the truth if it walked up to her and slapped her in the face."

"Well, she told me that he screwed her in the back of their transit van. She described the sex in great detail."

"Great detail which she probably got from the Cathy and Claire page in *Jackie*," added Alice.

Jackie magazine was essential reading for all the teenage girls at their school. It gave them tips on how to deal with the important things in life like fashion and make-up. More importantly, it answered their questions about boys through its Cathy and Claire problem page.

"No, I mean really great detail," Penny replied, before tapping her nose, "Describing things that they'd never be able to publish in *Jackie*."

"Okay, which member of the group did she do it with then?"

"She said she didn't ask him his name."

"Rubbish, she's making the whole thing up," scorned Alice, "and even if she did do it, I bet it was with one of the roadies rather than with one of the group."

Penny nodded in agreement.

"Which of the girls in our class do you think have done it?" asked Alice.

"I bet more than half have," Penny replied.

"Okay, let's go through the register," suggested Alice.

Penny and Alice were sixth formers, so they no longer had the class register read out every day. Despite this, they could both remember how it went and reciting it was a surefire way to guarantee they didn't miss anybody out.

"Sheila Armitage," said Alice.

"Definitely," replied Penny. "She's been going out with her boyfriend for over a year now. They must have done it, otherwise he wouldn't still be with her."

"She told me she only gives him blowjobs," added Alice.

"Bloody hell, I wouldn't fancy having a cock in my mouth. I wonder what … you know, what it tastes like?"

"What, spunk?" replied Alice. "She says it's like rinsing your mouth in sea water."

"Aargh, that's disgusting. Anyway, blowjobs count as having done it. So that's one-nil."

"You're next on the register and I reckon you've definitely done it," said Penny.

"No, I haven't," Alice replied.

"What about that boy you met on holiday last summer?"

"We only snogged."

"Okay, what about Chris Wallace? You went out with him for three months at the end of last year."

"He was boring. Anyway, he finished with me because I wouldn't let him do it."

Alice could feel her face turning red, which prompted Penny to stop teasing her.

"That's alright, Alice, don't worry, I believe you. I know you're like a modern-day Elizabeth Bennett waiting for Mr Darcy to come along and pop your cherry. I was only winding you up."

"Sandra Bates," Alice continued.

"She's got acne and I've never seen her with a boy," said Penny. "I can't see her having done it. So that's 2-1 to the virgins."

"Dorothy Bland."

"She's too fat. She'll never get a boyfriend."

"I heard she's started going out with Larry Gunn."

"You are joking, not lardy boy Larry? He's grosser than she is. Can you imagine them at it? It would be like Big Daddy jumping on top of Giant Haystacks on World of Sport."

"Stop it, Pen, you're so wicked," said Alice before bursting out laughing.

"Anyway," she said between giggles, "I don't think they've had it off. Do you?"

Penny shook her head before saying, "That's 3-1 to the virgins then."

"Angela Brown," Alice continued.

"Definitely," said the two girls in unison.

"She's had more cock than all the hens in Thornhill's poultry factory."

That last statement caused even more laughter from the two of them. They were both in stitches and, having finished their sandwiches, decided it was time to set off again. Their discussion continued whilst they were walking.

"Pamela Camplin," said Alice.

"No chance," replied Penny. "And if you asked me the same question in twenty years' time, the answer would still be the same. She thinks a shag is a type of carpet and sex is a number between five and seven."

That caused even more hysterics from the girls.

"Elaine Copson," Alice continued.

"Not pretty enough and too tall," stated Penny with confidence. "And with those goofy teeth she'd need to put a bag over her head if she ever wants to have a shag."

"Well, a packet of Durex fell out of her bag when she was getting changed for netball the other week."

"You are kidding me?"

"Straight up, I saw it with my own eyes."

"That doesn't mean a thing. She has a Saturday job in Boots and probably just bought them to impress everybody. Believe me, she is definitely a virgin."

"Okay, well that's 5-2 to the virgins."

"Julia Dyke."

"Dyke by name Dyke by nature," commented Penny. "You know she's seeing Dawn Watson, don't you? Karen Rossington saw them snogging behind the caretaker's shed."

"Never. You're having me on."

"No, I'm not, and it brings a whole new meaning to the phrase 'up at the crack of dawn'."

"That's terrible, Pen," said Alice who was starting to laugh again.

"I don't think I could ever be a lesbian," said Penny. "I wouldn't know who does what or where or with what."

"Does lesbian sex count?" asked Alice.

"Absolutely," replied Penny. "But that's still 5-3 to the virgins."

"Anyway, you're next," commented Alice, "and I know you've definitely done it."

"I have not," replied Penny. "What makes you say that?"

"Because you've had more boyfriends than any other girl in our class."

"That doesn't mean I shagged them though," replied Penny. "I'll have you know that I'm still *virgo intacta*, but don't tell anybody. It would ruin my reputation."

"What about Jonathan Stoppard then?" asked Alice.

"Ah, Juicy Jonathan with his deep blue eyes. I can't say I wasn't tempted, but the closest we ever got, was a bit of fumbling on the front seat of his mum's Triumph Herald. It's difficult to get too passionate when you've got a gear stick rammed up your arse. Anyway, he got the hump and finished with me when I refused to let him put his hand down my knickers."

By this time, they had arrived at the road that led to Bleckley, the worst of the climb now behind them.

"Christine Garvey," Alice continued.

"She is a definite yes," replied Penny. "Did you see all those love bites on her neck the other day?"

The girls continued their discussion and were disappointed to come to the final conclusion that the virgins were still in the majority amongst their classmates. In fact, the final score was 19-13.

It was just after two o'clock when they finally arrived in Bleckley. Strictly speaking Bleckley wasn't a village. It didn't have a church or a post office, which made it a hamlet. It also contained only a handful of dwellings, one of which was the youth hostel, and another was the Three Tuns, the village pub.

"Thank God for that," said Penny. "I was worried you really had brought me to the arse end of nowhere. But thankfully there's a pub. So no guessing where we're going tonight."

"Well, I will be," said Alice. "I'm eighteen, don't forget, but you'll have to wait for another two months before you can get served."

Alice had turned eighteen back in November and had celebrated it with a party in the upstairs room at the Terminus Hotel. Penny, however, was one of the youngest girls in the upper sixth and her birthday wasn't until June, a fact that Alice loved to tease her friend about.

"You may be older than me, Alice Barlow, but you look about twelve whereas I look like a sophisticated 21-year-old."

"Yes, but I've brought my passport with me, which proves I'm eighteen," Alice replied.

"And I will blag my way into getting them to serve me," Penny stated with confidence.

The youth hostel was only a couple of minutes' walk from the pub. It was small by YHA standards and relatively new. But despite its modernity, it still had a somewhat Spartan interior. There were two dormitories. One of them was for men and slept eight and the other was for women and slept six, all in bunk beds. There was also a communal kitchen, a dining room and a TV lounge containing a few sofas.

As they entered the building, Mervyn Baston, the warden, greeted them. He was the type of man who, when talking to young women, never made eye contact with them. He was far too busy looking at their breasts.

"Hi, I'm Alice Barlow. We're booked in for three nights."

"Please, will you sign the book, ladies?" he replied. "I need your full names, home addresses and telephone numbers."

"I bet you do," muttered Penny whilst smiling at him.

The girls did as he requested and entered their contact details into the youth hostel's guest book.

"Right, I'll show you to your dorm," he announced as soon as they had finished.

Without further ado, he took the girls down the corridor and showed them where they were sleeping.

After he'd gone, Penny turned to Alice and said, "He's weird."

"What makes you say that?" Alice replied.

"Well, for a start, he's got to be at least forty, yet he dresses like a hippy and has his hair in a ponytail. Did you see how he looked at us? It was as if he was transfixed by our tits. Not only that, but he lives all by himself in a youth hostel in the middle of nowhere. Now that's what I call weird."

"How do you know he lives by himself?"

"Because no self-respecting woman would want to live here with him. You see if I'm not right."

"Just ignore him," said Alice. "Perhaps there'll be a real hunk in the other dorm to take your mind off him. Anyway, I've been sweating like a pig on the climb up here. So I'm going to take a shower."

The dormitory had a small bathroom, which Alice immediately took advantage of. Meanwhile, Penny lay on her bed listening to the radio and looking at the Ordnance Survey map, planning the route for the next day.

A few minutes later, Alice came back with her hair wrapped in a towel. She was using a second towel to dry herself.

"It's quite nice here," said Alice. "I thought there wouldn't be any hot water, but there's plenty. Are you also going to have a shower, Pen?"

Penny was just about to answer when the door opened.

"Girls, I'm afraid you aren't allowed to use a radio in the dormitory," Mervyn announced.

Alice tried to cover as much of her naked body as possible. But unfortunately for her, she wasn't quick enough. Mervyn had caught sight of one of her bare breasts before she was able to cover it with the towel. Alice was absolutely horrified.

"Sorry," said Mervyn without taking his eyes off Alice's chest. "I didn't realise that you weren't fully dressed."

He slowly turned and closed the door behind him.

"See, I told you he was weird," said Penny, "and a pervert. I bet he was looking through the keyhole just waiting for you to come out of the shower. I wouldn't be surprised if it was the highlight of his year. Mind you, it's a pity it was your left jug he copped an eyeful of. I think that out of the two of them, your right one's the best."

"It's not funny," said Alice. "I've a good mind to report him to the YHA authorities."

Despite what had just happened to her friend, Penny also decided to take a shower. However, she made sure she got dressed before coming out of the bathroom.

When she re-entered the dormitory, she discovered that Alice had been joined by another couple of girls. They were slightly older than them and were from Germany. Mind you, they spoke good English, far better than many people from Derbyshire, in fact.

The four of them got talking. The German girls were on an eight-week holiday, touring the national parks of northern England.

They had started off by spending three nights at the youth hostel in Castleton before moving on to Bleckley. Their plan was to stay two nights in Bleckley, and then go to the hostel in Hartington.

"We're going to the pub later," said Penny. "Would you like to come with us?"

"Thank you, but we've just finished a long walk carrying heavy rucksacks," one of the girls replied in perfect English. "I think we'll get an early night if that's okay."

Penny and Alice were slightly disappointed by the German girls' reply. Deep down, however, they were relieved that there were now four of them in the dormitory. It meant that Merv the Perv, as they had christened him, was less likely to try it on with them. Also, the German girls were quite meaty and looked as if they could take care of themselves. In fact, it wasn't long before Penny started referring to them as Valkyrie and Brunhilda, even though they'd told them their names were Claudia and Hanna.

Residents of the youth hostel have to complete a daily chore and Penny and Alice's task for the day was to help prepare the evening meal. Neither of them was looking forward to it, as it brought them back into contact with Merv the Perv again. Still, he obviously realised he'd upset them earlier and for the most part, he stayed out of their way.

The meal was a disappointment. Not because the food was bad as the homemade chilli con carne was actually quite good. No, it was the moment when the girls were introduced to the people who were staying in the men's dormitory that proved to be the big let-down. Six of them were fifteen-year-old boys spending their first holiday together without their parents. The other two were men in their fifties who, like Penny and Alice, were on a walking holiday.

"I thought this was a youth hostel," said Penny, "for young people, not geriatrics. They shouldn't be here. They should be in an old folk's home."

"Keep your voice down, Pen," said Alice. "They'll hear you."

"I doubt it," replied Penny. "They probably haven't switched on their hearing aids."

"Anyway," she added, whilst looking at her watch. "It's now cider o'clock and time for the pub."

"Thank God for that," said Alice. "At least we won't have to put up with Merv the Perv undressing us with his eyes for the rest of the evening."

"Undressing me, perhaps," replied Penny. "I seem to remember that he didn't need to do very much to undress you this afternoon."

"That's not funny, Pen," said Alice. "I'm still furious about it. Why is it that blokes are so obsessed with ogling women's chests all the time?"

"It's because deep down they're all like little babies wanting to be breast-fed," Penny replied.

Alice's comment had given Penny an idea.

"Excuse me for a minute, Alice," she said. "There's something I need to do back in the dormitory. It won't take long."

After a few minutes she returned. Alice was horrified.

"Why have you taken your bra off?" she asked.

"It's simple," Penny replied. "Nobody will ask how old I am if I haven't got a bra on under my T-shirt. That's because they won't be looking at my face."

"Bloody hell, Penny," said Alice. "It's bad enough having Merv the Perv ogling us, without you encouraging all the red-blooded males in the village to do the same."

Chapter 2
Wednesday evening, December 13th, 1978

"When the angels had left them and gone into heaven, the shepherds said to one another, 'Let's go to Bethlehem and see this thing that has happened, which the Lord has told us about.' So, they hurried off and found Mary and Joseph, and the baby, who was lying in the manger. When they had seen him, they spread the word concerning what they had been told about this child, and all who heard it were amazed at what the shepherds said to them."

DI Diane Rothwell finished her reading from the Bible and returned to her seat near the bar. For this particular service wasn't taking place in a church. It was actually being held in the lounge of the White Hart in Walton, one of Diane's favourite pubs.

The vicar stood up for the final prayer:

May God himself, the God of peace,
make you perfect and holy;
and keep you all safe and blameless, in spirit, soul and body,
for the coming of our Lord Jesus Christ.

"We will now finish by singing carol number eighteen on your hymn sheet, *Hark! The Herald Angels Sing.*"

Once the service had finished, Frank McKinley approached Diane and thanked her for agreeing to do one of the readings.

Frank was the tenant of the White Hart and the chairman of Chesterfield Licensed Victuallers Association. Diane was a detective inspector with Derbyshire Constabulary based in Chesterfield. She and Frank were jointly in charge of the Chesterfield police/licensee forum, a body that had been set up to tackle crime involving the licensed trade.

It had only been running for eight months, but both parties considered it to be a success. But over this time, Frank and Diane had come to enjoy each other's company and both of them held the other in high regard.

"Well, I have to admit, Frank," said Diane, "it's a first for me. I've never been to a carol service in a pub before."

Frank had bought Diane a Babycham, which she gratefully accepted.

"Diane, let me introduce you to the Reverend Nicholas Bash," said Frank as the vicar came over to join them.

"Nick the Vic," said the reverend.

"Why, what have you done?" she asked. "Interfered with the choirboys?"

He looked at her and raised an eyebrow.

"Sorry, that was very vulgar of me," Diane added quickly, a tad embarrassed.

"That's okay," the Reverend Bash replied. "Nick the Vic is the name that most of my parishioners at St John's know me by."

Nick was a good-looking man, over six feet tall with dark curly hair. He looked more like a model than a vicar. Diane put his age at about 35.

"I wonder if he's married," she thought. But instead of asking him, she said, "Are you one of these new trendy vicars then, Nick?"

"I wouldn't describe myself as trendy," he replied. "Although I do feel I am more in touch with the younger members of my parish than some of my older colleagues. Also, I believe in taking God's message of love out to people who normally wouldn't go to church, which is why I asked Frank if we could hold a carol service in his pub."

"Frank tells me that you are a police officer," he continued. "Our jobs are similar in many ways, you know."

"Yes," Diane replied. "You look after our souls, whilst I lock up arseholes."

"Very witty, Diane. No, what I meant was that we are both in the business of protecting the public from evil."

He smiled at her and said, "Anyway, I can tell from your accent that you're not from around here."

"No," Diane replied. "I'm from Guildford originally."

"You're joking, I went to school near there, Charterhouse in Godalming."

"Never! My last boyfriend went there as well. Perhaps you knew him, Ricky Mountstevens, Rick the Prick?"

"It doesn't ring a bell. How old is he?"

"He's 33, but he usually acts as if he's thirteen," Diane replied.

Nick smiled. "Well, he'd be two years younger than me then. I didn't really know the names of the younger boys unless they were in my house. You don't know which one he was in, do you?

"Sorry," Diane replied. "I didn't know him when he was at school. We met when we were at Cambridge University together."

"You went to Cambridge?"

"Don't sound so surprised," Diane replied.

"No, what I meant was that I went to Cambridge as well. I studied theology at King's College before graduating in 1966. Which college were you in?"

"I studied psychology and criminology at Newnham College and I graduated in 1968."

"We were there at the same time then," added Nick. "We could have passed each other in the street and never realised it. It's a small world, isn't it?"

"I suppose it is," Diane replied. "So, Charterhouse, Cambridge and then the church. Don't tell me. I bet you're the third son. The first runs the family estate, the second went into the army, which left you to go into the church."

"I think you just about summed up my family," Nick replied. "Anyway, how come you ended up in Chesterfield?"

"Well, to start off I went back to Guildford. Ricky was articled to a firm of solicitors in the town, and I got a job with Surrey police. Then over the years Ricky and I grew more and more apart until one day I asked for a transfer, both from Surrey police and from him. The Derbyshire force was looking to appoint its first female inspector. I applied and got the job. I love it here. The countryside and the people are fantastic and, more importantly, it's 170 miles away from Guildford. Anyway, enough about me, how about you?"

"Well, I worked in a mission in Botswana for five years after leaving university," he replied. "I loved Africa, especially the vistas, the wildlife, and the people. However, I could never get on with the heat, and so I returned to the UK in 1971."

"How did you land in Chesterfield then?" Diane asked. "It's a bit different from Africa."

"As a priest in the Church of England you have to go where you are needed. To start off, I was a curate in Norwich before

I was offered the parish of St John's in 1975. Like you, I also love it here. I couldn't have wished for a better parish. You'll have to come along to one of our services on a Sunday."

"I might just do that," said Diane. "You don't do those happy clappy services, do you? I can't get used to all that shaking hands with the people sitting next to you. When I was young, the church we went to was very traditional. It was all bells, incense, over the top regalia and people singing out of tune."

"You might notice a few changes, but you won't feel out of place. It's a traditional service, although we don't use incense anymore, I'm afraid."

"How did your wife like all that moving around and living in the third world without modern facilities? That's East Anglia I'm talking about by the way, not Botswana."

Nick laughed. "It's precisely because I've moved about a lot that I've never married. I guess I haven't met the right woman yet. Either that or nobody wanted to live with me. Mind you, most of the women in my parish want to marry me off. I think that providing a matchmaking service for the vicar is a favourite pastime of women of a certain age, that and flower arranging."

Diane had ascertained by now that Nick was two years older than her, single and available. All she had to do was to prove to herself that he wasn't gay, and romance could be on the cards.

"I know," Nick said. "Why don't you come to midnight mass on Christmas Eve? Then you can see me on home turf. That's providing you're not going anywhere for Christmas."

"No, I've decided to stay in Chesterfield this year," she replied. "In fact, I volunteered to work on Christmas Day. It's only fair. After all, I'm single, whereas most of the other officers have families they want to be with. I've only got my mum and dad and I don't want to spend the whole of Christmas Day being grilled by them. All they ever want to talk about is when I am going to get married. This is usually closely followed by when they can expect to become grandparents."

"What time do you get off on Christmas Day?" Nick asked her.

"I'm on an early shift. So I get off at 4pm," Diane replied.

"Well, why don't you come to the vicarage for Christmas dinner? There's no point in us both eating by ourselves. I can delay the meal until after you get there."

"Nick, are you chatting me up?"

"I might be," he replied with a twinkle in his eye.

"Well, that's a first for me," added Diane.

"What, you've never been on a date with a vicar before?"

"Absolutely not, and as well as that, I've never been on a date with a man who wears a dress before."

"It's not a dress, Diane. It's a cassock and I can confirm that I definitely won't be wearing it for Christmas dinner. In fact, I won't be wearing my dog collar either."

"How extraordinary," she added whilst taking a sip of her Babycham, "an invitation to have Christmas dinner with a naked vicar. It's definitely a new one for me."

"Naked except for my jeans and T-shirt. Anyway, you don't know how good my cooking is. I might be totally useless. You really ought to find out before you commit yourself to spending Christmas Day with me. So why don't you come around this Friday? I can cook you my signature dish of *coq au vin*. Call it 'a try before you buy' night."

"You really are chatting me up, aren't you?"

"What can I say? Most of the women I meet are middle-aged and those who aren't are usually more interested in the lifestyle they might have as a vicar's wife than they are in me as person. You're different, you've got a career and I can't see you ever giving that up to arrange afternoon teas at the vicarage for the ladies of the parish. That appeals to me. Not only that, but you're intelligent and beautiful. Why wouldn't I try to chat you up? I'm a man as well as a vicar, you know. Tell me you'll accept."

"How can I refuse?" Diane replied before adding, "especially since I was only going to have a Vesta curry this Friday."

"Great, let's say seven o'clock. You know where the vicarage is, don't you? You can't miss it. It's directly opposite the church."

"Seven o'clock it is then."

"Diane, if I can just pull you away for a minute," interrupted Frank. "There's somebody I'd like you to meet. This is Bernie Sanders, the licensee of the Old Bulls Head in Little Hucklow."

Diane turned around and noticed a short, rotund man wearing a bow tie standing next to Frank.

"Pleased to meet you, Mr Sanders," she said, whilst at the same time wondering if he was related to Colonel Sanders, the founder of Kentucky Fried Chicken. In fact, all he needed was a red apron and he could have passed for the Colonel's twin brother.

"Bernie is the chairman of the Derbyshire Dales Licensed Victuallers Association," added Frank. "He's heard what we've been doing in Chesterfield and wants to set up a similar forum on his patch."

The area that Diane covered in her specialist role had recently increased. She was now responsible for all the licensed trade crimes in a large part of rural Derbyshire, in addition to those occurring in Chesterfield. Diane's boss may have increased her responsibilities, but he'd failed to match this by increasing her pay, her rank, her budget or the headcount of her team. It had really pissed her off, which was something she'd mentioned to Frank. He'd obviously wasted no time telling Bernie about it.

"Thanks, Frank," she thought to herself. "I hope you didn't invite me here tonight just to ambush me."

"Frank's been singing your praises and told me that you're now covering the Derbyshire Dales," said Bernie.

Diane turned to Frank and forced a smile.

"A police/licensee forum is just what my publicans need," he continued. "We might be a rural area but, unfortunately, we are not immune to crime. In fact, I was robbed myself only two weeks ago."

"Really?" said Diane. "Did you report it to the police?"

"Yes, and a uniformed copper came out to see me and gave me a crime number. But I'm not at all hopeful that anybody will be brought to justice over it. And I'm not the only one. Three of my members have also been robbed over the past two months, and all the robberies followed a similar pattern."

"That's very interesting," said Diane. "Tell me what happened."

"Well, it was about half past two in the afternoon, and there was only one punter in the bar. He wasn't a regular customer. I'd only seen this man once before. Anyway, the draymen arrived and started making their delivery. So I went into the cellar to check it in. When I returned to the bar, the punter had gone and so had the contents of my till."

"Was there anything distinctive about this man? Could you describe him to one of our photofit artists?"

"He was just a bloke with thinning hair in his late thirties," Bernie added. "I'm not that good at recalling faces, but I could have a go at doing a photofit for you."

"That would be most helpful of you, Mr Sanders."

"Please call me Bernie," he replied.

"Bernie, I presume most of your customers come to you by car?"

"That's right, Little Hucklow is only a small village, so I don't get many locals drinking in the pub. Most people come from Manchester, Sheffield or Chesterfield by car. Although we do get quite a few ramblers and cyclists as well."

"And did you notice if this particular man came by car?"

"Well, I presume he did but, to tell you the truth, I didn't notice. The pub's car park is on the other side of the road and I can't see it from the bar."

"And what brewery are you with, Bernie?"

"I'm a free house, so I deal with more than one. But it was Northern United that were delivering that day."

"Thanks for that, Bernie," replied Diane. "I will get somebody to phone you about the photofit and I will try to make it either at Buxton or Bakewell stations as they are both closer to you than Chesterfield. Could you let me have the names of the other publicans who've been robbed by this man?"

"Yes, they are Jim Knott at the Crown Inn, Wensley, John Higgins at the Plough Inn, Flagg, and Jasper Stenson at the Bulls Head in Wardlow," Bernie replied.

"You can add a couple more to that list, Diane," added Frank. "I was going to mention it to you at the next meeting. Only I've had a couple of similar robberies reported to me, one at the Nettle, Fallgate and the other at the Three Horseshoes, Spitewinter."

"Right," said Diane, "leave it with me and I will visit all those pubs tomorrow."

Turning to Bernie, she added, "And I will contact you after Christmas about setting up another liaison group. But in the meantime, I think I'll have another drink."

"Here, let me get this," said Nick.

"Thanks very much, Nick. I'll have a Babycham."

"Frank tells me you're partial to a spot of brandy in it," he added. "Shall I make it a brandy and Babycham?"

"Go on then," Diane replied. "You know what they say, whisky makes you frisky and brandy makes you randy."

"In which case, we'd better make it a double Courvoisier and Babycham for you and a large Bell's for me."

Chapter 3
Monday evening, April 11th, 1971

"Are you girls going out?" asked Mervyn.

He was completely mesmerised by Penny's chest.

"Yes, we are just popping out for our early evening constitutional," Penny replied.

"You're definitely popping out all right," said Mervyn who couldn't believe his luck. "Well, make sure you're back by ten o'clock, because that's when I lock the front door. If you return after that, you'll have to pay a forfeit if you want to come in."

"In which case, we will definitely be back by then," replied Alice who realised only too well what Mervyn was implying.

"He makes my flesh creep," said Penny once they were out of the door.

"You make him worse by going bra-less," Alice reprimanded her friend.

"Hey, don't forget it's your bare breast he's seen, not mine," Penny replied.

It was a lovely spring evening and quite a few people were sitting outside the pub, taking advantage of the view over Bleckley Edge and the valley beyond. Being a bank holiday, many of them had driven out from the cities that surround the Peak District and had parked their cars opposite the pub. The pub's car park was squeezed in on a thin strip of land between the road and a sheer drop down to the villages of Eyam and

Foolow below. All that somebody needed to do was to put their car into the wrong gear, and there was every chance they would do a swan dive over the cliff edge.

Penny and Alice entered the pub and went straight up to the bar.

"Two halves of Woodpecker Cider, please," said Alice.

"And how old are you, miss?" asked the publican.

"I'm eighteen and I've got my passport to prove it," said Alice, at the same time taking her ID out of her handbag.

"And I've forgotten mine but I'm older than her," added Penny.

Mind you, the landlord wasn't interested in what Penny was saying or in Alice's passport. He was too busy looking at Penny's chest.

"Ah… ah… I'll get the dr… dr… drinks for them l… l… lasses, Matt," said a scruffily dressed man who was standing at the bar.

He had a bad stammer and was obviously a local since he knew the landlord's name. Unless he'd merely read it from the notice above the door that said Matthew Yates, licensed to sell all intoxicating liquor for consumption both on and off these premises. Penny presumed it was the former since he looked as if he was too stupid to read.

"No, thank you," she said. "We'd prefer to pay for them ourselves."

"In which c… c… case would your p… p… p… puppies like a drink?"

"What are you talking about?" Penny asked.

"Those t… t… two p… p… puppies f… f… fighting in that s… s… sack there," he said, pointing intently at Penny's chest.

Matt thought this was very amusing. But when he'd finished laughing, he said, "Pay no attention to him, miss, he's soft in the head."

He turned his back on the girls and went to pour their drinks.

"That'll be 32 pence, please," he said as he passed the ciders to them.

Penny gave him a fifty pence piece and waited for her change. As Matt was getting it for her, a young lad came up to the bar. Penny recognised him as one of the six boys from the youth hostel.

"He'll never get served," she thought to herself, and it wasn't long before she was proved right.

"I'm not serving you," said Matt. "How old are you?"

"Nineteen," the lad replied.

"And I'm Albert Einstein," said Matt.

"Pleased to meet you, Mr Einstein," said the lad holding out his hand.

"You cheeky monkey," added Matt. "Get out of here."

The lad knew that he was fighting a lost cause. He meekly turned around and went out of the door. He'd try the same thing again tomorrow night at a pub in Castleton with the same result.

Penny and Alice meanwhile wandered over to one of the tables by the window. The inside of the pub contained all manner of polished brass, especially around the fireplace, which was close to where the girls sat down.

"I wouldn't like to be the person who has to polish that lot," said Penny taking a sip of her cider.

"I think you've made a friend there," commented Alice whilst looking at the man at the bar. "It's a pity he smells of horse piss and can barely string a sentence together."

"And did you see his hands?" added Penny, "as big as shovels and as rough as sandpaper. I wouldn't like to bump into him on a dark night."

"He's harmless," said a lad who was sitting at the next table and had overheard their conversation. "He lives in the village. He and his brother are both coal merchants, and their parents run the stables. He's just a bit simple. We call him Daft Dave."

"He reminds me of Lurch from the Addams family," said Penny. "Are there many others like him around here?"

"Just Daft Dave," replied the lad. "Everybody else around here is perfectly normal and I should know as I've lived here all my life. Bleckley's a small place with just fifteen inhabitants. We've only got one nutter and we certainly don't have any pretty girls like you two living here. By the way, my name's Brian Law and this is my twin brother Andy. We live at Barn Farm on the edge of the village."

"Village? I've been in bigger model villages than this place," replied Penny.

"It may be small, but we like it here," said Brian. "Do you mind if we join you?"

"You can if you want to," Penny replied. "We're not going to object."

So the two boys moved to sit at the same table as the girls.

"Are you sure you are twins?" asked Alice. "You don't look the same."

"We're not identical," said Brian before winking at his brother and adding, "I got all the good bits and Andy got the bits that were left over."

Looking at the two of them, you could see what Brian meant. He was a good-looking lad, over six feet tall with dark hair and a wonderful smile. It was obvious that he was the more outgoing of the two brothers. Andy hadn't said a word yet. He was also quite a bit smaller than his brother, with greasy hair and spots. His look was made all the worse by the pair of round bottle-end glasses perched on the end of his nose.

"Anyway, you haven't told us your names yet or where you're from."

"I'm Penny Foster and this is Alice Barlow and we're both from Chesterfield."

"P… P… Penny's p… p… puppies," came a shout from the bar.

Daft Dave was pointing at Penny's chest.

"Shut it, Dave," Brian shouted back. "Otherwise I'll tell your mam and dad that I saw you having a wank at the back of one of the stables yesterday."

Two middle-aged ladies sitting opposite looked horrified by Brian's comment. Matt, the landlord, didn't like it either. Mind you, he was fully aware that Brian, as a local, would still be visiting the pub in November after all the tourists had left.

With this in mind, he just said, "Keep it down, Bung, will you?"

"Bung?" said Penny.

"It's my nickname," Bung explained. "It's short for Bungalow Brian."

"Why Bungalow Brian?" asked Penny.

"It's because he's got nothing upstairs," Andy cut in.

"Shut it, Bonar," said Bung. "I was given the name by my classmates. They were being ironic because I was the cleverest boy in the class."

But Penny wasn't listening. Instead, she had picked up on Andy's nickname.

"Why do you call him Boner?" she asked. "Don't tell me, it's because he's got a permanent hard-on?"

"No, it's Bonar with an a not an e," Bung replied. "I started calling him that after the former Prime Minister Andrew Bonar Law. See, I told you my classmates were being ironic."

"I think my explanation was better," replied Penny as she glanced at Bonar.

"So what are you girls doing here?" asked Bung, changing the subject.

"We've just taken a few days' holiday before we start our A levels," Penny replied. "We are staying at the youth hostel next door."

"And what are you going to do whilst you're here?"

"Alice has planned a few walks for us."

"That sounds a bit boring to me."

"Says the lad who lives in one of the most boring places in Britain."

"Hey, at least we aren't all bent and twisted like everybody in Chesterfield."

"Ha, ha, I haven't heard that one before," said Penny. "Anyway, it's not the people who are crooked, it's the church spire."

"And this area isn't boring, there's plenty to do. In fact, Bonar and I are going to the races tomorrow."

"What, you've got a racetrack around here?" asked Penny in utter amazement.

"We certainly have," answered Bung. "It's Flagg point-to-point races tomorrow. Why don't you come with us?"

"That's very good of you to offer," Alice cut in. "But we've got a walk planned."

"Flagg races will be much more fun," Bung added. "There will be stalls selling all sorts of stuff, food vans, a beer tent and, of course, you can bet on the horses. The races only take place once a year on Easter Tuesday. If you don't come tomorrow, you will have to wait for another year."

"Oh Alice, let's go," pleaded Penny.

Alice, however, was adamant that she wanted to go for a walk. So Bung proposed a compromise. Since the races didn't start until half past twelve, the girls would still be able to go for a walk in the morning as long as they were back by eleven o'clock.

Seeing that she was outnumbered, Alice gave in and reluctantly agreed to Bung's proposal. The boys arranged to pick the two of them up at a quarter past eleven the next day.

The chitchat between them continued for the next two hours with the girls having several more drinks.

Everything was going swimmingly until Alice realised it was five to ten.

"Shit, Pen," she said. "We'd better get back sharpish. Merv the Perv locks the front door in five minutes' time."

They both downed their drinks and quickly said goodbye to Bung and Bonar before heading out of the pub.

To their dismay, it was teaming down with rain.

"We can't wait," said Alice. "Otherwise, we'll be locked out and you'll have to pay a forfeit to get Merv the Perv to unlock the door.

"What do you mean, I'll have to pay a forfeit?" Penny replied. "Don't think for one moment that he won't make you pay one as well. He'll probably want to have a look at your other tit."

But Alice wasn't in the mood for discussing the situation with her friend.

"Let's make a dash for it," she said.

They made it just in time. Mervyn was waiting for them and he tapped his watch as they came through the door.

"You've made it with one minute to spare," he said.

He looked at Penny, grinned and added, "I didn't know they were holding a Miss Wet T-shirt competition in the pub tonight."

His eyes were transfixed on Penny's chest and as she looked down, she was horrified to see that her rain-soaked T-shirt was now completely see-through.

Chapter 4
Thursday morning, December 14th, 1978

"So you're going on a date with Nick the Dick then," commented Spencer as he sat in the passenger seat next to Diane.

Spencer Spooner was Diane's bagman, her sergeant to be precise. He was seven years older than she was and married with two kids. He was more worldly wise than his boss and not afraid of telling her what was what. Spencer was also not averse to the odd sarcastic comment or joke at Diane's expense. Despite this, the two of them got on well together and both respected the other's professionalism and integrity.

Diane would often confide in Spencer. But after details of her date with the Reverend Bash had slipped out, she was beginning to regret mentioning it to him.

"It's Nick the Vic, not Nick the Dick," she corrected him.

"That's not what I've heard," Spencer replied.

"Come off it, Spencer," said Diane. "You don't even know him. You haven't been to church since they stopped doing mass in Latin."

"That's not true," replied Spencer. "I'll have you know that I went to my niece's wedding at his church only last May."

"That hardly qualifies you as the fount of all knowledge regarding the Reverend Bash."

"No, but Elsie who lives next door to me is a member of his congregation and she tells me he's tried it on with all the unmarried women under thirty in his congregation. I heard he's had more pussy than my sister's tomcat."

He looked at Diane and added, "Mind you, it looks as if he's raised his maximum age requirement this time."

"Fuck off, Spencer," Diane replied.

The two of them were heading towards the Three Horseshoes at Spitewinter, the first pub on their list. It was the type of crisp December morning when the bare branches of the trees glinted in the sun with their coating of frost. Mind you, Diane was acutely aware that country roads didn't get gritted as much as the roads in town. She was keeping her speed down, while at the same time looking out for patches of black ice. She was driving her Ford Capri John Player Special, with its black paintwork and gold piping – the flying ashtray, as some of her colleagues called it.

"What are we trying to achieve today?" asked Spencer.

"The main thing is to establish whether there is any pattern to these robberies," Diane replied. "In particular, I want to find out whether they were all committed by the same person. I also want to discover what time the robberies took place, whether the thief had ever been seen in each pub before, and if anybody has any details about him or his car."

Spitewinter is a small hamlet just outside Chesterfield on the Matlock Road. The pub itself is located on the brow of a hill and, on first inspection, it didn't appear to have too much going for it. There were very few houses nearby and it wasn't old and quaint or new and contemporary. It was positioned at the top of the long climb out of Chesterfield, at the start of the 'flying mile', a straight stretch of the A632 popular with boy racers. This made it extremely dangerous to enter the pub's car park when turning across the lane of traffic coming from Matlock.

It was obviously a well-kept pub as the paintwork was immaculate. It was nicely decorated for the festive season with fairy lights draped just below the roofline and a large external Christmas tree. Given its location at the top of a hill, all those bulbs must have made the pub visible for miles around once it got dark.

Diane took her life in her hands and turned right into the car park. They hadn't informed anyone they were coming and a gentleman who was busy emptying a container full of bottle tops into the outside bin looked around as they pulled to a halt a few feet away from him.

"We're not open yet," he shouted at the two officers.

"I should hope you're not," replied Diane. "Otherwise, I'd have to do you for serving before your permitted hours and that would be a first for me. I've charged a few in my time for serving after hours, but I don't think even DS Spooner here wants a drink at ten o'clock in the morning."

Diane and Spencer showed him their warrant cards and, after briefly inspecting them, he introduced himself to the two officers as Ian Garvey, the licensee.

He ushered them inside, saying, "So what brings a detective inspector out here? Surely, it's not the robbery I reported two weeks ago. I thought that was gathering dust at the bottom of your heap of unsolved crimes. I only reported it so I could get the money back on my insurance. You've got to have a crime reference number before you can make a claim these days."

"You obviously don't have a very high opinion of the police, Mr Garvey," Diane replied. "DS Spooner and I specialise in crimes involving the licensed trade and let me tell you, we treat any crime on licensed premises very seriously indeed. That's especially true of crimes that form part of a crime wave."

"He's robbed other pubs then?" queried Mr Garvey.

"That's correct, there's been five other very similar robberies reported to us recently. That's why it's important that we find the person responsible."

"I didn't know Derbyshire police had a specialist licensed trade team," he continued. "How long has that been in place?" .

"We started earlier this year," Diane replied. "Chesterfield's Licensed Victuallers Association members are working with us, and we hold a joint meeting once a month. Their chairman should have informed all their members. Didn't you get the message? "

"I don't get too involved with the LVA," Mr Garvey replied. "I'm a member, of course, and I know most of the people on the committee, but I don't really have the time."

"It's only a couple of hours on a Thursday at Frank McKinley's pub, the White Hart in Walton. Come along, you might pick up some useful tips about crime prevention. After all, it's less than a mile away from here."

"I'll think about it," Mr Garvey replied.

Diane guessed he'd only said this to placate her. She knew he wouldn't bother, which was why she decided to press him for details of the crime instead.

"Mr Garvey, I want you to tell me precisely what happened on the day you were robbed."

"Well, it was two weeks ago last Tuesday and it was about a quarter past two in the afternoon. We'd had a few in for lunch, but they had all gone by then. I was thinking about closing early when this bloke comes in, sits on a barstool and asks for a half of mild."

"Now, Mr Garvey," Diane interrupted, "can you tell me if you'd ever seen this man before and can you describe him to me?"

"I don't think I've seen him before. I only saw him briefly because straight after I'd served him, the brewery delivery arrived. But I'd say he was about forty, going bald, and wearing a check jacket, if that's of any use to you?"

"That's really helpful," Diane replied. "Can you tell me which brewery it was that made the delivery? I noticed that the signs outside say Sheffield Brewery. Was it one of their drays?"

"Yes, but they call themselves Northern United these days. They've got around to repainting their drays, but God knows when they'll get around to repainting my signs."

"And you went into the cellar to see in the delivery?" Diane continued.

"Yes, there used to be a lot of problems in the past with draymen stealing. The buggers would deliver twelve kegs, ten of which would be full and two would be empty. If you didn't notice at the time, there'd be nothing you could do about it once you had signed for your order. That problem was largely solved when the brewery went over to fixed runs."

"Can you explain what you mean by a fixed run, please?" asked Diane.

"A few months ago, the brewery introduced a new system whereby we get the same draymen delivering at approximately the same time every week. Under the old system, a crew might only visit us two or three times a year. Consequently, good customer service wasn't top of their agenda, and they'd try to rip you off. With fixed runs, we get the same crew every week. The idea behind that is that they are less likely to get up to any monkey business if they know they'll have to come back and see you the following week. Mind you, even with the new fixed run system, I still wouldn't dream of letting them deliver without checking everything in."

"So you just left the man alone in the bar?"

"Yes, and when I came back, he'd gone, as had the contents of my till. To make matters worse, the lowlife scum had also pinched our two charity boxes. It's ironic really when you think about it. There was I worried about the draymen nicking, when I should have been more concerned about the customer I'd left alone in the bar."

"Where was your wife whilst all this was happening, Mr Garvey? Couldn't she have looked after the bar for you whilst you saw the delivery in?"

"She was in pot wash doing the dishes after the lunchtime session."

"You didn't happen to notice anything else about this man?" Diane continued. "Did he have a local accent, for example, or did you notice what car he drove?"

"You can't see the car park from the bar, Inspector, and as for accents, I've never been very good at identifying them. But if I had to have a go, I'd say he came from Sheffield."

"One final question, Mr Garvey, do you know how much he got away with?"

"I don't know how much was in the charity boxes, but we took £110.62 during the lunchtime session and, when you add that to my £50 float, it makes £160.62."

"Thank you very much, Mr Garvey. Sergeant Spooner will keep you informed about any progress we make with the investigation."

Diane and Spencer both shook his hand and left.

"I don't want to jump to any conclusions until we've spoken to all the other licensees," commented Diane once they were back in the car. "But isn't it strange that both robberies so far have taken place whilst Northern United were delivering?

Perhaps one of the draymen is involved. He could be tipping off our thief about where and when they are going to deliver."

"However, the robber could just be following the brewery dray," countered Spencer.

"In which case, how come he's arrived at the pub before the dray at both the Old Bulls Head and the Three Horseshoes?"

"Good point, ma'am," Spencer replied. "But as you say, we shouldn't jump to any conclusions until after we've interviewed the other landlords."

Diane started the car and turned right out of the car park towards Matlock. The next pub they were due to visit was the Nettle in Fallgate, which was a short drive away.

Fallgate was another small hamlet, located close to the much larger village of Ashover.

"One thing all these pubs have in common is that they are in isolated locations," commented Spencer. "Do you think this is a reason for the robber targeting them or is it just a coincidence?"

"I think our thief is deliberately targeting rural pubs because it is far less likely there will be any witnesses. A husband and wife team runs most country pubs and the majority of them have to do food these days in order to make ends meet. That's why our thief targets pubs just before closing time when a delivery is being made. Not only will the till be full of the lunchtime takings, but all the customers would have left. Then when the delivery arrives, the husband and the draymen go into the cellar whilst the wife will probably be in the kitchen tidying up."

"But how does he know which pubs to target?"

"That, Spencer, is what we have to find out," Diane replied.

The Nettle was a pub renowned for its food. If it had been the weekend there would have been quite a few staff working.

The Sunday carvery was particularly popular. But this robbery had taken place on a Wednesday lunchtime, just before closing time, when the only people working were the licensee, his wife and one waitress.

Mr Scott, the licensee, clearly had a good memory for faces as his description of the robber was very similar to those given by Ian Garvey and Bernie Sanders. In other words, he also described the robber as a man in his late thirties or early forties with thinning hair.

Even though the Nettle was a free house, and Mr Scott dealt with two different breweries, the thief had chosen the day when Northern United was delivering. Furthermore, the delivery in question was made just before closing time.

There were small differences between the robbery at the Nettle and the robberies at the Three Horseshoes and The Old Bulls Head though. Diane had never been to the pub in Little Hucklow, but she understood it was quite small. The pub in Spitewinter wasn't particularly large either and certainly was not that busy during lunch in the middle of the week in December.

The Nettle, in contrast, was quite a big pub. Despite not being as busy on weekdays at lunchtime as it was on a Saturday or a Sunday, they still had enough customers to warrant them employing a waitress. Diane hoped that she might have noticed something. But at 2.45pm when the robbery had taken place, she had been with the owner's wife in the kitchen clearing up.

Despite this, the waitress was still able to give the officers a description of what she thought was the thief's car. While the draymen had been delivering the beer, she'd gone to the dry goods store opposite the pub. At the time, Mr Scott's Jag and one other car were the only ones in the car park. It was an orange Ford Escort and she remembered it because the owner had parked it too close to the store, making it difficult for her to open the door.

"Some people are really inconsiderate," she told the two officers. "There's a sign on the store door which says, 'No Parking'."

She didn't take down the car's registration details, but it was still a lead that could be followed up.

The thief had gotten away with over £230 at the Nettle, plus a charity box and the contents of the tip jar that was on a shelf behind the till.

When Diane asked Mr Scott if he had ever seen the thief before, she was surprised to discover that he had been to the pub at least twice prior to the robbery.

"He may have been more often," said Mr Scott. "But I've only noticed him twice before. On both occasions, he arrived just before Northern United started delivering, just as he did on the day of the robbery. The only difference was that there were still quite a few customers left in the bar by the time the dray arrived."

"Was the dray crew the same for all three deliveries?" Diane asked him.

"They're the same every week," answered Mr Scott. "We are on a fixed run. So we always get the same draymen. Except if one of them is on holiday or off sick."

"Do you know their names?" asked Diane.

"Sorry," he replied. "You must think I'm awfully rude, but I've never asked them, and they've been delivering here for the past six months. Mind you, the driver always signs the delivery note. I can show you his signature if you like."

Diane was keen to have a look at one of the signed delivery notes but was disappointed when Mr Scott got the latest one from his office.

"This drayman must have a secret desire to become a doctor," she commented. "I can't make his signature out at all. What about you, Spencer?"

Spencer had a look, but he couldn't decipher the signature either.

"Never mind," he said, "I'm sure the brewery will be able to tell us who the driver is."

"Thanks for your help, Mr Scott," said Diane. "We need to get an image of this man. Can you come to Chesterfield police station tomorrow and sit down with one of our photofit artists?"

Bernie Sanders had already volunteered to try and give the police a description of the man involved. But if Mr Scott really was as good at remembering faces as he said he was, then it wouldn't hurt to have two photofits of their suspect.

"Only if it's early morning before we open or after we've closed in the afternoon," he replied.

"I'll arrange for him to see you at nine o'clock tomorrow morning then," said Diane. "It shouldn't take more than an hour. You should be back by half past ten. Is that okay?"

"Nine o'clock is fine by me," he replied.

Having concluded their business, Diane and Spencer left the Nettle for the next pub on their list, the Crown Inn at Wensley.

"I wonder how many times our thief would visit a pub before he gives up?" muttered Spencer as Diane was driving out of the car park.

"I can't believe that he'd go more than three times," replied Diane. "Otherwise it becomes too risky. He's already made a mistake by going to the Nettle three times. That has resulted in his car being identified. What is more, we'll hopefully get a good photofit out of Mr Scott."

"Well, Mr Scott did say he's very good at remembering faces, ma'am," said Spencer. "Let's just hope that between him and Bernie Sanders we can get a good likeness."

"You know, Spencer," added Diane, "I'm pretty certain I know what's happening here. The brewery's decision to go over to fixed runs has reduced the opportunity for some of the draymen to steel from the publicans they are delivering to. So instead, they have invented a new way to do it. They identify suitable pubs and tell an accomplice when they are going to deliver. Then, when they have the licensee with them in the cellar checking the delivery, their accomplice robs the till."

"It all sounds very feasible to me, ma'am," said Spencer.

"Of course, the one thing they can't predict is whether there will be any other customers in the bar when they deliver. They can be fairly certain that any other staff will be in the kitchen. But just in case they aren't or if there are still any customers around, our thief then takes the decision to go back the following week. That's why it took him three attempts to rob the Nettle, two attempts to rob The Old Bulls Head, but with the Three Horseshoes he got lucky and was able to carry out the robbery there on his first visit. I fancy we will wrap this case up tomorrow when we visit Northern United's depot in Staveley and find out who these draymen are."

Although Diane had already decided what was happening, she and Spencer still went to visit the other three pubs. She was nothing if not thorough with her investigation. However, none of the other licensees were able to add any further details about their suspect. Mind you, all three of them did reinforce the picture that Diane had already built up, namely that their suspect was somehow linked to the draymen at Northern United.

Diane went home in a very good mood that evening. After all, she was convinced that she would identify precisely who was carrying out this spate of robberies the next day.

"Clearing up six crimes in one go is bound to be a feather in my cap and go down well with Superintendent Barker," she thought to herself as she settled down to watch the evening news.

Chapter 5
Tuesday morning, April 12th, 1971

Penny and Alice got up early the next morning determined to fit in a two-hour walk before the boys picked them up and took them to the races. But they soon changed their plans when they realised that the rain from the previous night hadn't ended. In fact, it had turned to sleet.

"Bloody hell," said Penny as she and Alice were looking out of the window at the murky conditions. "Anybody would think it was January rather than April. Can you believe it? Yesterday, I was sweating my socks off. Today, I'm so cold you could hang a brace of pheasants from my chest, one on each nipple."

The girls decided to have breakfast and then to sit around reading for two hours instead. However, the peace and quiet of the youth hostel's lounge was soon shattered.

"Hi girls, not going out today?"

Merv the Perv had slipped into the room whilst their backs were turned.

"Yes, but not until 11.15," Alice replied. "We're off to Flagg races. Mind you, we were thinking of going for a short walk this morning, only the weather has put us off."

"It always snows for Flagg races," Merv replied. "That's one thing you can bet on and guarantee a win, which is more than you can say for most of the horses running at Flagg."

"Will you and your wife be going?" asked Penny.

"Hey girls, I'm not married, I'm young, footloose and fancy free. Just like you two."

"Shouldn't that be old, toothless and smelling of pee," muttered Penny under her breath. She smiled insincerely and said, "Really? You do surprise me. I'd have thought all the ladies in Bleckley would be lining up."

"In case you hadn't noticed, there aren't any single women in this village," he replied. "So there's plenty of time for you two to get to the front of the queue."

He was blissfully unaware that Penny was taking the piss.

"I'm going to Flagg races myself," he continued. "Why don't you tag along?"

"Oh, we'd really like to," replied Penny. "But Bung and Bonar from Barn Farm have already asked us. We'd much rather go with you, but we promised them, didn't we, Alice?"

"I'm afraid we did," replied Alice. "Unfortunately, we can't back out now, even though we'd both like to."

Mervyn looked crestfallen, which was why the girls decided to torment him a bit more.

"If only you had offered earlier," added Alice. "It would have been such fun, just the three of us together in your car with the windows all steamed up."

"Still, you can always ask Claudia and Hanna to go with you," said Penny. "I promise we won't be jealous. Those two are such fun, always laughing and joking. As for some of the things they get up to, well it makes me blush just thinking about it. Yesterday, they were telling us about all the threesomes they've had, back in Germany. It sounded such fun. I could always ask them if they'd like to go with you. That's provided you want me to, of course."

"No, it's alright, thank you," said Mervyn who by this stage was aware that the girls had been taking the mickey out of him. He quickly added, "Anyway, I'd better get back to my office."

Once he'd gone, Penny turned to Alice and said, "See, I told you he wouldn't be married. Nobody in their right mind would want to get hitched to an old pervert like him."

"Mind you, I don't think we should have wound him up like that," added Alice. "What if he takes us seriously and tries to chat us up?"

"After what I've just told him, I think it's Valkyrie and Brunhilda who'll have to watch out, not us," Penny replied. "Besides, if he tries it on again, I'll get Bung to sort him out. I'm sick of the way that pervert looks at us. He never takes his eyes off our tits. He's probably in his office right now playing with himself."

"Urrh," replied Alice, "please don't, Pen. I think I'm going to be sick."

Fortunately, Merv the Perv didn't reappear that morning and, at 11.15, the boys turned up in their 1950s Land Rover.

"It stinks in here," said Penny in disgust as she was getting in.

"Of course it does," replied Bung. "We've been using it to transport sheep and they aren't pets you know. None of them are house-trained."

It wasn't the most comfortable of journeys as Alice and Penny were sitting on a couple of bench seats facing each other in the back. The Land Rover's suspension had seen better days and the girls were bounced all over the place as Bung drove over the many potholes in the road.

By the time they reached Flagg, the sleet had changed to snow.

"It always snows for Flagg races," said Bung.

"So we understand," Penny and Alice replied in unison.

"Despite the weather, the whole of Bleckley will be here," Bonar chipped in, "apart from Matt, as he's got to open the pub at lunchtime."

"That means there'll be at least fourteen people in the crowd then," Penny replied sarcastically.

"Eleven," added Bonar, "Matt's family won't be here either."

The racecourse was a little way out of the village of Flagg itself. It was just off the A515 on Flagg Moor, close to the Bull i'Thorn Inn. Bung turned off the main road and, after paying the entry fee, he proceeded into the field which acted as the car park for the day.

"I'm glad we came in the Land Rover," commented Bung. "I wouldn't like to be in a two-wheel drive car today. This field will be well and truly churned up by the time it comes for us to leave."

The four of them got out of the Land Rover and walked over to where most of the stalls were located. By this time, the snow was coming down horizontally and the girls were really pleased they were both wearing warm waterproof clothing. It had been a last minute decision to pack their thick winter coats. After all, it had been touching twenty degrees the previous day and they had set off wearing just shorts and T-shirts. However, they had lived in Derbyshire all their lives and were fully aware of how rapidly the conditions could change, especially in the Peak District in April. As a result, they had decided to be prepared for every type of weather, and now concluded it was one of their better decisions.

"Bloody hell, it's absolutely freezing," said Penny. "Why don't they hold the race meeting during the summer?"

"It's a point-to-point meeting organised by the High Peak hunt," Bung replied. "In order to take part, a horse must have been hunting at least once during the season. That's why Flagg races always takes place on Easter Tuesday. It's right at the end of the hunting season."

Penny was going to reply, but despite her thick winter coat keeping out the worst of the winter weather, her lips were starting to go blue and her teeth were chattering.

"It's very exposed on Flagg Moor," said Bung. "Let's go into the beer tent and see if this weather blows over."

Bung led the way to a large marquee. There was a banner outside with the words, 'Whitbread Tankard sold here' printed on it.

Lots of other people obviously had a similar idea as the marquee was heaving with racegoers. Mind you, Penny and Alice didn't care about how full it was as the temperature inside was considerably warmer than it was outside in the snow and wind. Several Calor Gas heaters warmed the tent, and these were augmented by the body heat emanating from the numerous farmers, most of whom were knocking back pints of weak keg bitter. The smell inside the marquee could best be described as ripe, as wet tweed jackets were starting to dry out in the heat. Penny guessed that it was a long time since any of these jackets had been to the dry cleaners, if indeed they had ever been.

"What can I get you girls?" asked Bung as he fought his way to the bar.

"We'll both have half a cider," Alice replied not wanting to order anything too exotic. The chances of the bar stocking anything other than bitter on draught and the odd bottle of lager and cider were virtually non-existent.

Bung eventually caught the barman's eye.

"Two pints of Tankard and two halves of agricultural chardonnay," he said.

"What did you ask for?" exclaimed Penny.

"Agricultural chardonnay," Brian replied. "It's what we call cider around here."

Alice hadn't stipulated whether they wanted sweet or dry cider, since she was doubtful whether the bar stocked a choice of two different varieties. In fact, the only drinks where they did offer a choice were the wines, where they offered either red or white, or indeed a bit of both if you wanted rosé.

In the end the cider was dry, which wasn't Alice's favourite, but she didn't care. At least she was indoors and had a glass of alcoholic liquid in her hands.

"Hey, it's Daft Dave," said Bonar who'd noticed him waving at them from the other end of the bar.

"Please don't," said Penny. "I don't want that simpleton ogling me again."

"And he smelt bad enough yesterday," added Alice. "God only knows what he'll be like in here today with the heaters drying all that piss and shit on him."

"Excuse me, miss, but I'd ask you not to talk about my son in that manner. He's a bit slow but he's got a heart of gold and he's worth two of you any day of the week."

The man who was addressing Alice had presumed it was her who had made all the derogatory comments about his son. Penny wasn't going to put him straight that it had actually been her who'd referred to him as a simpleton. She just went quiet and disappeared into the background.

"I'm sure she didn't mean any harm, Mr Hallsworth," said Bung trying to calm the situation down. "It's easy to get the wrong impression about Dave until you get to know him. Here, let me get you and your wife a drink."

But Mr Hallsworth could not be bought so easily, and he took his wife and wandered over to where Dave was standing. At the same time, he muttered, "bloody townies" just loud enough for the girls to hear.

"You could have told us that Daft Dave's dad was behind us," said Penny who had reappeared now that Mr Hallsworth was out of earshot.

"I didn't even notice him," Bung replied. "I knew he was coming, of course. His son Frank is riding in the second race. He also looks after some of the other horses that are taking part. I told you everybody from the village would be here today. I guess I should have kept an eye open for him. And talking about people from the village, there's Hugh Stanton over there. You don't want to bump into him on a dark night."

Penny and Alice followed Brian's line of sight and could see a man in his late fifties with a ruddy complexion. He was dressed like a typical farmer in a flat cap, an old tweed jacket and a green jumper full of holes. This was complemented by a dirty pair of moleskin trousers tucked into green wellies. He was deep in conversation with a group of men who were similarly dressed. All of them were drinking pints of bitter with whisky chasers, despite the fact it wasn't twelve noon yet.

Bung could tell that Penny and Alice were dying for him to explain a little more about what he meant, and he didn't disappoint them.

"Hugh is a heavy drinker," he said. "And when he drinks, he gets violent. He used to beat his wife until she left him, and he's been arrested several times for being drunk and disorderly. He always goes to Bakewell on a Monday because it's market day and the pubs are allowed to open from eleven in the morning until eleven at night. On one occasion, he was sitting on a barstool in the Anchor Inn and was so drunk he couldn't stand up, let alone walk to the toilet. So he just unzipped his fly and pissed all over the bar."

"That's too much information," said Alice. "Can we change the subject, please?"

But Bung hadn't finished. He'd got numerous stories in his locker about Hugh Stanton, and he wanted to tell them all. Like, for example, the time Hugh had shat himself whilst in the lounge bar of the Bulls Head in Eyam. Or the time when he'd fallen asleep in the toilets at the Rutland Arms in Baslow and had been locked in when the landlord had closed for the night. Despite yelling the place down, he hadn't been let out until the cleaner went in at nine o'clock the following morning. Needless to say, Hugh wasn't best pleased by this and threatened to sue for false imprisonment. However, the landlord knew this was an idle threat and responded by barring him for life. In fact, Hugh was barred from most of the pubs in North Derbyshire. But not the one in his home village of Bleckley, despite numerous threats by various landlords over the years to do just that.

These were some of the stories that Bung wanted to tell the girls. But at this point, he was interrupted.

"Ah, there you are Brian," said a middle-aged lady who was accompanied by a man who Penny presumed was her husband.

He was dressed in the obligatory tweed jacket, just like most of the other men in the marquee.

"I suppose these must be your latest girlfriends," the woman continued. "Are you going to introduce us?"

"Mum, you are embarrassing us, they are just friends," Bung replied.

Then seeing his mum was still waiting he continued, "Mum, Dad, this is Penny and Alice from Chesterfield. They are currently staying at the youth hostel."

"Chesterfield's not very far away. Maybe these two will last more than a few days this time," commented his mother.

"Mum," shouted Bung in disgust.

Bonar obviously thought it was all very amusing and was trying hard not to laugh. Bung just smiled and turned to the girls

"Anyway, the weather's improved," he said. "Why don't we go outside and have a look at the stalls?"

The fact that it had stopped snowing wasn't the real reason he'd suggested going outside. It was in order to get the girls away from his mother.

"That's a good idea," Penny replied as she drained the last of her cider and followed Bung towards the exit.

"What did your mother mean when she said she hoped we'd last more than a few days?" asked Penny once they had left the beer tent.

"Well, in case you hadn't noticed there aren't any girls of our age in Bleckley. In fact, there are only five other properties in the village in addition to our farm. One is the youth hostel where the only permanent resident is Mervyn, and one is the pub with Matt and Helen. Now, they do have two daughters, but they are only aged five and seven. So they're a bit young for Bonar and me."

"That shouldn't worry you," said Penny, "it still leaves several hundred sheep to choose from."

"Ha, ha, very funny. But seriously, the only other people who live in the village are Mike and Jenny Hallsworth who have two sons and Hugh Stanton who's only son left after falling out with his father. Finally, there's James Hargreaves, an author who moved to the village ten years ago. He keeps himself to himself and we don't see much of him. He moved here because he likes the peace and quiet and he lives by himself."

"He's hardly likely to have moved to Bleckley because he likes clubbing," added Penny.

Bung decided to ignore her snide comment this time.

"As you can see then," he continued, "there isn't much in the way of girls where we live. But there is the youth hostel and the girls from all over the world who come to stay there. Sometimes, Bonar and I get talking to one or two of them for a bit of female company. That was all my mum meant. It's never serious, of course. After all, how would we start a full-time relationship with a couple of girls from Norway or even London for that matter?"

"And is that what Alice and I are? A bit of female company?"

"No, you too are very different," Brian replied. "For a start, you are the only girls we've met from the hostel who live in Derbyshire. That makes you two local. We could easily drive over to Chesterfield in order to see you."

Penny seemed quite pleased with that idea. But not Alice. There was no way she wanted to start a relationship with someone whose nickname made him sound like an erect penis.

Chapter 6
Friday morning, December 15th, 1978

"I have a good feeling about today, Spencer," Diane announced. "I can feel it in my water."

"You ought to get that checked out, ma'am," Spencer replied. "You may have a touch of cystitis."

Diane merely pulled a face at him. The two of them were driving to Staveley where the new delivery depot for Northern United Brewery was located. It was the first time either of them had visited this particular site, although both of them had visited the company's head office in the past. They had also been to their old premises in the centre of Sheffield before it had closed down. Sheffield Brewery had been brewing on the same site there for ninety years before it became surplus to its new owners, United Breweries' requirements. They had closed it in order to make way for a mixed development of retail outlets and loft apartments.

Although the address for the new depot was Staveley, it was actually some way away from the town itself, close to junction 30 on the M1 on a new industrial estate. That was why United Breweries had chosen it. They no longer brewed beer in Sheffield. Therefore, it made sense for them to be close to the motorway. It made it easier for the large articulated lorries known as trunkers to get in and out. Sheffield had been one of their three smaller breweries and, shortly after it had closed,

United Breweries had closed their Cardiff brewery, with Plymouth following three months later.

The depot itself was not easy to miss. It was massive, totally dwarfing everything around it. To the casual observer, it was difficult to work out what the purpose of the building was. In fact, if it hadn't been for the three-metre-high letters spelling out the words 'Northern United', it could well have been a delivery depot for one of the supermarket chains or one of the big retailers.

Diane pulled up at the security gatehouse and showed her warrant card to the guard. The man in the gatehouse pointed the way to the visitor car park and she easily found a space that wasn't too far away from the door marked 'Reception'.

The reception itself was a bland functional area with two receptionists dressed in blue blazers sitting behind a laminated desk. Diane and Spencer introduced themselves and told one of them they had an appointment with Alan Fisher, the distribution manager. After being given a couple of badges with 'Visitor' printed on them, she and Spencer took their seats whilst they waited to be collected.

Diane noticed that one of the pamphlets on the table was entitled *Wilson and Bush, great people make a great company.* Imbra plc, the parent company of United Breweries, had recently been taken over by Wilson and Bush of America. This pamphlet, which contained photos of all the senior people in the group, had been produced to replace the old Imbra one.

"It's not surprising really," Diane thought to herself, "especially since so many of the old senior executives fell on their swords at the time of the takeover. If they hadn't produced it, nobody would have been able to put a face to who was shafting who in the organisation."

The two officers didn't have long to wait until Suzy, Alan Fisher's secretary, came to collect them. Alan's office was on the top floor and had a large glass window overlooking the warehouse. He was in his fifties with grey hair and a moustache, immaculately dressed in a pinstripe suit. He shook their hands and offered them some coffee.

Diane remembered that the coffee they'd given her on her previous visits to the company had been very good. So she gratefully accepted, as did Spencer, who secretly hoped they'd be offered biscuits as well.

"I understand this isn't the first time you've been to visit us, Inspector," said Mr Fisher by way of an opening.

"It's the first time I've been to this site though," Diane replied. "I did visit your old premises in Sheffield city centre earlier this year and I've also been to your head office in Burton upon Trent."

"I know a lot of people mourn the closure of the old brewery," Alan continued. "But this site far better suits our needs in the modern era. It is specifically laid out for modern distribution, whereas our old site was originally planned for horse-drawn drays. Here we are close to the M1, which is ideal for us, as all our beer is transported by road these days. We also operate on a 'just in time' basis. The beer arrives overnight and is loaded onto the drays. It's then distributed to our customers the following day. That way we keep our stock levels to a minimum and our best-before dates to a maximum, which is good for both our customers and for ourselves. New legislation dictates that we have to put best-before dates on all our beers nowadays. Life was a lot easier when the only thing we had to put on a keg was a gyle number."

"I don't have a clue what a gyle number is, Mr Fisher," said Diane.

"Sorry, Inspector," he replied, "it's easy to fall into the trap of using jargon when you've been working in the industry for as long as I have. You tend to forget that people who don't work for a brewery don't always understand what you're on about. A gyle is the unique number that we give to a brew."

"Thank you for explaining that, Mr Fisher," added Diane. "Please continue telling us about this site."

"This warehouse has got 25 purpose-built loading bays," he continued. "It makes it easier to load up our drays than if we had to use forklift trucks. Not only that, but we only need half the warehouse staff compared to the old site in order to run the place."

"Very efficient, I'm sure," replied Diane. "Can you tell me how many people transferred here from Sheffield?"

"Our Free and Tied Trade departments transferred in total. They are on the floor below, as is our telesales department, although most sales staff are new. We had to recruit them locally as many of the old telesales operators didn't want to make the move. Credit control is the only part of the old finance department to come here. That's because most of the finance jobs were centralised in Manchester when the Yorkshire Brewery region merged with Watson's of Manchester. About half of the credit controllers made the switch and about half are new recruits. They are on the ground floor along with our admin department, all of which are new apart from their manager."

"And what about the delivery and warehouse staff?" asked Diane.

"About two-thirds of the draymen made the transfer and just less than half the warehouse operators, which was ideal, being as though we only needed half the original number. In total, we've currently got 114 people working onsite, but that number is set to rise when our new bottling and canning plant opens next year."

"Really," said Diane, "I had no idea you were going to produce packaged beers here?"

"Yes, the warehouse here is pretty large, but the new bottling hall next door will be twice as big. It will replace four smaller bottling and canning lines elsewhere in the country and will satisfy all the company's packaged beer requirements."

At this point, Suzy reappeared with the coffee. Things had definitely changed at United Breweries and not for the better. The coffee now came from a machine in a little plastic cup. Mind you, they were soon extremely grateful that the cups were so small. The coffee was disgusting and had blobs of undissolved powdered milk floating on the surface. Diane tried to make them dissolve but only succeeded in chasing them around the top of her coffee with a small plastic stirrer.

"Anyway, Inspector, enough about us," said Alan after taking a sip from his red-hot coffee. "What can I do for you?"

"There's been a spate of robberies from pub tills reported to us recently," said Diane. "These robberies all have one thing in common. They occurred whilst one of your drays was delivering."

"And you think some of our draymen may be involved?"

"Not directly," Diane replied. "The thief is a man with thinning hair aged about forty. He arrives at the pub just before the dray gets there and waits until the publican goes into the cellar to check in the delivery. That's when he nips behind the bar and helps himself to the contents of the till, plus anything else he can lay his hands on. He always chooses deliveries that are taking place just before closing time, as that is when there will be the most money in the till. It's also when there is a good chance that there will be no other customers in the bar. What we were wondering is if one of your draymen could be tipping this man off about which pubs to target."

"He could just be following one of our drays," Alan Fisher replied.

"But that wouldn't explain how he always manages to get there before the dray."

"It would if he'd also followed them the previous week. You see all our deliveries are now made on a fixed run basis. As a result, each customer gets its delivery from the same crew at approximately the same time every week."

"Several of your customers have told me about your new fixed run system," said Diane

"In which case you'll know that all someone has to do is to follow a dray, see which pubs the crew deliver to just before closing time and then visit one of those pubs slightly earlier the following week."

In truth, neither Diane nor Spencer had realised just how easy the fixed run system made it to predict when a dray would arrive at an outlet.

What Alan Fisher was saying was perfectly feasible, but Diane's gut instinct still told her that somebody on the inside was tipping off the thief.

"Well, in order to rule out any of your draymen, we need to establish which crews delivered to the affected outlets," Diane explained to him and produced a list with the names of the six outlets on it.

Alan Fisher put his reading glasses on and examined the list.

"If you were hoping they had all been delivered by the same crew, then I'm afraid you are going to be disappointed,

Inspector," he announced. "Only two of these outlets are delivered from here. The other four are delivered from our satellite depot in Bakewell."

"A satellite depot? What's that?" asked Diane

"Let me explain," Alan Fisher continued. "We've always had delivery issues in the Peak District. Originally, our deliveries were made from Sheffield, and it took quite a long time for our drays to get there from the city centre. However, a number of our customers wanted an early morning drop, especially in the summertime when there were lots of tourists about. The main reason for this was that a dray turning up later than that was likely to have access problems, which would make it difficult for the crew to make the delivery. There might be cars parked in narrow streets, caravans blocking the road and that sort of thing. Customers who were affected by this problem just had to grin and bear it unless they were free-trade accounts. They could take their business elsewhere and, believe me, we lost a lot of accounts due to this issue back in those days."

"Yes, but you don't deliver out of Sheffield anymore. You deliver from here. Surely, that solved the problem for you."

"Not really. This depot is further away from the Peak District than the one that was in Sheffield. Not only that, but we also had to negotiate the traffic in Chesterfield in order to get there. We had another problem at the time. You see, back in 1970, Bakewell Town Council introduced a delivery restriction, whereby all vehicles that were delivering to outlets in the town centre had to be finished and gone by 8.30 in the morning. The Council introduced this by-law in order to counter congestion in the town centre when the tourists started arriving. This caused a major headache for us, as it usually took our drays about an hour to get to Bakewell from Sheffield. Since all our draymen started work at 7am, this only gave us a thirty-minute window in which to make all our Bakewell deliveries."

"Surely, there was a simple solution to your problem," said Diane. "You could have gotten some of your crews to start earlier."

"I can see that you've never had to negotiate with any shop stewards from the Transport and General Workers' Union, Inspector. They would have wanted too many concessions from us in return. That was why we decided to open a satellite depot on a small industrial estate in Bakewell instead. It might be called a satellite but it's actually a lock-up garage with one dray in it."

"I don't understand how it works," Diane interrupted.

"The lorry is loaded up with that day's deliveries during the early hours of the morning, once the trunkers have delivered to the depot. It's then driven to Bakewell where the driver leaves it in the lockup. At the same time, he collects the lorry full of empties that's been left there following the previous day's deliveries and drives it back to the main depot. Then at seven o'clock in the morning, two local draymen pick the new lorry up and begin their deliveries."

"And that solved the problem, did it?"

"The customers loved it and I'm not just talking about the customers with delivery restrictions. What they all really liked was the fact that the same crew delivered at virtually the same time every week. It was the forerunner of the fixed run system we use today. Of course, it was far more difficult to introduce fixed runs into a major depot like this one with 25 drays. It wasn't as flexible as the previous system, you see. But we are a customer-led business, Inspector, and we introduced it because our customers wanted us to."

"What a load of bullshit," Diane thought to herself. "He did it because it was the cheapest solution to his problem."

"Anyway, looking at your list, I can see that the pubs in Little Hucklow, Flagg, Wardlow and Wensley are all delivered by the Bakewell satellite whereas the other two are both delivered directly from here. The Nettle is one of Richardson and Adlen's drops and the Three Horseshoes is one of Ainsworth and Jones's, both of whom are new recruits who joined us here after our move. I would personally vouch for both crews. Their customer focus is excellent, far better than the militant sods they replaced."

"What about the satellite crew?" Spencer asked.

"Stenen and Hancock are the only permanent draymen at the Bakewell satellite. They've been with us since it was established, in fact, even longer in the case of Cec Stenen. We've never had a serious complaint about either of them. Furthermore, if you think there's a conspiracy going on here then let me tell you that Stenen and Hancock have never even met the other two crews. After all, why would they? They work out of different sites. In fact, neither Stenen nor Hancock have been to our new depot in Staveley yet."

"Thanks for that, Mr Fisher," said a disappointed Diane. "We may want to interview all three crews in order to see if they noticed anything when they were delivering to these pubs."

"That's not a problem, Inspector," replied Alan Fisher. "The best time would be 6.30 in the morning, both here and in Bakewell, just before the crews go out. Let me know when you want to see them, and I'll make sure they are available for you."

Diane thanked him, before she and Spencer shook his hand and made their way back to reception where they handed in their badges.

"Shit," said Diane once they were out of the building. "I was convinced we'd tie this one up today, Spencer. Why are things never that simple?"

"It's a good job they're not," replied Spencer. "If they were, then we wouldn't need as many police officers."

Chapter 7
Tuesday afternoon, April 12th, 1971

Penny and Alice weren't too impressed by the variety of the stalls selling goods at Flagg races. Most of them were selling country items such as wax jackets, flat caps and brown ladies' hats resplendent with pheasant feathers. There were also numerous pairs of corduroy and moleskin trousers, various items of clothing made from tweed, as well as any colour of wellington boots you wanted, just as long as they were green.

At one stage, the girls had a narrow escape as they spotted Mervyn examining a rack of fleeces. They hid behind a row of quilted jackets until he eventually disappeared.

"That was close," said Alice trying hard not to giggle. But Penny wasn't listening.

"Well, this goes a long way to explain why everybody dresses the same around here," she exclaimed. "They must shop for clothes at the races every year. It's probably the only occasion during the year when they all get away from their farms."

However, it wasn't just stalls selling clothes that were there that day. There were also a few vans selling food, including one that tried optimistically to sell ice cream.

"If only the races had been a day earlier, he would be doing a roaring trade," Penny thought to herself.

Both of the girls were hungry, so they decided to buy a pork cob with stuffing and apple sauce from one of the vans, along with hot Bovril in a paper cup.

"Where's the loo?" asked Penny when they had finished.

"I think we passed it on the way in," replied Alice.

"Right, let's meet back here in a little while," said Penny as the two girls left Bung and Bonar and went in search of the toilet.

It was twenty minutes before they returned, and Penny was fuming.

"What's the betting that the organising committee for this race meeting doesn't have any women on it," she fumed. "That's why you can walk straight into the gents but if you're a woman, you have to queue for nearly half an hour before you can get into the ladies."

After she had calmed down a bit, Bung suggested they go over to the parade rink to look at the runners and riders in the first race. But when they got there, they were surprised to discover there were no horses to be seen.

"I wonder where they are?" he said with a bemused look on his face. "The first race starts in less than fifteen minutes."

After looking at his programme, he realised why there were no horses.

"Ah, that explains it," he said. "The first race is a traditional point-to-point race. It starts in Flagg village one and a half miles away and ends on the racecourse. The riders are free to take any route they want."

"I presume that's why it was called a point-to-point race in the first place," said Penny.

"You're absolutely right," Bung replied. "Point-to-point races got their name because the horses didn't use to race on a circuit, but between two points on a map. However, that wasn't particularly interesting for the spectators, which is why most changed to the circuit racing we see today. It's far better for the crowd, you see. I'm pretty sure that Flagg is the only race meeting to keep the tradition alive."

Changing the subject, he asked, "Have you girls decided which horse you're going to bet on?"

"Not yet," said Penny.

"Well, study the form before placing your bet. You've got the choice of either placing it with one of the bookmakers or with the Tote."

"What's the difference?" asked Alice.

"With the bookmakers, they write the odds on their board and those are the odds you get. With the Tote, you don't know what you're going to win until the race is over. That's because what the Tote pays out is proportional to the amount in bets that they've taken. Sometimes that can work to your advantage and sometimes it can work against you. One other thing is that a Bookmaker keeps his profit whereas the Tote's profits all go to the race organisers."

"In which case, I think I'll bet on the Tote," said Alice.

"And so will I," added Alice.

The girls headed towards the Tote, whilst the boys went to look at the bookmakers' odds. The marquee housing the Tote had four windows in it. Three of the windows had '£1 bets' written above them and had massive queues whilst the other said '£5 bets' and had no one waiting.

The girls decided a £1 bet was enough for them and went to stand in one of the queues. Fortunately, the queue moved pretty quickly and soon there was only one person between them and the window. He was a large farmer dressed in the mandatory tweed jacket and moleskin trousers. Penny and Alice intended to pay particular attention to what he said, as neither of them had ever bet on a horse race before and didn't really know what to do.

"A pound to win on Likely Lad and ten bob each way on Houston Flyer," said the man who then produced the largest wedge of cash either girl had ever seen. Decimalisation may have taken place two months previously, but it had yet to reach the farming community in the High Peak. The farmer peeled off a £5 note and gave it to the lady on the other side of the window. She gave him a betting slip in turn and £3 in change.

Neither girl knew what a bet each way meant. So they both placed a single bet on a horse for a win.

When they returned to where the boys were standing, Bung asked them which horse they had bet on.

"I've placed a £1 bet on Pretty Penny," replied Penny.

"I wonder why you chose that horse?" said Bung sarcastically.

"And I've picked Wonderland Wish," said Alice. "You get it don't you? Alice in Wonderland?"

"Jesus," said Bung whilst looking to the heavens. "The first rule of betting is never back a horse because of its name. However, there is an additional rule for betting at Flagg races. That's because each race only has two good horses in it. The rest of them are just there to make up the numbers. As a result, whenever you place a bet at Flagg you should only ever bet on one of the favourites."

"Outsiders can sometimes win, though," said Alice. "My mum won £200 on Foinavon when it came in at a hundred to one."

"That was in the Grand National," replied Bung. "And it only won because all the other horses fell. This is Flagg. Things are slightly different here. Pretty Penny has no chance of winning as the jockey is a woman riding sidesaddle. As for Wonderland Wish, it should be renamed 'I wonder how it will get to the finish' as it is ridden by Ken Astle, a fat farmer from Great Longstone. He's giving away 48 pounds. In other words, his horse is carrying the equivalent of one and a half jockeys on its back."

"How do you know all this?" asked Penny.

"Because I've read the form guide in the programme," Bung replied. "There are only two horses that can win this race and they are Houston Flyer and Likely Lad and we got 7 to 2 and 4 to 1 on them from Honest Sid Roberts, the third bookmaker from the left over there."

"Let me get this straight," said Penny, who was beginning to get the hang of it. "If you placed a one pound bet on Likely Lad and it won, you'd get four pounds back. Am I right?"

"Plus you'd get your stake back, so you'd get five pounds back in total," Bung explained.

"So a one pound bet on Houston Flyer would net you four pounds fifty?"

"Provided it won, yes."

"What's an each way bet?" asked Alice.

"That's where your bet is split. A bet of a pound each way will cost you two pounds. One pound is bet on the horse coming first. The other pound pays out if the horse is placed."

"What does placed mean?" she asked

"Jesus Christ, you don't know much about betting, do you?"

It was obvious that Bung was getting frustrated.

"I'm not going to explain it to you in minute detail because it depends on the number of horses taking part. But since all the races at this meeting have between twelve and fifteen runners in them, it means you'll get paid out if the horse finishes in the top three. But you'll only receive a quarter of what you would have gotten if the horse had won."

Alice wasn't completely clear about all the intricacies involved in each way betting. But she decided that she'd better leave it for now, especially since the race was about to start.

They wandered over to a small hill above the finish line from where they had a good view of the race. Penny and Bung were hand-in-hand. Alice was keeping a healthy distance from Bonar.

Penny could see what Bung had meant when he'd said that the traditional point-to-point races weren't particularly interesting for the spectators. She could barely see the horses as they set off, as they were so far away. There was no way she could tell which one was winning. Things became clearer, though, as the horses drew nearer.

The jumps were all made of dry stone walls apart from the last one, which was on the racecourse itself and was a proper fence made from brush wood.

It is one thing to jump fences made from brush wood and quite another to jump drystone walls that don't give an inch if you hit them. It was too much for Wonderland Wish with his enormous load and he refused half-way between the village and the finish line.

Of those that did manage to finish, Pretty Penny came last some four minutes behind the eventual winner Likely Lad. Mind you, at least she finished, which was more than Houston Flyer did. He fell at the last fence whilst contesting the lead with Likely Lad.

"That's £5 we'll get back," announced Bung. "We had two £1 bets on both the favourites. In total, we're £3 up."

From then on, the girls decided to follow the boys by betting on the same horses as them. They were rewarded straight away as Frank Hallsworth won the second race on the favourite, Dave's Dash.

"What's the betting his parents named the horse after his brother?" said Alice.

"In which case, they should have called it Dave's Daft rather than Dave's Dash," announced Penny.

"Don't speak so loudly, Pen," said Alice as she looked around. "Dave's parents might overhear us again."

That didn't stop the two of them from giggling, though.

The rest of the meeting saw win after win for the four of them. Mind you, in each case the amount of money they got back was relatively small. In the remaining five races, they had four winners and both girls ended the day £7 up.

"I like horse racing," announced Penny. "I think I'll come again."

"You know, winning is the worst thing you can do at your first race meeting," said Bung. "It is a lot easier to pick winners at Flagg than it is elsewhere, and the Flagg meeting only happens once a year. Don't go thinking it's always as easy as it is here. Remember there's only one group of people who win all the time at race meetings, and they're called bookmakers."

"And there endeth today's lesson," replied Penny sarcastically.

After collecting their winnings from the last race, they wandered back to the Land Rover where they noted that Bung's prediction was coming true. Several of the two-wheel drive vehicles were going nowhere as their wheels spun around in the mud. Others were waiting to be pulled out of the field by tractors.

There was no such problem for the Land Rover, however, and, as a result, they were soon on the tarmac road heading home.

"Do you don't mind if we go via Monsal Head?" asked Bung.

"Go any way you want to," Penny replied.

Monsal Head was a well-known Derbyshire beauty spot, popular with courting couples, which Penny was fully aware of, but Alice was not.

When they arrived, the view wasn't at its best. It hadn't snowed again since they'd been in the beer tent, but it was still a grey overcast day. You could still see how magnificent it must be in the summer with Monsal Dale and the old railway viaduct laid out before them.

"My dad used to bring us here to see the trains when we were boys," said Bung. "Barbara Castle closed it down three years ago, another nail in the coffin for the countryside, I'm afraid."

Then turning to Alice, he said, "You don't mind if Bonar and Penny swap places, do you?"

"No," she replied a little hesitantly.

Alice was surprised by Bung's request and wondered why he wanted them to swap seats. Mind you, she didn't have long to wait and suddenly she realised how innocent she'd been as Bung and Penny started snogging.

However, worse was to come, because it was at that moment that Bonar started to kiss her. She felt pressurised into kissing him back even though she didn't really want to. Then things got even worse when she suddenly felt his hand on her breast.

"No, you don't," she shouted as she went to slap his hand away.

But she'd misjudged her stroke and her hand ended up hitting the lump in his lap instead.

"Oh no," she thought to herself. "Bonar's got a boner."

Chapter 8
Friday afternoon, December 15th, 1978

"Shit," said Diane once again as soon as she and Spencer were back in the car heading towards Chesterfield. "It serves me right for assuming that a drayman was responsible for these robberies. You know, I was so convinced that one of them was involved, I forgot to look at other possibilities."

"Perhaps it is just like Alan Fisher says it is," replied Spencer. "In other words it's somebody who just follows a dray in order to decide which pubs to target the following week."

"In which case, why are only deliveries made by Northern United involved?"

"Maybe they're the only brewery who operate fixed runs," suggested Spencer.

"Or maybe somebody who works for Northern United is telling our thief which pubs to target," replied Diane. "After all, it could be anyone who knows about the fixed run system. It doesn't necessarily have to be a drayman. That thought was only put into my head by Ian Garvey of the Three Horseshoes, when he told me that the draymen were notorious for stealing. Thinking about it, though, Northern United got rid of most of their problem draymen when they moved sites. So maybe it isn't one of them. Maybe it's another employee?"

"It could be," replied Spencer. "The entire site in Staveley knows about the fixed runs, not to mention any former employees. But then again, it could just be somebody following a dray. He could have heard about the fixed runs from a publican and decided it was a golden opportunity for him to get away with daylight robbery."

"Okay, let's see what our two photofit artists have come up with. If we don't recognise the culprit, let's get the team to interview the draymen on Monday morning."

During her last major investigation Diane had been given temporary command of a team of five additional officers. One of them, Constable Claire Adcock, had been on secondment from uniform. She had returned to her normal role as soon as the investigation was completed. The others, however, were all detectives. Diane's boss, Superintendent Barker, had been so impressed that three murders had been solved, he'd decided to keep the team together for future operations.

That said, DS Webb had retired shortly afterwards and, after passing his sergeants' exam, Alan Bateman had been promoted to take his place, much to the annoyance of his colleague Colin Wallace. Webb's retirement and Bateman's promotion had meant there was now a vacancy in the team for a detective constable and Diane was instrumental in ensuring that Claire Adcock fulfilled her dream of joining CID. The final member of the team was DC Nigel Rose who was teamed up with DC Adcock.

When they got back to the station in Beetwell Street, the two photofits were waiting for them. Diane had a look at them.

"Well, you can just about tell they are the same person," she said. "But the one I'm going to choose is the one by Mr Scott from the Nettle. He's the only person to have seen our suspect on three separate occasions and he's also the only person who says he's good at remembering faces."

"Choose it for what?" asked Spencer.

"For a 'wanted dead or alive poster'," Diane replied.

Diane wasn't really going to produce a wanted poster, of course. That was just her idea of a joke. What she really needed the photo for was to make a flyer she could send out to pubs in the area.

"Out of the six pubs he's visited so far," she continued, "he's visited one on three occasions and three on two occasions. So there's every chance he will do the same again in the future. Therefore, if we mailshot all the rural pubs in North Derbyshire with this photofit, we can ask anyone who sees him to phone us. Maybe, just maybe, we can lie in wait for him on that pub's next delivery date. It's a chance for us to get one step ahead of him."

"It sounds like a good plan to me, ma'am," Spencer replied.

The rest of the day was spent producing the mailshot, which was posted out to all the country pubs in the area, 121 of them in total. Not all of these would be customers of Northern United, but Diane had decided it was easier to do a blanket hit rather than run the risk of missing a crucial one off the list.

By the time her team had finished franking all the flyers and putting them in the post, it was gone five o'clock and time for them all to go home. But before Spencer left for the night, he approached Diane.

"I hope you enjoy your date tonight, ma'am," he said. "Mind you, I don't want to come in on Monday morning only to discover you've gone all religious and have joined a convent."

"No fear of that, Spencer," Diane replied. "I've got enough bad habits as it is. I've no desire to wear one."

"Well, enjoy your evening with Nick the Dick and remember, no sex. Mind you, as a former missionary, at least he'd get the position right."

Spencer left the room, but not before Diane had thrown her eraser at him.

About fifteen minutes later, she went home herself. She had decided to make an effort that evening and, after having a shower, she spent half an hour deciding what to wear. Should she dress to impress, or should she go casual? In the end, she remembered what Nick had said about wearing jeans and a T-shirt on Christmas Day and decided to wear a new pair of camel slacks and a blouse she'd recently bought from C & A in Sheffield. After deciding it was too cold to go outside dressed in only a blouse, she opted for a red cardigan as well.

"God, I look like a frump," Diane said to herself, before deciding to start again.

In the end, she plumped for a pair of Levi's with a pink striped shirt and a pink jacket.

"That's better," she thought to herself "just the right mix between casual and smart."

Next, she started on her make-up. She didn't want to look as if she'd made too much of an effort. That might give the impression that she was desperate. But at 33 years of age, she was acutely aware that some form of cosmetic enhancement was necessary if she was to look her best. In the end, she was pretty pleased with the results, especially now that she'd covered up the laughter lines around her eyes. Okay, she could have spent another hour or two perfecting the look, but she didn't have the time. Finally, she dabbed some of her favourite perfume, L'Air du Temps by Nina Ricci in a few spots, and was good to go.

"I'll knock him dead," she said as she gave herself one final look in the mirror.

Her final act before leaving was to take a bottle of Piat D'Or white wine from the fridge.

The vicarage was a massive house, far too large for a single man to live in and about four times the size of Diane's little semi. It was built during the age when vicars were expected to have large families and reminded Diane of the parsonage at Howarth were the Brontë sisters had grown up. She'd visited it on a school trip to Yorkshire when she was sixteen. It was still the furthest north she'd ever been.

She rang the doorbell.

"Look at you," said Nick as he opened the door and planted a kiss on her cheek. "You're looking absolutely gorgeous."

He was dressed in black trousers and a black polo-neck sweater that made him look a bit like the Milk Tray man from the TV advert. Well, he would have done if it hadn't been for the apron he was wearing with the words 'God sends meat. The devil sends cooks' written on it.

"I've brought a bottle of wine," Diane announced as she came through the door. "I didn't know if you preferred red or white."

"White is absolutely fine. Red always reminds me of Holy Communion. Let me put it in the fridge. I'm afraid I've already helped myself to a glass of Blue Nun. I like to have one whilst I'm cooking. Will you join me?"

"Is the Pope Catholic?" Diane replied, instantly regretting making such a crass comment.

Nick didn't appear to mind though, as he poured some wine into a Waterford Crystal glass for her.

"You've got a really nice place here," Diane said. "Do you look after it all yourself?"

"I'll let you into a little secret. I've got Mrs Williams who comes in five days a week and tidies for me. She also does my washing and cooking. Then there's Mr Williams who does my gardening. As you can see, I don't really have to do anything for myself except look after my flock."

"So how come you're cooking tonight, then?"

"Well, I've got two days a week when I have to fend for myself. Besides which, I believe every man should have at least one dish that he can make. Mine just happens to be *coq au vin*."

The food was actually very good, and the conversation was even better. Diane reminisced about growing up in Guildford as an only child with her over-protective parents. In reaction to their cautiousness, she'd gone a bit wild during her university days, taking part in several student demos and briefly joining the Communist Party. That was probably why most of her friends had been completely astonished when she'd decided to join the police force. They had all assumed that she'd do a law conversion once she'd graduated and then join Ricky as a criminal lawyer.

Nick's university days, in comparison, seemed a pretty tame affair. He hadn't even smoked a joint.

"You must be the only student who went to university in the 1960s who can claim that," she teased him.

Nick's memories of his time in Botswana seemed far more interesting to Diane than his life at university. He'd combined running a church with teaching duties. That said, he still had time for photographing the wildlife.

As the evening went on, Diane couldn't help but wonder if he wanted to spend the night with her. So far, they hadn't even kissed, well, not a proper kiss anyway. You could hardly count the peck he'd given her on her cheek when she arrived. Diane had consumed two-thirds of a bottle of wine, and she considered her options. Either she could spend the night in the vicarage, or she could walk home, which would take her at least three-quarters of an hour, or she could take the risk and drive.

She decided to press the matter.

"You can kiss me, you know," she whispered. "I won't bite, I haven't even brought my handcuffs and truncheon with me."

"That's a shame," he replied as he leant across and kissed her. The kiss went on for ages and got more and more frantic until eventually they broke away from each other.

"I would have kissed you as soon as you came through the front door," he panted. "Only, I have to be careful in my position. After all, women often pour their hearts out to me and it would be easy for me to get the wrong idea."

Diane tried to get the thought of Spencer's throwaway comment about the missionary position out of her head.

"You haven't got the wrong idea," she said whilst undoing her shirt to reveal her brand-new Marks and Spencer bra underneath.

It was her best one and she was glad she'd decided to put it on rather than one of her old ones that had gone grey in the wash.

"Let's go up to the bedroom," said Nick, taking her hand and leading her upstairs.

After kissing her once more he added, "You go and get into bed. I'll be with you in a minute. There's something I've got to do first."

"You're not going to do the washing up are you?" joked Diane.

"You'll see," he replied.

Diane stripped off and got in between the sheets.

A few minutes later, he reappeared completely naked with a packet of condoms in one hand and a bottle of wine in the other.

"What would you like, cock or *vin*?" he asked. "I told you that they were my speciality."

Diane sat up and let the bed sheet fall away revealing her naked breasts.

"Can I be greedy?" she said. "Can I have both please?"

Chapter 9
Tuesday evening, April 12th, 1971

"I don't know if I want to go to the pub tonight," said Alice.

Penny and Alice were back in the dormitory at the youth hostel and Penny was putting her make-up on.

"But Bung said that the night in the pub following Flagg races was one of the best nights of the year," protested Penny. "What do you mean, you don't want to go?"

"There's something not quite right about Bung and Bonar," said Alice. "Bung isn't too bad, I suppose, but Bonar puts the willies up me."

"He'd like to, I can tell you that much," Penny replied with a smile on her face. "Anyway, that didn't stop you from snogging him in the back of the Land Rover earlier."

"Yes, but he wanted to go much further, and I don't even like him. He's not my type. He's not exactly what you would call a conversationalist, is he? He very rarely says anything. It's Bung who does all the talking."

"I'm sure I can think of a way to shut Bung up," added Penny.

"I bet you can, Pen," Alice continued. "All I'm saying is that I don't fancy Bonar and I don't want to spend the evening with him. I'm beginning to regret coming here. The weather's crap, the warden's a pervert and the choice of boys is absolutely pathetic. No wonder this hostel is less than half full even though it's still the Easter holidays."

Alice was referring to the fact that the group of fifteen-year-old boys had moved on to the hostel in Castleton and nobody had moved into the men's dorm to replace them. As a result, the only residents, other than Penny and Alice, were the two German girls and the two middle-aged men.

"Can I just remind you that it was you who booked this hostel?" said Penny indignantly. "Anyway, I'm going to the pub. You can stay here with Merv the Perv, Valkyrie and Brunhilda and the two extras from *Dad's Army* or you can come with me."

Put like that, Alice didn't really have a choice, which is why, at half past seven she found herself in the bar of the Three Tuns alongside her friend.

Bung had been correct. The bar was absolutely heaving. In fact, it was just as if the whole beer tent at Flagg races had decamped to Bleckley with the odd tourist thrown in for good luck.

Alice noticed that Hugh Stanton was in the bar, still drinking as heavily as he had been all day. He was slurring his speech, banging into people and basically being a pain in the arse. She secretly prayed that he wouldn't come over to where they were sitting.

The pub was doing a fair amount of food as witnessed by a flustered looking Helen Yates, Matt's wife. She would occasionally appear from the kitchen holding basket meals in her hands, shouting out "one chicken and chips" and "two scampi and chips" to the expectant diners.

"We've saved some seats for you," yelled Bung from the other side of the room and, after getting served, the two girls made their way over to them.

Alice was embarrassed that Mr and Mrs Hallsworth were sitting at the next table along with Daft Dave and another lad who she presumed was Frank, their other son. Frank was nothing like Dave. He was quite good-looking and smelt of

Brut aftershave rather than horse piss. He smiled at her as she sat down next to him.

"Perhaps tonight isn't going to be such a chore after all," she thought to herself.

Pretty soon, it was Penny's turn to be embarrassed as Daft Dave started barking at her.

"That's enough, Dave," said Frank who apologised to Penny on his brother's behalf. He introduced himself to them.

"I'm Frank Hallsworth," he said, "Dave's older brother."

"You were riding today, weren't you?" Alice replied. "I won £2.50 when you came first in the second race."

"That's right, I was riding Dave's Dash, one of Dad's horses. Our family owns the riding stables across the road and Dave and I supplement our income from the stables by delivering coal in the winter."

Alice and Frank continued their conversation for the next hour and a half. By this time, Frank's parents and brother had left and Bonar was becoming annoyed about being snubbed.

Penny was also getting on well with Bung. At one point, the two of them had popped outside for some 'fresh air' and, when they returned, Penny was buttoning up her blouse.

"No prizes for guessing what you two have been up to," whispered Alice in Penny's ear.

"Well, you seem to be getting on just fine with the galloping coalman over there," came the reply. "Anyway, Bung told me not to go out alone in case the beast gets me and drags me off to its lair."

"What on earth is the beast?" asked Alice.

"Tell her, Bung," replied Penny.

"You haven't been spinning her that load of old crap, have you, Bung?" cut in Frank.

"It's not a load of old crap, it's the truth," protested Bung. "It's the Beast of Bleckley, a massive wolf which escaped whilst being transported to the zoo at Riber Castle. It now lives on Bleckley Moor. Many attempts have been made to catch it, but nobody knows where its lair is. It regularly comes down to the village for food. We've lost at least twelve sheep over the past few years, their throats ripped out by the beast."

"What a load of rubbish," commented Frank. "Your sheep have all been killed either by foxes or by the dogs of city folks who haven't got the common sense to keep them on a lead."

"But it's not just sheep that the beast is after," Bung continued, "because his favourite meal is human flesh."

"What a load of old tosh," remarked Frank.

But Bung was unperturbed by his interruption and continued dramatically.

"Firstly, there was a potholer who reckoned he'd discovered the entrance to a massive cavern complex nearby. He was going to announce his discovery to the world, but before he could do that he was attacked by the beast and dragged off to its lair."

"What actually happened is that this guy probably became trapped in one of the caves he was exploring," added Frank. "And because he was so secretive about where the new caverns were, nobody knew where to find him. Anyway, that was eight years ago. Tell me, how old is this wolf supposed to be, Bung?"

Bung just ignored his question and continued.

"Then three years ago, the body of a council workman was discovered nearby. He'd been savaged by the beast."

"No, he hadn't, he'd been savaged by a couple of pit bulls," Frank interrupted. "They belonged to a man who was camping in Hugh Stanton's field. It made the TV news. The man was convicted of keeping dangerous dogs and received a suspended sentence. In fact, the only reason he escaped prison was because someone had untied the dogs and it was argued in court that he couldn't be expected to control them because of this. The pit bulls were subsequently put down."

"Ah, but the man concerned always protested the dogs' innocence. He claimed they were family pets, particularly good with children and they were more likely to lick someone to death than to savage them."

"Which is why one of them bit a police officer who was investigating. Honestly, Bung, you do talk a load of bullshit sometimes."

"Then there was Hugh Stanton's son who wandered off one day never to be seen again."

"He wandered off because he'd had enough of his old man," interrupted Frank again. "He wanted to get as far away from him as possible and didn't want him to know where he was. He's living in Kent according to Mildred Brown at the post office in Eyam."

"The following year, his mother disappeared as well."

"But we all know what happened to her," Frank protested. "Old Hugh had got pissed up once too often. She'd had enough of his drunken beatings, which was why she upped and left him, just like her son. She didn't want to be found either. She probably went back to Ireland where she came from. Either that or she's down in Kent living with her son."

"All I'm saying is that, with one death and three people disappearing in suspicious circumstances, I wouldn't venture out alone after dark around here."

"Which presumably is why you let Alice and me walk back alone to the youth hostel last night," added Penny sarcastically.

"Ah, but it was raining last night," Bung replied. "The beast never ventures out when it's raining. He stays in his lair. We knew you'd be safe, didn't we, Bonar?"

His brother started nodding.

"Do you know what?" said Penny. "I think you're making this up as you go along. You told us about Hugh Stanton's wife and son earlier today and you just said they'd left him. You never mentioned a beast."

"I didn't want to frighten you," Bung protested. "It's the truth, scouts' honour, and furthermore I've seen the beast. He was by the stone circle on Bleckley Moor, howling his head off and guess what? It was a full moon that night."

"Okay, Bung," said Frank, "I think you've said enough. As for not wanting to frighten anyone, well, that's a load of crap and you know it is. Otherwise, why mention it this evening? Can we just change the subject, please?"

As Frank was speaking, a man with a dog entered the pub. He was dressed in a wax jacket and a pair of green wellies. He was in his early forties and had a guarded look about him.

Despite his dress, it was obvious that he wasn't a farmer. For a start, he didn't have the ruddy cheeks of someone who spends all his days outdoors.

"Ay up, that's a rarity," said Bung. "It's not every day that James Hargreaves comes into the pub. You're honoured, girls. That means you've now met everybody who lives in the village, apart from Matt and Helen's girls."

"That's hardly an achievement," commented Alice. "This place only has a population of fifteen, it's not like saying we've met the entire population of Manchester, is it?"

"Anyway, we're in for some fun now," said Bung. "Watch this."

Hugh Stanton had started to lurch over to where James Hargreaves was standing. He was swearing and pointing his finger at him. But before he could reach him, Matt had moved out from behind the bar and intercepted the staggering local drunk.

"Come on, Hugh, I think you've had enough," he said whilst putting a hand on Hugh's shoulder. "Isn't it about time you went home?"

Hugh removed Matt's hand with an angry swipe and staggered backwards, before falling and sending a table full of glasses flying in the process.

"Bloody hell, Hugh," said Matt who tried to pick him up.

But Hugh had badly cut his hand and after wrapping a towel around it and sitting him in a chair, Matt phoned for an ambulance. Meanwhile, Helen appeared with a dustpan and brush and started to clear up the broken glass.

"See, I told you we were in for some fun," said Bung. "You can probably tell that Hugh and James don't exactly get on."

"Does anybody get on with Hugh?" Alice asked. "He looks like a complete tosser to me."

"No, but not many of them have come to blows with him," Bung continued. "James accused Hugh of poisoning his last dog by leaving meat laced with rat poison outside one of his fields. Hugh said he'd done it in order to poison whatever was killing his sheep. James said Hugh was irresponsible. That was when Hugh called James an outsider, saying, 'there's a lot you need to learn about living in the country sonny'. That riled James and he shouted back 'so, that's why it's called the country, is it? I always wondered. Now I know it's because it's got cunts like you living in it'."

"There's no need to use words like that, Bung," said Frank. "There are ladies present."

"I was just painting a picture," Bung replied before continuing. "Now, Hugh's a big bloke, handy with his fists and not used to being spoken to like that and he went to hit poor James. Well, that was what he tried to do, only James floored him with a single punch. It all happened right here in this bar. I've never seen anything like it. It was the most entertainment we've had around here in years."

"Why didn't Matt bar them both?" asked Alice.

"Because he's not daft. As you've already pointed out, there are only fifteen people living in this village. He'd be cutting off his nose to spite his face if he banned the two of them, especially when one of them is a big drinker like Hugh Stanton."

Whilst Bung was telling them about James Hargreaves, Penny and Alice's eyes were transfixed on him. He didn't look like the type of man who'd get into a fight in the local pub. He looked more like the type of man who would shy away from violence. However, looks can often be deceiving.

After paying for his drink, he went and stood by himself in a corner of the bar. Alice remembered he was an author and she wondered what type of books he wrote in an isolated village like Bleckley.

"Is he a novelist or does he write cookery books?" she asked Bung.

"I'm told he writes novels about the Cold War," he replied. "He's supposedly outstanding in his field."

"A bit like you then," added Penny. "I heard someone say that you were outstanding in your field as well. I presumed they meant the one at the back of your farmhouse."

Unfortunately for Penny, her comment went straight over Bung's head.

"He used to be a sergeant in the army before he came here," Bung continued. "So he's gone from being the new John Le Mesurier to the new John le Carré, if you get my drift."

Alice looked across to where James Hargreaves had been standing. But he wasn't there anymore. He'd obviously finished his drink and had left without anyone noticing.

"I'm afraid I've got to love you and leave you," Frank said.

"What? So soon?" said Alice, who was obviously disappointed. "Penny and I don't have to be back for another half an hour yet."

"I'm afraid so," Frank replied. "I promised Mum and Dad I'd be back by half past nine as one of our mares is giving birth and it's my turn to keep an eye on her. Dave could do it, of course, only Mum doesn't trust him."

"How many horses do you have at the stables?" asked Alice.

"Just eight at the moment," Frank replied. "Four belong to us and the other four are stabled on behalf of other owners."

"I had a go at riding when I was about twelve, but I never kept it up," commented Alice.

"Well, why don't I give both of you a lesson? We've got a couple of really placid horses that would be ideal. Don't worry about riding hats as we've got plenty at the stables."

"That sounds really great. Are you up for it, Penny?"

"Hey, I'm easy," Penny replied.

"That's why I like you," commented Bung, causing Penny to give him a really hard slap on his leg.

"Let's make it sometime tomorrow then," added Frank. "What time do you want to come around?"

"Well, we are going for a walk in the morning, as we didn't go for one today," said Alice. "Would it be possible to do it tomorrow afternoon, say after three o'clock?"

"No problem," Frank replied before getting up. "Let's make it half past three, then. Now, if you will excuse me, I really must be going."

Frank downed his pint and left.

"You know the weather forecast for tomorrow is really bad again," said Bung. "If I were you, I'd give up on the idea of going for a walk. Why don't you come to our farm, and I'll show you around instead? We've got some newborn lambs and some baby calves in one of the barns. We are having to hand-rear them. Why don't you come over and help me feed them?"

"It's very kind of you to ask, but we came here with the intention of going walking," Alice replied. "And so far, the only walking we've done is between the bus stop and the village."

"Oh, go on, Alice," said Penny. "It will be fun and if the weather is as bad tomorrow as it was today, it will be pretty miserable to go for a walk."

But Alice had made up her mind and nothing Penny could say was going to convince her to change it.

It was now a quarter to ten and, not wishing to cut it as fine as the previous night, the girls decided it was time to leave.

Well, that was why Alice decided to leave. Penny wanted to leave because it gave her fifteen minutes of snogging time with Bung.

Now that his rival had left, Bonar thought he'd have another go at Alice and tried putting his arm around her. However, it wasn't his lucky day as she just shrugged him off.

As soon as they got back to the hostel, Alice said she would see Penny in the dormitory, and she went inside leaving Bung and Penny outside. Meanwhile, Bonar was hanging around the front of the hostel acting like the proverbial spare prick at a wedding.

As she entered the youth hostel, Alice was shocked to see Mervyn sat in the lounge with the two German girls. All three of them were in a state of semi-undress.

"I'm just teaching Claudia and Hanna some traditional English games," said Mervyn. "We're currently playing strip poker. Do you want to join in?"

Alice hurried past them into the dormitory without saying a word.

"Bloody hell," she thought to herself. "Penny didn't know how right she'd been when she told Mervyn that he wouldn't believe some of the things the two German girls got up to."

Meanwhile, Bung and Penny were kissing in the entrance to the youth hostel. Bung had his hand inside Penny's bra and was feeling her left breast.

He suddenly stepped away from her and said, "What's the matter with Alice? It will be really fun at the farm tomorrow. If she doesn't want to come, why don't you come by yourself?"

"A bit like you're going to do tonight, you mean?" Penny replied with a wry smile on her face.

"That's as maybe, but rest assured it will be you I'm thinking of whilst I'm pulling my plonker," Bung replied.

"Leave it with me," said Penny. "I'll speak to her in the morning. I'll try to convince her to come."

"And I'll make you come tomorrow," he replied before kissing her again.

"But not tonight," said Penny as she broke away from him. "It's nearly ten o'clock and I've got to be back inside."

"And tomorrow I'll be inside you," Bung thought to himself as she closed the door.

Chapter 10
Tuesday morning, December 19th, 1978

"Guv, we've got a response to our mailshot."

It was Alan Bateman calling across the room. He'd acquired the annoying habit of referring to Diane as guv rather than ma'am after being promoted to sergeant. She'd told him off about it before, but he appeared to take no notice. That was why she'd made a note to raise it at his annual appraisal, which was due in January.

The previous day, he and DC Colin Wallace had visited Bakewell in order to interview Stenen and Hancock. At the same time, Nigel Rose and Claire Adcock had been to Staveley to speak to Richardson, Adlen, Ainsworth and Jones, the other four draymen who'd been delivering when the robberies had taken place. However, none of the crews had noticed anything untoward. Therefore, the news that a licensee had responded to Diane's 'wanted dead or alive' poster had come as a welcome potential breakthrough.

"I've just taken a call from a Matthew Yates," Alan continued. "He's the licensee of the Three Tuns in Bleckley, and he reckons our suspect paid him a visit yesterday. He didn't think anything about it at the time. It was only later when he opened his post and read our mailshot that he realised it was our man. He said our suspect arrived at 2.30, had half a pint and left. He'd got a party in from the Chesterfield Ramblers

Association at the time, so he didn't really notice too much about him. In fact, he was so busy he even had to call his wife from the kitchen to see the delivery in."

"That sounds like just the news we've been waiting for," Diane announced. "Spencer, grab your coat. We are going to pay Mr Yates a visit."

The journey took a little over half an hour going through Baslow, Calver and Stoney Middleton before they turned off the A623 towards Eyam.

"I never asked you how you got on the other day with Nick the Dick," said Spencer as they headed up the hill that led to the village of Eyam.

"Oh, you know, it was pretty good. We sang a few hymns and took Holy Communion together."

"So, Nick the Dick dipped his wick, did he?"

"Honestly, Spencer, I don't know why I tolerate you," Diane scowled. "I bet you've been waiting all morning with bated breath to say that"

"Perhaps it's because I'm the older brother you never had, ma'am."

"No, Spencer, you're more like the itchy arse that I need to scratch."

They carried on through Eyam and began the climb up to Bleckley.

"The Three Tuns is one of my favourite pubs in Derbyshire," said Spencer as they were getting closer. "It's quite difficult to get to, especially in the winter. It's really high up, the highest pub in the county, and one of the highest in England. It used to be on a drovers' road between Great Hucklow and Grindleford. But the Grindleford section of the road was closed years ago. The only way to get to it nowadays is to climb up from Eyam or Foolow or come cross-country from Great Hucklow."

"From the sound of it, I'm surprised they get any customers," added Diane.

"Well, it's worth it as the views are spectacular and the pub itself is really great with oak beams and horse brasses. It's a quintessentially English pub, which is why it gets so busy in the summertime, even though it is off the beaten track."

"You've obviously got a great future writing guide-books when you finally decide it's time to hang up your truncheon," replied Diane.

A few minutes later, Diane and Spencer arrived at the Three Tuns and Diane parked her car across the road from the pub. Unfortunately, she couldn't appreciate the view. It was too misty that day. But she could see what Spencer had meant about the pub itself. It was absolutely beautiful, especially as it was festooned with Christmas lights and had no fewer than three external Christmas trees.

It was just past eleven o'clock in the morning and the pub wasn't open yet. The door wasn't locked and so the two officers let themselves in. The pub smelt of disinfectant and all the chairs were upturned on the tables as the cleaner mopped the flagstone floor.

Diane couldn't help but wonder where the Three Tuns got its staff from in such an isolated location. However, once she started chatting to the cleaner, a lady called Lauren, she soon discovered that she drove in daily from the village of Foolow, one and a half miles away.

"This job suits me down to the ground," Lauren explained. "I've got two children aged six and nine. I can drop them off at school, drive to the pub, do the cleaning, remake the letting bedrooms and return home again in time to pick them up again."

"So you've got letting bedrooms here?" asked Diane.

She was thinking that perhaps she and Nick could come here for the weekend. Then she remembered that Nick worked every Sunday. Mind you, there was no reason why they couldn't come mid-week. The pub would probably be less busy then.

"Only two double rooms, both ensuite," Lauren replied. "They provide a useful source of extra income for Matt and Helen, especially during the summer months."

Lauren left to go and see if she could find Matt Yates whilst Diane and Spencer waited in the bar.

The pub was nicely decorated for the festive season with a holly wreath draped across the inglenook fireplace and a Christmas tree in one corner of the room. This one had gift-wrapped boxes made to look like Christmas presents underneath it.

A few minutes later, Matt finally appeared from upstairs, where he had been in the office.

"Inspector," he said to Spencer.

Diane responded, "Good morning, Mr Yates. I'm DI Rothwell and this is my sergeant, DS Spooner."

Matt went red and apologised to her for assuming that the senior officer would be male. He began to tell her what had happened.

"The man came in yesterday at about 2.30," he said. "A Monday lunchtime is usually very quiet. I've even considered closing on Mondays during the winter. But yesterday was different. I had a party of ramblers in for a meal following their Christmas walk. There were 23 of them in total. So as you can see, we were absolutely heaving."

"What did the man do?" asked Diane.

"He sat at the bar and ordered half of mild. Knowing what I know now, he was probably hoping that the walkers would leave. But just as the delivery arrived, they came to pay the bill and they wanted it split between them. I was forced to call Helen out of the kitchen to see the delivery in. Dividing a bill between 23 ramblers is not easy, I can tell you. Some had a dessert, others had coffee, some of them had their wives with them and wanted to pay for two meals. By the time I'd finished dividing it all up, it was ten to three and the man had left."

"And you are sure this was the man?" asked Diane whilst showing Matt a copy of the photofit.

"That was definitely him," replied Matt. "I didn't open my post until after service had finished, which was when I saw your letter. I am absolutely certain it was him, aged about forty with thinning hair. He arrived just before Northern United. It all fits, doesn't it?"

"I don't suppose you spotted his car, did you?"

"Sorry Inspector, the walking party had asked if they could leave their cars in our car park from nine in the morning and I agreed they could. After all, it was no skin off my nose. We weren't likely to get many other customers on a Monday lunchtime. It really didn't matter that the car park was full. I can only presume that he must have parked on the road."

"And it was definitely Northern United that were delivering?"

"Yes, we're a Northern United pub," Matt replied. "They are the only brewery that deliver here. Only, they don't normally deliver on a Monday afternoon."

Diane immediately saw the implication behind what Matt was saying. In other words, if his delivery wasn't normally on a

Monday afternoon, then someone must have known it was going to be at a different time from what it usually was, and that somebody almost certainly worked for the brewery.

"But I thought all the brewery's customers were on fixed runs now. Doesn't your delivery come at the same time on the same day every week?"

"Normally, that's true," replied Matt. "In fact, we've been on a fixed run since 1970 when the Bakewell satellite was established. But they can't stick to the normal delivery pattern over the Christmas period. There are three bank holidays, and it is always the busiest time of the year. That's why they send out a separate delivery schedule for the month. Would you like to see it?"

Diane was definitely keen to see the schedule and Matt pulled a leaflet out from behind the bar to show her. It was printed on glossy paper with Christmas scenes around the edge and had 'Northern United Xmas Delivery Schedule' written across the top.

There were two columns headed 'normal delivery date' and 'actual delivery date'. Diane could see that the first delivery day highlighted was Wednesday, December 6th, and there was a comment alongside which said, 'last orders for wines and spirits'. After that, the delivery days kept on being pulled forward by a day. The next delivery, which should have been made on Wednesday, December 13th, was actually made on Tuesday, December 12th, and had 'last orders for bottled beers' printed next to it. The next should have been made on Wednesday December 20th, but was actually on Monday, December 18th, and had 'stock up with draught' next to it. The last scheduled delivery that month should have been on Wednesday, December 27th, but Diane saw it was due to be made on Saturday, December 23rd instead, and had 'final orders for Xmas and the New Year' next to it.

The three working days between Christmas and the New Year all had 'Emergency Top Up' orders next to them. Those three days were obviously intended to get beer to those pubs where the Christmas trade had been better than anticipated. Finally, all the deliveries during the first week in January were put back by a day, due to the New Year's Day bank holiday. Everything then returned to normal from January 8th.

"The brewery likes us to get our orders in for wines, spirits and bottles as early as possible, being as though they have the longest shelf life," explained Matt. "I don't really mind as I don't have to pay for my December deliveries until the 20th of January, no matter when it's delivered during the month."

Diane continued to look at the leaflet and couldn't help thinking that she didn't like it when people shortened the word Christmas to Xmas. It was so sloppy. Then she pulled herself together after realising that she wasn't there to comment on Northern United's style of writing.

"So your next delivery is due this Saturday," she said.

"That's right. In the run-up to Christmas and occasionally in peak times in the summer, the brewery will also deliver on a Saturday. I don't have the largest cellar in the world here. I will definitely need my empties clearing away and another delivery before Christmas."

"Any idea what time it will be due at?" she asked.

"Not really," Matt replied. "My normal delivery window is between nine and ten in the morning. But during December you have to take it whenever it arrives. One year, it didn't get here until half past five in the evening. Mind you, the brewery should be able to let me know the day before. You see, I'll get my telesales call on Thursday. The delivery is then planned the following day and delivered on the Saturday."

Diane knew exactly what she was going to tell Matt to do next. She took a business card from her handbag and gave it to him.

"Right, sir," she said. "What I need you to do is to phone the brewery on Friday and ask them what time your delivery is due to arrive. When you've done that, I want you to phone me on this number and let me know when it will be here. DS Spooner and I intend to come to the pub next Saturday. We will wait in the bar until our man arrives and the two of us will leave and wait for him outside by the door. You need to see the delivery in as normal and allow him to rob the till. We will then arrest him as soon as he leaves."

"What if there are other customers in the bar?" asked Matt.

"I'm afraid I'm going to have to ask you to tell any customers you get in that you are going to close early. It is vitally important that Sergeant Spooner and I are the only people still in the pub when our suspect arrives, otherwise he won't try to rob you. Is that clear?"

"Crystal clear," he replied.

Diane shook his hand. She and Spencer returned to her car.

"I'm not a betting person," said Diane as they were heading back to Chesterfield. "But if I was, I would bet on his delivery on Saturday being scheduled for just before closing time."

"I was going to buy our Rachel's Christmas present on Saturday," Spencer replied. "It was supposed to be my day off."

"Never mind, Spencer," added Diane. "You can always buy your wife something from the Three Tuns. I'm sure she'll really appreciate getting a jar of pickled onions, a bottle of Mackeson and a packet of salt and vinegar crisps for Christmas."

Chapter 11
Wednesday morning, April 13th, 1971

"You cannot be serious about going for a walk in this weather," pleaded Penny.

The girls had woken up the following morning only to discover that a thick blanket of fog was covering the moors and farmland around Bleckley. It was the third day of their holiday and, so far, they had experienced the weather of three different seasons. Today was the turn of autumn, which meant the only one they hadn't experienced was spring. Which was ironic, being as though that was the season they were actually in.

"Okay, it's not raining or snowing," Penny continued. "But you can't see your hand in front of your face."

But Alice would not be moved.

"Penny, I know you want to go to the farm to see Bung," she replied. "But I've already told you that I don't want to go there. I really don't fancy a morning of being chased around a hayloft by Bonar and his boner. Besides which, I thought we came on this holiday to do some walking, to get some exercise and fresh air after weeks spent with our heads buried in books."

"But we can get plenty of exercise on the farm," pleaded Penny.

"Yes, and we both know what type of exercise you're talking about. Anyway, if you're so keen to go, why don't you just go by yourself? You can shag Bung and then meet up with me later for our riding lesson. That's providing you're not too sore to go riding."

"Ho, ho, very funny," said Penny. "Just for your information, I am not going to shag Bung. Anyway, you should talk! What about you and your friend, the jump jockey? What's the betting that it's you he really wants to jump? Riding lesson, my arse. It's just an excuse. The only filly he wants to ride is you."

"Frank and I only met last night and, unlike the aptly named Bonar, he hasn't tried it on with me. Bung is a creep who thinks he's God's gift to women, but I'll give you one thing. He's the picture of normality compared to his brother. He's strange."

"He's strange? Don't make me laugh. Haven't you noticed Frank's brother? I'd watch it if I were you. They say madness runs in families. In which case, you'd better make sure you don't get pregnant."

"There's no chance of that happening. You, on the contrary, is the one who needs to be careful. You and Bung were virtually doing it in the doorway last night."

The row got more heated as it went on. It was a good job that Claudia and Hanna were out of the dormitory helping to lay the table for breakfast. At least, they were able to miss the shouting match between Penny and Alice.

Eventually, the two girls went to join them in the dining room, although by this stage, they weren't talking to each other, a situation that didn't change over breakfast.

After they'd finished, they both went back to the dormitory to put their outside gear on, and Penny thought she'd make one more attempt to persuade Alice to change her mind.

"Come on, Alice, it's shit weather for walking. Nobody in their right mind would want to go for a hike on a day like this. Perhaps it will be better tomorrow."

But Alice's mind was made up.

"Nobody in their right mind, eh? So why is it that Private Godfrey and Lance Corporal Jones are going for a walk, and why are Valkyrie and Brunhilda about to set off for Hartington?"

"I think that proves my point," Penny replied. "None of that lot are in their right minds anyway."

Alice just folded her arms and didn't say anything.

"Please come with me, Alice," said Penny

"No," she replied, and after she had finished tying her boots and putting her rucksack on, she stomped off towards Great Hucklow.

"You'll probably end up in a ditch," Penny shouted after her before setting off Barn Farm.

The farm was located on a small lane, which left the main road between the pub and the youth hostel. The lane made it look as if Bleckley was located on a road junction. However, the only purpose of this lane was to lead to a couple of farms. After that, it was just a rough track, eventually looping back onto the main road again.

The first farm belonged to Hugh Stanton, although he had sold off most of his land after his son had left home. In fact, he'd only kept two fields, which he had originally used as a campsite. Not only was this far more profitable for him than farming, but it also required far less effort.

But Hugh's fields lacked facilities. There was only one solitary tap and nothing else. Eventually, the competition from other, better-equipped sites had forced him to give up. He still used the fields, but now only for producing silage, which he sold to other farmers in the area.

The Laws' farm was the second one down the lane. If Penny had feared she would find it difficult to locate Bung in the fog, she need not have worried. As she entered the farmyard, she spotted him walking towards the milking shed.

"Hi, Bung," she shouted out.

"I'm just about to start milking the cows," he shouted back. "Do you want to come and watch?"

"I'd love to," she replied.

Penny followed him into the milking parlour. This was in a room adjacent to a large barn, where all the cows were waiting. It contained twelve milking stations all with large glass milk collection jars above them. Once each cow had finished, its milk was transferred to a chilled stainless-steel tank in the room next door.

"You couldn't persuade moaning Minnie to come along then?" asked Bung adding, "Bonar will be really disappointed."

"Bonar would have been disappointed even if Alice had decided to come," Penny thought to herself.

"No, she was adamant that she wanted to go for a walk," she replied. "I don't know why, being as though she won't be able to see anything. But that's typical Alice."

Bung opened a galvanised steel gate and the first of the cows wandered in. He was standing in a sunken walkway, which made it easier for him to put the teat cups onto the cow's udders.

"It's all very organised," said Penny. "The cows just wander in and let you milk them."

"They love it," Bung replied. "Their udders get really full, and they would be in great pain if they didn't get milked. You have to know what you're doing when milking cows, you know. For a start, you have to have soft hands. You can't be rough when handling titties."

"I hope you're not implying that my tits are like cows' udders," Penny replied.

"I'll do the comparison later," commented Bung who had to move out of the way quickly as one of the cows lifted her tail sending a stream of steaming shit into the well where Bung was standing.

"A hazard of the job," he said ruefully.

It didn't take long for all the cows to be milked and Penny was amazed how, once one lot were finished, they just moved through the exit gate letting another group take their place.

"It's just like the queue for the log flume at Blackpool Pleasure Beach," she laughed.

When the entire herd had been milked, Bung said, "Right, I promised I would show you some baby animals and we'll do that next."

Bung climbed out of the sunken walkway and grabbed hold of Penny's hand, before leading the way into a small stone barn. Inside were two animal pens, one of which contained six calves and the other four lambs.

Each pen had an infrared lamp suspended over it in order to keep the young animals warm and, as a result, the barn was pleasantly hot inside.

"Oh, they are so cute," said Penny looking at the lambs.

"Hold your fingers out and they'll suck them," replied Bung. "Don't worry, they won't hurt you. They haven't got any teeth yet."

Penny did as she was told and giggled as the lambs sucked on her fingers, their little tongues tickling her as they did so.

"You can do the same with the calves," said Bung.

Penny repeated the exercise in the other pen with exactly the same result.

"And now I want to show you one of the best sights on the farm," said Bung. "It's in the loft."

"You are joking," Penny replied. "I bet there's nothing up there apart from pigeon shit."

"No, honestly, there's something I want to show you."

Bung took Penny's hand and led her up the stone stairs to the upper floor of the barn.

"See, I told you there was nothing up here," said Penny.

She looked around, but could only see bare floorboards, some bales of hay and a couple of old horse collars on the wall.

"What I'm going to show you in a moment will make your eyes water," replied Bung taking Penny in his arms. "And it'll make other parts of you moist as well."

They started kissing, and as they lay down in the hay, Bung started unbuttoning Penny's blouse and put his hand inside her bra.

They kissed some more and then Penny felt him unzipping her jeans.

"Do you know that girls' fannies only come in two sizes?" he said. "They are either horse's collars or mouse's earholes. My betting is that yours is the latter."

Penny didn't think that Bung's joke was particularly amusing, and she sat up and fastened her jeans.

"Easy tiger," she said. "Unfortunately, it's the wrong time of the month."

"Who do you think you're kidding?" Bung replied, whilst trying to undo her jeans again.

"No, Bung, the painters are in, honestly."

Bung was clearly annoyed by what Penny was saying, and he got up and stood over her.

"Penny, I have to tell you something," he said. "When I told you the reason why my classmates called me Bungalow, I wasn't telling you the truth."

"Really?" replied Penny who was now getting quite concerned about being all alone with Bung.

"No," he replied. "The reason they called me that isn't anything to do with having nothing upstairs. The reason is because I'm really big downstairs."

Bung dropped his trousers revealing he'd gone commando that day. His dick was hanging only a few inches from her face.

Penny froze on the spot before finally pulling herself together and shouting, "Stop it, Bung. Put that thing away. It's gruesome."

"That's right," he replied. "And once you and I get started, it will grow some more."

"You're not bringing that thing anywhere near me," shouted Penny who had risen to her feet and had started to make a dash for the stairs.

But Bung was too quick for her, and he grabbed her wrist. However, he'd forgotten his trousers were around his ankles and as he fell forward, he let go of her again in order to break his fall with his hand.

Penny saw her opportunity and ran down the stairs whilst Bung shouted after her.

"You little prick teaser," he yelled.

Once out of the barn, Penny ran headlong into Bonar. Mind you, he didn't have time to say anything before Penny kneed him straight in the balls, leaving him doubled up in pain as she ran back down the lane towards the youth hostel.

Her pulse was racing, and she was breathing hard as she slammed the youth hostel door behind her.

"What have you been up to in order to get so out of breath?" asked Mervyn as Penny came through the door. As usual, his eyes were focused on her chest, and he was treated to a view of

Penny's bra. In her haste, she hadn't had time to do up her blouse.

"Don't you fucking start," snapped Penny. "Or I'll rip your dick off and ram it up your arse. And you can stop staring at my fucking tits, you fucking pervert."

Mervyn was not expecting such a reaction and he took a step backwards. But Penny hadn't finished with him yet. She was angry and her anger boiled over.

"For fuck's sake, Mervyn," she said. "Don't be a cunt all your life, try taking a day off for once, will you?"

Penny ran into the girl's dormitory and slammed the door, leaving a bemused Mervyn to wonder what precisely he'd done to upset her.

She sat on her bed crying and wishing she'd gone with Alice instead of going to the farm by herself. Alice had always been the sensible one. She had a nose for sniffing out danger, which is why she'd been right to be wary of the Law brothers.

Anyway, there was nothing to do now except to wait for her friend to return. It was only eleven o'clock and Alice had told her that she wouldn't be back until three in the afternoon. Penny had already decided that the two of them wouldn't be going to the pub that night just in case they bumped into Bung and Bonar again. Then in the morning, they'd be off to the youth hostel in Elton, leaving Bleckley behind for good.

"Thank God for that," thought Penny as she looked out of the dormitory window.

She spent a couple of hours reading her book, until eventually she closed her eyes and went to sleep.

Finally, she was woken up by Mervyn knocking gently on the door. His earlier encounter with her had made him somewhat reticent about confronting her.

"Sorry, Penny," he said apologetically. "Only, I've got Frank Hallsworth in reception. He wants to know if you and Alice are okay, as he says the two of you were due to have a riding lesson at half past three."

Penny looked at her watch and saw that the time was a quarter to five.

"Shit," screamed Penny. "Where the hell could Alice have got to?"

Chapter 12
Saturday morning, December 23rd, 1978

"What did you get Rachel for Christmas then?"

Diane had let Spencer take the previous day off as she expected him to work on Saturday.

"I've pushed the boat out this year and I've bought her a Kenwood Chef food mixer."

"And they say romance is dead," said Diane sarcastically. "And how busy were the shops yesterday?"

"It was fairly quiet, actually."

"So when you bear in mind that today is the busiest shopping day of the year, I think I did you a favour. I hope you're going to thank me, Spencer."

"Thank you very much for moving my day off, ma'am," replied Spencer sarcastically.

The two of them were heading back towards Bleckley. Diane was in a good mood because Northern United had confirmed the day before that The Three Tun's final delivery before Christmas would take place at approximately two o'clock that day. As a result, both she and Spencer intended to be at the pub by twelve noon at the latest.

"And what have you bought the boys?" Diane asked.

"I leave all that sort of thing up to Rachel," Spencer replied.

"Bloody hell, Spencer, you have things easy in your house. I bet poor Rachel's in the supermarket right now fighting over the sprouts and parsnips, trying to get all the ingredients for your Christmas dinner."

"Well, I can hardly go with her, can I?" Spencer replied. "I'm with you all day."

As usual, it was Diane who was driving, and the conditions were not good. It had been snowing, but not settling when they left Chesterfield. However, by the time they'd reached the village of Wadshelf and started crossing the moors, it was blowing a blizzard. Worse than that, it was now settling on the road despite the fact that the A619 had been gritted.

Diane pushed on and conditions got slightly better by the time they reached Baslow. But then things got decidedly worse again when they turned off the main road towards Eyam. Diane could feel her car's wheels skidding as she proceeded up the hill towards the village. She prayed she wouldn't come across any obstructions, such as an abandoned vehicle. If she had to slow down, she knew she wouldn't have the momentum to continue up the hill.

Fortunately, she was in luck, and she managed to get through without any mishaps.

Eyam resembled a winter wonderland, covered in a thick blanket of snow. Most of the residents were safely locked indoors. The only people the two of them spotted whilst proceeding cautiously through the village were a group of children having a snowball fight.

"If you don't mind me saying," commented Spencer, "you should have put winter tyres on."

"Thanks for that, Spencer," Diane replied. "That's really useful. How about telling me before we set off next time?"

"Do you really think our man is going to turn up in this weather, ma'am?" he asked her.

"He may already be there, Spencer. He may be waiting outside the pub until just before the delivery arrives. Anyway, this is our best chance so far to capture him in the act. We can't just assume that the weather will put him off."

If the road between the A623 and Eyam had been bad, Diane knew the road between Eyam and Bleckley would be even worse. But fortunately for her, a snowplough had passed through just before they got there and had cleared a track.

At the Bleckley turnoff, their luck ran out as the snowplough had carried on towards Grindleford, whereas they needed to turn left. There were no steep hills on this particular bit of road but, even so, it was treacherous. Progress was painfully slow as Diane fought to keep the car on the road.

When they finally arrived in Bleckley, it was half past one, an hour and a half later than they had planned.

Diane's original instruction to Matt about telling the other customers that the pub was closing early that lunchtime clearly hadn't been needed. For there were only two cars in the car park, a silver Vauxhall Viva and Matt's old Jaguar XJ6.

Diane and Spencer entered the pub after banging their feet to remove any snow and, once inside, they were treated to a roaring log fire. Mind you, the bar itself was totally devoid of customers.

"I'm afraid you've had a wasted journey, Inspector," said Matt, who was behind the bar. "Actually, I'm surprised to see you. We've had nobody in this lunchtime, and I'd be surprised if my delivery turns up, let alone your thief. Not only that, but Lauren phoned in earlier to say she couldn't get here because the road from Foolow is closed."

"Well, if he does turn up, at least we'll be waiting for him," Diane replied.

Matt's wife Helen made coffee for the two officers, which they drank while waiting by the fire.

They waited and waited but nobody came. Finally, when it got to three o'clock Matt came over and said, "I think we have to accept that both my delivery and your wanted man have been defeated by the weather. I've got 22 booked in for dinner on Christmas Eve and another 26 for lunch on Christmas Day and without my delivery, I'll almost certainly run out of beer. Fortunately, all my food deliveries came this morning before the worst of the snow. But without beer, I don't know what I'm going to do. I guess I'll have to phone the brewery and see if there's anything they can do for me. Perhaps they'll be able to get me a wholesale delivery tomorrow, but I'm not optimistic. After all, it's a Sunday, as well as being Christmas Eve."

At that moment, however, there was the faint rumble of a diesel engine and looking through the window, they could see a lorry with Northern United Brewery written on it pulling up outside.

"Hallelujah," said Matt. "I don't think I've ever been so pleased to see anyone in my entire life."

"Well, your delivery may have turned up but, unfortunately, our suspect hasn't," commented Diane.

The draymen entered the pub and went up to Matt who was still behind the bar.

"All I can say is thank fuck we've got no more deliveries to make after this one," said one of them, before noticing Diane and apologising to her for his bad language.

"The conditions are absolutely hell out there," he added.

"If I'm honest, I'm surprised you made it," replied Matt.

"I wasn't going to let you run out of beer over the Christmas period, Matt," he continued. "You'd never have forgiven me."

"Inspector Rothwell, Sergeant Spooner, I'd like to introduce you to Robert Hancock and Cec Stenen. Robert's a local lad. He lives down the road in Foolow, and I've known him since he was in short trousers."

"And I'm a foreigner," Cec said, "not from Holland despite my Dutch name. I'm originally from Sheffield, but I live in Monyash these days."

"So Stenen is Dutch, is it?" asked Spencer. "What's your connection with Holland?"

"My father is Dutch. He moved to Sheffield just before the war and started working for the brewery. That's where he met my mother."

"So you've followed your father into Northern United then?" Spencer continued.

"Not exactly," Cec replied. "My father worked for the opposition at the Cannon Brewery. He said I was betraying my family when I joined Sheffield Brewery as it was back then. He was only joking, of course."

"If you don't mind, Inspector, we'd better start unloading," Robert cut in. "We had a difficult enough journey getting here and I don't want to leave it any longer than absolutely necessary before we head back."

"No, you get on with your delivery," said Diane.

"By the way, if you're planning on going back via Eyam, you can forget about it," Robert continued. "The road is closed after a car skidded on some black ice. It's now completely blocking the traffic. He couldn't have done it in a worse place as it happened about 400 yards after he'd turned off the Eyam to Grindleford road. Nobody can get past and quite a few motorists have had to abandon their vehicles and walk back to Eyam. They couldn't turn around because the snow was too deep and the road too narrow. At least that was what the copper by the roadblock told me. We had to go via Great Hucklow in order to get here. There was no point trying to go via Foolow, as the road is too steep and is always the first to get closed in bad weather. That was why we were so late getting here."

"Thanks for that," said Diane. "I'll take your advice and go back via Great Hucklow."

"You can follow me back to the main road if you want to," added Robert. "After all, the snow is pretty deep out there, and our lorry will at least have more traction than your car. It should be a lot easier for you if you drive in my tyre tracks."

"Thanks again," said Diane. "I'll do as he you suggest."

Matt went to open up the cellar flaps whilst Robert and Cec undid the curtain on the side of their lorry.

It took the two draymen about twenty minutes to complete the delivery, after which they got back into their lorry and Robert switched the engine on. Diane and Spencer got into their car and the small convoy of brewers' dray and Ford Capri headed off towards Great Hucklow.

The roads towards Foolow and Great Hucklow separate shortly after leaving the village. But the two vehicles never made it as far as that. Bleckley is an exposed village, high up in the Peak District and, whilst the draymen had been delivering, the wind had whipped the snow up. It had formed a large drift, which now blocked the road out of the village. Not even a ten-ton lorry could get through, although they did try, only to get stuck.

"Fuck, there's no chance we'll get out of here tonight, especially since it's starting to go dark," said Spencer. "It looks as if we'd better reverse back to the pub, ma'am."

"I hope they can clear the road tomorrow, Spencer," replied Diane. "Otherwise, you're going to be spending Christmas with me rather than with your family and the new food mixer."

"Worse than that ma'am," Spencer replied. "It would mean that you would have to spend Christmas with me rather than with Nick the Dick."

Chapter 13
Friday evening, September 14th, 1973

Bung and Bonar were in the bar of the Three Tuns trying to chat up a couple of blonde-haired South African girls who were staying at the youth hostel. As usual it was Bung who was doing all the talking whilst Bonar merely hung onto his coattails, hoping he'd be able to pick up the girl Bung didn't fancy.

However, Bung was struggling to make any headway with either of them. That was why he decided to try a joke.

"There was a party of tourists going around Chatsworth House the other day and the guide wanted to get to know the people in his group. 'Do we have any Americans here today?' he shouted out. A group of Americans started whooping and hollering. Then he said, 'Do we have any Japanese here today?' And a small party of Japanese tourists timidly put their hands up. Finally, he says, 'Are there any South Africans here today?' To which a couple of girls towards the back of the group shouted out, 'Yes, we are from South Africa.' The guide turned to them and said, 'I'm told that South Africa is famous for two things, its rugby and its beautiful women'. Then he paused and added, 'So what team do you girls play for?'"

"Do you get it?" asked Bung.

"*Jy's 'n regte windgat,*" replied one of the girls in Afrikaans.

"That sounds so sexy," replied Bung. "What does it mean?"

"It means I think you are really funny," she replied as she turned her back on him.

Bung couldn't see her wink at her friend, nor the sign she made with her hand, indicating that she thought he was a wanker. Instead, he caught a glimpse of a tattoo on the base of the girl's back as her T-shirt rode up.

Still wanting to engage her in conversation, he asked, "Hey, what's with the tattoo?"

"I had my name tattooed just above my bum," the girl replied. "It says Yolanri."

"I'd like to get a tattoo of my name. Only Brian isn't exactly a sexy name like yours, and my nickname is even worse. It's Bung, short for Bungalow."

"He got called that because he's got nothing upstairs," jumped in Bonar, right on cue.

"Really?" said Yolanri. "I wouldn't tell anyone that if I were you."

"They were being ironic," commented Bung. "They called me that because I was the cleverest kid in my class. That's why I gave my brother the nickname 'Bonar'. His real name is Andy Law and I decided to call him Bonar…"

"… after Andrew Bonar Law, the British Prime minister in the 1920s," cut in Yolanri.

"How the hell do you know that?" commented Bung. "You're not even British. Nobody knows that. Bonar Law is the unknown prime minister. He's famous for being the least famous Prime Minister ever. He's even less famous than Sir Alec Douglas-Home and nobody remembers him."

"I've got a first-class honours degree in European History from Stellenbosch University," Yolanri replied. "You see, I was also the brightest pupil in my class. Except there were 32 other pupils in my class. I wasn't home-schooled like you and your brother."

"We weren't home-schooled," said Bung indignantly. "We went to Lady Manners in Bakewell."

"I was only joking," added Yolanri. Anyway, if you are serious about getting a tattoo of your name done you can always get it written in Afrikaans. *Draadtrekker* is the Afrikaans for bungalow. Here, I'll write it out for you.

Yolanri produced a notepad and wrote '*draadtrekker*' on it in her neat handwriting.

"How long are you girls staying here?" asked Bonar.

"We move on tomorrow," Yolanri replied.

"'Why don't you come to our farm before you go?" suggested Bung. "We've got some newborn calves. You can feed them if you like."

"I was brought up on a farm," replied Yolanri. "Newborn calves are nothing new to me, and we've got to walk to Youlgrave tomorrow. So we won't have time."

Yolanri was obviously becoming bored with Bung's attention.

"Anyway," she added, "we've got to be back at the youth hostel shortly. So we'll say goodbye if that's okay."

"You don't want to go back to the youth hostel by yourself, girls," said Bung as his final throw of the dice. "The Beast of Bleckley might get you."

"The what?" asked Yolanri.

"The Beast of Bleckley," repeated Bung. "It's killed at least five people and twenty sheep to my knowledge. First, there was a potholer from Sheffield. The beast dragged him back to his lair and ate him. Then there was a council workman. The beast ripped his throat out and left his body near the road through the village. Two people who lived on the farm down the road from ours were next. First, the son disappeared as he was out walking one day, and then a year later, the beast came back and took his mother. Finally, two years ago the beast claimed its fifth victim, a girl who was staying at the same youth hostel as you two. One day, she went for a hike by herself, and the beast got her. She wandered off into the mist and was never seen again. If I were you, I'd let Bonar and I walk you back to the youth hostel. You don't want to go out there by yourself. Not if you want to remain safe, you don't."

"And what type of animal do you think this beast is then?" asked Yolanri.

"It's a massive wolf," replied Bung.

"What a load of *kak*," said Yolanri. "There aren't any wolves in the UK."

"Ah, but this one escaped whilst being transported to the zoo at Riber Castle during the big freeze of 1963 and he's been living on the moors around here ever since. Sometimes when the moon is full you can hear him howling."

"And nobody has been able to capture this wolf in the past ten years, have they?"

"Many people have tried, but he's always been too cunning for them."

"Really?" said Yolanri. "And tell me, do you know what age wolves live to in the wild?"

"No," Bung replied.

"A maximum of eight years," Yolanri continued. "Even if your story were correct, your wolf would be long dead by now."

The two girls got up and left the pub. Bung and Bonar had failed on this occasion, but they both knew there would be many more girls and many more opportunities in the future.

"Still, it would have been nice if the girls had played ball," thought Bung. "Even nicer if they had played with my balls."

His chat-up lines having failed him, it was a dejected Bung who went up to the bar to buy another couple of pints. As he was waiting to be served, a man approached him. He was aged about twenty and was wearing a T-shirt, which said 'Journalists don't live by words alone. Although sometimes they have to eat them.'

"Here, let me get these," he said.

Bung had never seen him before, but he wasn't going to turn down a free drink.

He passed the drinks to Bung and introduced himself.

"My name is Jonathan Stoppard," he said. "I'm a reporter for the *Derbyshire Times*, and I must apologise. I couldn't help but overhear your conversation just now."

"You don't look like a reporter," replied Bung. "You look as if you're just out of nappies."

"I'm a cub reporter," Jonathon explained. "I only started in March, although I've been working for the paper for two years. I'm still looking for my first big story and the Beast of Bleckley could be just the thing I'm looking for. Do you know why nobody has ever picked up on it before?"

"It's common knowledge in these parts," replied Bung. "But we don't get many reporters around here. I guess that was the reason why it never made the newspapers."

"I knew Alice Barlow, the last girl who disappeared. A group of us used to hang out together when I was at school. I remember that her disappearance made the national newspapers. It even featured on *Look North*. They never mentioned the beast though."

"That's because they thought she'd run away. She'd had a row with her friend and just walked out into the fog. The police interviewed her as they thought she might have had something to do with her disappearance. She couldn't account for her whereabouts, you see. In fact, the only person who'd seen her was Mervyn from the youth hostel, who said she was in a really bad mood. Anyway, they let her friend go in the end, as they didn't have any evidence."

"Did the police have any theories about what had happened to her?" asked Jonathon.

"They reckoned she was getting a lot of pressure from home to do well in her A levels. The police thought it was that, combined with the argument she'd had with her friend, which probably caused her to snap and, she just upped and left. She was over eighteen, of course, and so she didn't have to tell anybody where she was going. In the end, the search for her was called off, but mark my words, the beast got her."

"What about the others?" enquired Jonathon. "Why haven't any of their deaths or disappearances been attributed to the beast?"

"Because the police don't believe the beast exists. They've always come up with alternative explanations. The first man, the potholer from Sheffield, well, they reckon he must have gotten trapped underground and was never found because he hadn't told anyone where he was going."

"I thought potholers always told people where they were going, just in case they got stuck."

"That's normally the case. But this guy was nervous about sharing his big find with anyone."

"And what big find was that?"

"It's rumoured that he'd discovered a massive cave system under Bleckley Moor. Other people have looked for it since then. But nobody's ever been able to find the entrance."

"So he was the first to disappear. You said that a council workman was next."

"That's right. The police reckoned he'd been savaged by dogs from the campsite. They had the poor buggers destroyed. Mind you, the man who owned them said they weren't vicious at all and would never do such a thing."

"And then you said that there were two people from a local farm."

"Yes, they were Hugh Stanton's wife and son. The police thought they weren't dead but that they'd just left Hugh because he was a drunk with a violent temper. They never tried to find either of them as they said they were both adults and they probably didn't want to be found. They also said there was no evidence of foul play in either disappearance. In fact, one of the coppers was heard to say that he was surprised both of them hadn't run away years before. Run away, my arse. Believe me, the beast got them both."

"Okay," said Jonathon. "If a beast was responsible, what was it and where did it come from?"

"Oh, we know the answer to that," Bung explained. "It was a wolf, which escaped when the lorry crashed that was transporting it to the zoo at Riber Castle."

"Go on."

"It was early in 1963 when they were stocking the new zoo and wildlife park at Riber Castle near Matlock. The zoo was due to open in time for the Easter holidays and exotic animals were arriving virtually on a daily basis. Now, the winter of 1963 was one of the worst on record and, on one fateful day, a lorry transporting a wolf from Chester Zoo skidded on the ice and crashed near Foolow. The lorry was badly damaged, and the wolf escaped."

"But wolves are dangerous animals. Didn't they try to recapture it?"

"They went after it alright, but the wolf had been injured in the crash and when they couldn't find it, they presumed it had crawled into the cave system under the moors in order to die. Mind you, that all happened only two months before the potholer from Sheffield went missing. Need I say any more?"

"It's an intriguing tale," said Jonathon. "It would definitely make a good article for my paper. But I'll have to go away and do some research before I can publish anything. Can I contact you again if I need some more background information?"

The boys seemed hesitant and so Jonathon told them that it could turn out to be a really big story. In which case, *Look North* might even want to interview them about it. That seemed to settle any worries they may have had. But just to be on the safe side, he bought them another beer each.

"By the way," Jonathon added pointing at the piece of notepaper on the table. "I wouldn't get that word tattooed on your arm if I were you. I might have been born in Chesterfield, but I lived in Johannesburg between the ages of three and fourteen. *Draadtrekker* doesn't mean bungalow. It's the Afrikaans word for wanker."

Chapter 14
Saturday afternoon, December 23rd, 1978

There was a blizzard outside and Diane and Spencer were resigned to the fact that they weren't going anywhere that night, and neither were Cec and Robert, the two draymen. This was particularly galling for Robert, as he only lived a mile and a half down the road.

"Still, there could be worse places to get stuck than in a pub that's just had a delivery," said Diane. "By my calculations, it will take us at least a couple of months to drink all the stock. Then there's all the food that'll need eating."

"Tell me about it," said Matt. "I can only hope they clear the road tomorrow, otherwise it'll all be going to waste. Mind you, I'm not worried about the beer. The locals will drink that. If there's one thing you can guarantee, it's that they will all come to the pub whenever we get snowed in. It's the siege mentality, you see. There's not many of them, mind you, but they'll all be here, even James Hargreaves and he only comes to the pub once in a blue moon."

"How often do you get snowed in up here?" asked Spencer who was sounding quite apprehensive about the prospect of spending the night away from his family.

"It's only happened four times since we've been here."

"And how long have you been in the pub?" Spencer continued.

"Six weeks," Matt replied.

Spencer went white, and Matt, Cec and Robert all started laughing.

"I'm only joking," said Matt. "We took over the pub in 1966, just after Lucy, our second daughter, was born. It wasn't an ideal time really, but it was the first time the tenancy had become available in 25 years. It was a case of take it whilst it was available or miss out completely."

"Do pub tenancies really come on the market that infrequently?" asked Spencer.

"Yes, providing it's a good pub," Matt replied. "Not only that, but you can also usually pass the tenancy on to one of your children when you retire. It may surprise you to hear that here are some pubs around here that have never been on the market whilst I've been alive. At the time this tenancy became available, I was a coach driver living in Grindlow and working for a firm in Tideswell. I'd had my eye on this pub for years. So Helen and I had a long conversation about it before finally deciding to take it on. We've never regretted it. Although I have to admit that it was a lot easier back in the 1960s, as we didn't do food back then."

"I love it when he says 'we'," said Helen. "What he really means is that I slave away in the kitchen doing all the cooking, waitressing and washing up, whilst all he does is take the orders and the money."

"Okay, when it comes to food, I'll admit that you do ninety percent of the work. But country pubs have to do food these days. We do basket meals at weekends and during the school holidays. We also do a roast dinner on Sunday at lunchtimes. As well as that, we do turkey with all the trimmings in the run-up to Christmas and, this year, we've even decided to do food on Christmas Day. We are charging £20 a head, so it's good money, far more than we could charge on any other day of the year. It may be expensive, but there aren't many places open on Christmas Day around here. In fact, we've been fully booked since the end of September. I'm not worried yet about the weather as it is notoriously fickle in these parts. We could wake up tomorrow and discover the snow's all gone. On the previous occasions when we've been snowed in, the road was cleared within 24 hours."

"Except for 1963," added Robert. "Even Foolow was cut off for five days that year and it's nowhere near as high up or exposed as Bleckley. It's also far closer to the main road."

"But the winter of 1963 was exceptional," Matt replied, "the type we only get once in a hundred years. I wouldn't worry about the snow if I were you. Things will be back to normal tomorrow, you see. But in the meantime, we have a problem, because there are four of you and we've only got one room free."

"I thought you'd got two letting bedrooms?" added Diane.

"That's right. However, one of our letting bedrooms is taken by a lady who's staying here for Christmas. Hers is the other car in our car park. That's why we've only got one double room spare."

"I'm not sharing a double bed with Robert," joked Cec, "not unless he kisses me first."

"It may be okay for Morecambe and Wise," Robert added. "But it's not okay for Cec and me."

"Right, I've got two ideas," said Matt. "Either you can sleep down here on a couple of the benches, or you can sleep in the youth hostel around the corner, where you'll have a proper bed."

"I don't much fancy the youth hostel," Cec replied. "I vote we stay here."

"I've got another suggestion," added Robert. "Why don't I just walk down the hill to Foolow."

"Don't be a twat," commented Cec. "It's dark, there's a blizzard blowing and there's two feet of snow outside. That's where it hasn't drifted. We'll stay here where it's safe and warm. We'll have a drink with Matt and then go home tomorrow. After all, Christmas is still two days away. Go and phone Ellen. Tell her that you're okay and not to worry."

Robert still wasn't very happy, but he did what Cec said and went and phoned his wife.

"I think you'd better do the same as soon as he's finished," Diane told Spencer. "And whilst you're at it, you'd better phone the station and tell them where we are."

"Will do, ma'am," Spencer replied

"If Robert and Cec are sorted, it means that you two can have the bedroom," said Matt.

"What it actually means is that I can have the bed and you can have the floor," said Diane, looking at Spencer.

"I was going to be a gent and offer," replied Spencer.

"Oh, it's got nothing to do with you being a gent, Spencer. I'm just pulling rank on you."

"We do have a spare mattress and quilt upstairs, which the girls use when they've got friends for a sleepover. I can put it on the bedroom floor for you."

"I'd really appreciate it if you could do that," said Spencer.

And without further ado, the sleeping arrangements for the night were now sorted.

"Right, we may as well have a drink then," said Diane.

"Actually," said Matt. "It's only 4.30 and we aren't allowed to open until five o'clock. I don't want to lose my license. You know what the police are like."

"Yes, they are dying of thirst," Diane retorted. "So stop moaning and get serving. I'll have a Babycham, Spencer will have a pint, get Robert and Cec whatever they want and one for yourself. It's Christmas after all. Let's start making merry."

"I always do what I'm told by the police," said Matt as he was pulling the first pint. "Except that on this occasion I can't as we don't have any Babycham. We ran out yesterday and it was missing from today's order."

"It was out of stock," Cec confirmed.

"Bloody typical," said Diane. "Out of all the pubs I could have chosen to get stuck in, I have to choose one that's run out of my favourite drink."

Chapter 15
Monday morning, September 17th, 1973

Jonathon was looking through back editions of the *Derbyshire Times*. He'd discovered an article about the escaped wolf and the story was pretty much the same as the one Bung had told him. The wolf had been in transit between Chester Zoo and Riber Castle, when the lorry transporting it had left the road and collided with a tree. This happened on February 11th, 1963. The *Derbyshire Times* of that week contained an article saying that police armed with rifles were trying to track down the escaped wolf. They also urged anyone who lived in the vicinity to stay inside and to lock their doors until the animal had been tracked down and shot.

The following week's edition contained the headline, 'Police call off search for escaped wolf'. It said there were traces of blood in the wolf's cage and since there'd been no sign of the animal, they presumed it had gone to ground in order to die. They didn't know how badly injured it had been because it was snowing heavily when it had escaped, which had obliterated any trail. But the blood stains they had discovered in the lorry suggested it had been quite badly hurt. The newspaper featured an interview with one of the zookeepers from Riber Castle who said that the wolf concerned was seven years old and had been bred in captivity. She also said that wolves were pack animals and that a lone wolf, which had lived its entire life in a zoo, wouldn't stand a chance of surviving for even a week in the frozen uplands of the Peak District.

Jonathon decided to phone Riber Zoo to ask how old wolves get. The gentleman he spoke to was most helpful and told him they lived to a maximum age of eight years in the wild or fourteen in captivity.

Given all these factors, Jonathon was convinced that there was no way an injured seven-year-old wolf, bred in captivity, could evade capture for more than eight years, and then kill Alice Barlow and drag her body off to its lair. Consequently, there had to be another explanation, one that probably involved murder.

After his phone call to the zoo, Jonathon turned his attention to the supposed victims of the beast. The first of these was Grant Cartwright, the potholer from Sheffield. An article written at the time of his disappearance said he was an experienced caver. Despite being young, he had been caving for several years and had even discovered a new chamber in the cavern system in Castleton.

Just before his death, he'd become obsessed with the notion that there was a vast underground cave system below Bleckley Moor. He was determined to find the entrance. When he'd disappeared, it was presumed that he'd discovered something, but had become stuck underground. The British Caving Association always recommends that people go potholing with at least one other experienced caver. But Grant Cartwright was a maverick, who was driven by the desire always to be the first. He didn't want to share his glory with anybody and that had probably led to his downfall.

The story behind Colin Loggenberg, the council workman, who was the second alleged victim, interested Jonathon a lot.

This case was quite clearly different from the rest. All the other potential victims of the beast had gone missing, but Colin's body was discovered where he died. Not only that, but the subsequent autopsy showed he'd been killed following an attack by a large dog.

Colin had been capping old mine shafts throughout Bleckley Moor at the time of his death. Lead mining used to be a major industry in the Peak District, but it went into decline during the nineteenth century with the last mine closing in 1939. Most of the mines were relatively small-scale operations and were either drift mines, where a tunnel was cut into a hillside, or else the lead veins were accessed by a mine shaft. The latter usually had a steam engine onsite to transport the miners up and down the shaft.

When these mines closed, the steam engines were removed. After all, they had a scrap value. The mine shafts were covered with a padlocked iron trapdoor. This was the cheapest way of making the shafts safe and, at the same time, leaving them intact in case it was ever feasible to reopen them again.

By the 1960s, many of these metal trapdoors had rusted and become unsafe. The local council, worried that people might injure themselves, decided to fill the shafts with rubble from nearby quarries and to put a concrete cap on top in order to seal them. Most of the shafts were only a few metres deep and it wasn't a big job. In fact, it was a job that one man and a dumper truck could do by himself, which is what Colin Loggenberg was doing before he died. He had six old lead mines to cap, and he had just finished capping the last one, Stanton Mine in Bleckley, when he was attacked and killed.

According to the newspaper article, the police had arrested a Stan Baxter who had been camping on Hugh Stanton's campsite with his girlfriend and his two pit bulls. On the day of Colin's death, the dogs had escaped. According to Baxter, they had been untied and when the body was discovered, it was assumed that the dogs had attacked and killed him. This was reinforced when one of them bit a policeman who'd been sent to investigate. It was further reinforced by the autopsy report. This said that the victim's throat had been ripped out, which suggested he'd been attacked by at least one vicious dog.

Stan Baxter was found guilty of keeping dangerous dogs and received a suspended sentence. His two dogs were destroyed.

Jonathon had less joy when looking up the disappearance of Hugh Stanton's wife and son, as there was no mention of either of them in the paper. He presumed this was because everybody had thought they had run away after suffering years of abuse. Because of that, neither disappearance warranted a mention in the paper.

Still, Jonathon thought he was onto something. Perhaps Grant Cartwright was nothing to do with any of the others. Perhaps he had died alone stuck in a pothole as the article in the *Derbyshire Times* suggested. The reason why Jonathon thought this was because all the other victims had one thing in common and that was Hugh Stanton.

Colin Loggenberg had been capping Stanton Mine in Bleckley. Now what was the chances that the old mine shaft was on Hugh Stanton's land? Surely, the name alone meant it would be too much of a coincidence to be anywhere else. A look at old maps of the area would answer that particular question. But even more interesting, the dogs that had allegedly attacked him belonged to a man who was camping in his field.

Also, the next two people who'd disappeared were Hugh Stanton's relatives. In fact, the more he thought about, the more he started to wonder whether he'd been right to discount Grant Cartwright's disappearance. What if he'd been camping on his field as well? The article didn't say he had. But it didn't say he hadn't. Of course, if he had been staying there, that meant Hugh Stanton was the common link between all four incidents.

That left Alice. Jonathon didn't need to look up Alice's disappearance in the paper. He remembered every detail about it as if it had happened yesterday. Alice had been a friend of his. Or, to be more accurate, she'd been friends with one of his ex-girlfriends. Her disappearance two years previously, just before her A levels, had shocked him to the core. One of the theories at the time was that she'd cracked under the pressure to do well in her exams. But Jonathon had never held with that idea.

On the day she'd disappeared, she had last been spotted heading into Great Hucklow. Two men who'd been staying at the hostel had walked with her for the first few hundred yards until they had taken the road to Foolow, and Alice had gone straight on towards Great Hucklow. They had chatted to her, and she'd seemed upset, which they presumed was because she'd had an argument with her friend.

The last person to see her was the landlady of the Three Tuns. She had been driving her children to school in Great Hucklow and had spotted Alice on both her outward and return journeys. The second time she'd seen her was by Hucklow Edge, about a quarter of a mile from the village itself.

The police had used tracker dogs to search for her, starting from the last place she'd been spotted. The dogs initially picked up her scent. But when they reached the village of Great Hucklow the scent disappeared.

This was all very good but there was nothing to link Alice's disappearance to Hugh Stanton. She hadn't been staying on his campsite and she hadn't disappeared on his land.

Nevertheless, Jonathon felt there had to be a connection with Stanton and he knew what he had to do next. He had to phone his former girlfriend, Penny Foster.

Chapter 16
Saturday evening, December 23rd, 1978

"Being as though they haven't got Babycham, what are you going to drink?" asked Spencer. "How about wine?"

"I like wine, but it doesn't like me. It's not something I want to drink all the time. I went on a wine diet once and I lost three days."

"You're not supposed to drink it by the pint, you know," said Spencer with a grin on his face. "What about gin and tonic?"

"It's not for me."

"How about beer then?"

"Too gassy. I've never quite worked out how you can drink pints of the stuff."

"I bet you haven't tried real ale, have you?" Matt interrupted. "Real ale's not gassy at all."

"And what is real ale when it's at home?" asked Diane.

"Real ale is beer made and served the way it used to be, cask conditioned in the cellar."

Matt saw the blank expression on Diane's face and started to explain.

"For hundreds of years, all draught beer was cask conditioned. Beer is made from water, malt, hops and yeast. It's the yeast that creates the alcohol in the beer by fermenting the sugars from the malt after they've been dissolved in water. The final part of the production process is when they pour the beer into casks and deliver it to the pub where it's put onto a stillage, a kind of wooden rack. The cask is left to settle before being tapped, allowing it to undergo a secondary fermentation in the cellar. This secondary fermentation gives off a small amount of carbon dioxide, which helps keep the beer fresh. It also gives it more flavour."

It was clear that Matt was a fan of real ale. He was almost evangelical in his description of the brewing process.

"Cask conditioning is an expensive, time-consuming process," he continued, "which is why the brewers started looking for something cheaper and, at the same time, idiot-proof. You see, cask conditioning requires skill if you are to do it properly. The solution they came up with was keg beer. Keg beer is filtered and pasteurised in the brewery. It doesn't need looking after in the cellar and can be served as soon as it arrives, under CO_2 pressure from a gas cylinder. The downside is that any flavour the beer might have had is largely removed during pasteurisation. In addition, the beer is served under pressure, which makes it very gassy."

"That explains a lot," said Spencer. "I always said my own pee had more flavour than Yorkshires Best."

"I agree with you," said Matt. "Mind you, Yorkshires Best is still Northern United's best-selling bitter by a long way. But from a position of nearly dying out, cask ale is making a strong comeback and even Northern United have had to stand up and take note. Six months ago, they reintroduced cask ale for the first time in more than twelve years and I was one of 25 pubs to trial it."

Matt proudly showed them his hand pump with a 'Great Northern Bitter' pump clip on it.

"I've always been interested in beer and brewing. I'm a CAMRA member and I was over the moon to discover that we got into the 1979 Good Beer Guide."

"I was with you up until that point," commented Diane. "What's a photography club got to do with beer?"

"It's CAMRA, not camera," replied Matt whilst showing Diane his copy of the *Good Beer Guide*. "CAMRA stands for the Campaign for Real Ale and is a pressure group set up seven years ago to promote cask ale. They produce a book every year highlighting the pubs serving the best quality real ale and we are in it this year."

"Okay, you've convinced me," said Diane. "I'll try a half."

"And I'll have a pint," said Spencer.

"Northern United haven't been able to go back to doing everything the way they used to do," Matt continued as he poured the beer. "For a start, they didn't have any casks. So they've converted some of their old kegs to take real ale instead. They've also devised the county handpump, which gets the beer out by blowing air into the top of the keg. It's the opposite of a traditional beer engine, which works by sucking the beer out. It's not ideal, but it works, and it has been accepted by CAMRA."

Diane and Spencer may have been prepared to give the new beer a try, but Cec and Robert were set in their ways. Both of them had a pint of Yorkshires Best instead.

"You know, I think you've converted me, Matt," said Diane as she downed her half. "I really like this beer and I think I'll have another one just to make sure. Only this time, you'd better make it a pint."

Diane took a few sips from her pint before starting a conversation with Cec and Robert.

"So do you guys enjoy working for the brewery?" she asked them.

"It's the best job I've ever had," Cec replied.

"Me too," said Robert. "I get to visit some of the best pubs in the UK, pubs located in stunning countryside and not only that, but they also pay me to do it.

"In addition, there's no foreman looking over your shoulder every five minutes," added Cec. "We just pick up the lorry in the morning and take it back at night when we're finished. We never get anybody from the main depot interfering with us. They just leave us to get on with the job and that's the way we like it."

"I wish Superintendent Barker would let me get on with my job without interfering all the time," Diane thought to herself.

"It was very different when I worked as a drayman at our old brewery in Sheffield," added Cec. "Everything there was checked and double-checked. They seemed to think that everyone who worked on the drays had a scam going. I'll admit that there were one or two bad apples, but the majority of us were just good honest working men trying to do a fair day's work for a fair day's pay."

"So you worked for the company before the satellite depot in Bakewell was established, Cec?" remarked Diane.

"That's right, I worked for two years in Sheffield, and I've now done eight years in Bakewell. I jumped at the chance to move when I heard that the company was establishing a satellite depot in Bakewell. I'd always liked the Peak District. My parents used to take me camping here when I was a boy. I may have been born and raised in Sheffield, but I always preferred the wide-open spaces of the Derbyshire countryside."

"I don't blame you," said Diane. "I absolutely love the Peak District. In my opinion, nothing can beat the Derbyshire countryside and I'm not even from around here. I'm a southerner from Guildford.

"We all have our cross to bear," said Cec. "Anyway, I consider myself very fortunate that the company agreed to transfer me. At the time, I didn't think I'd stand a cat in hell's chance of getting a move. I thought they'd want to recruit a couple of local lads like Robert here. However, the personnel manager who interviewed me told me he was really pleased that someone from Sheffield had applied for the job. They didn't need to train me, you see. I was already aware of all the company policies and procedures. In fact, he said that they were going to rely on me to train Robert."

"And you made a right pig's ear out of that, didn't you?" added Robert.

"I wouldn't say that mate. I reckon you're about halfway towards becoming as good a drayman as I am.

"Get out of here," Robert replied whilst doing a swatting movement with his hand.

"So Cec, I presume you relocated to somewhere near Bakewell," said Diane, "You didn't just commute from Sheffield."

"No, I rented a house nearby for the first year and a half. Then I bought a cottage in Monyash. I'm living the rural dream along with Angela, my wife, and Ross and Suzie, our two children."

"It sounds perfect. What about you, Robert? Have you always lived in Foolow?"

"I was born there, and I've lived there all my life," he replied. "When I left school, I went to work for Thornhills of Great Longstone and after six years with them, they agreed to train me as an HGV driver. But after five years of delivering poultry, I was starting to get bored. That was when I noticed the job as a drayman being advertised in the local paper and decided to apply. I was pleasantly surprised when I learnt I'd been successful, and I've been working for Northern United ever since."

A few beers and a lot of conversation later and it was half past six. There was a TV in the corner of the room and Matt put it on so they could see tomorrow's weather forecast.

It was not good news. There was a deep depression sitting over northern Britain. This was drawing in cold air from the east and wet weather from the southwest. They collided over the Pennines and the result was snow, lots of it.

"Shit, I might as well say goodbye to any profit this Christmas," said Matt. "Even if it's stopped snowing by Christmas Day, I still can't see any of our customers venturing out."

"Well, we can make a small dent into your food mountain," said Diane and ordered two turkey dinners, one for her and one for Spencer. Cec and Robert immediately ordered the same. It was not surprising really, since turkey was the only thing on the menu, just as it would be for the foreseeable future.

Whilst they were eating, Matt decided to keep the TV switched on in order to see if anything about the local area was mentioned on *Look North*.

As anticipated, the weather was the main item on the local news. There were several shots of cars sliding about in Leeds and Sheffield. They even had a report from the Tan Hill Inn, the highest pub in England. But there was no mention of North Derbyshire and no reference to the fact that the village of Bleckley had been cut off. Eventually, Matt turned the TV off in disgust.

"It's not even as if the Tan Hill Inn has been cut off," he said. "They've managed to get a bloody film crew there for a start."

Whilst she was tucking into her meal, Diane noticed that a woman in her mid-20s had joined them in the bar and had ordered a glass of wine. She had short blonde hair, and it was obvious she hadn't come in from outside. For a start, she was wearing ordinary shoes and was casually dressed in jeans and a cardigan. It was hardly the clothing of somebody who'd just braved the blizzard outside.

Diane was intrigued about who the woman was and her curiosity was soon satisfied. After she had finished her meal, she went to the bar to order drinks and Matt introduced them.

"Diane, I'd like to introduce you to Lydia Lopokova," he said. "Lydia's in our other letting bedroom and is staying here over Christmas."

Then turning to Lydia, he added, "Diane and the other three are all staying the night as well, although not through choice. They're all stuck here because of the weather."

"Well, I suppose you're lucky to be stuck in a pub rather than in your car," said Lydia.

"You're absolutely right," Diane replied. "We've got plenty of food and drink and a roaring log fire. Things could be far worse. Tell me, with a name like Lopokova I guess you must be Russian or have Russian parents?"

"Russian grandparents actually. They came over to escape the revolution in 1917 and settled in Norwich, which is where I still live."

"I hear it's a really nice city," Diane replied. "I've never been there myself, although my boyfriend lived there for a few years."

Spencer came to join them at the bar.

"Lydia, this is Spencer," said Diane.

"Diane was just telling me that you used to live in Norwich, Spencer."

"Sorry, Lydia," said Diane. "I should have explained better. Spencer isn't my boyfriend."

"No, I'm just the guy she's sleeping with tonight," said Spencer with a grin. "If you want to know who Diane's new boyfriend is, you can spot him at a distance because he always wears his collars the wrong way around."

"Just ignore him, Lydia, he's trying to be funny. Spencer is a work colleague who's going to sleep on the floor of one of the letting rooms tonight while I sleep on the bed on my own. What he's trying to say is that my boyfriend is a vicar. Anyway, are you staying here over Christmas by yourself?"

"Yes, I know it may seem a little peculiar. But I'm doing a PhD on nineteenth century lead mining and its effect on local communities. I came here in order to help with my research. Christmas may appear to be a weird time to do this. But to be honest, I've just split up from my boyfriend and I was looking for somewhere to go where I wouldn't be on my own. It was either here or my parents' house and here won hands down."

Diane knew exactly what Lydia meant. She had also looked for an excuse not to go back to her parents for Christmas.

At that point, a couple of men came into the pub, and unlike Lydia, there could be no mistaking the fact that they had come in from outside. They were both wearing thick winter coats covered in snow, which they removed and hung on the coat rack. One of the men went over to the inglenook fireplace and kicked his boots on the hearth causing most of the attached snow to fall off and hiss as it hit the hot stone. The second man did the same.

The two of them walked over to the bar and, as they approached, one of them put his hand on Lydia's backside and pinched her bottom.

As quick as a flash, she grabbed a canister from her handbag, turned around and sprayed something into his eyes.

The man immediately raised his hands to cover his face and sank to his knees in agony.

"You bitch," screamed the man. "You've blinded me."

"No, I haven't," said Lydia. "It's pepper spray. You'll be all right in a few minutes. Now don't you dare touch me again."

"That was interesting," thought Diane to herself. "I think Lydia and I are going to get along famously together."

Chapter 17
Tuesday morning, September 18th, 1973

Jonathon had phoned Penny and arranged to meet her the following morning. He hadn't spoken to her for more than two years since she'd gone off to college. In a few days' time, she'd be going back to the University of East Anglia in order to start her third year. So he was lucky to get her at home.

Jonathon hadn't gone to university. Instead, he'd joined the *Derbyshire Times*, starting as an office junior, where he demonstrated an aptitude for the newspaper industry. Two years later, he was promoted to the role of cub reporter. However, this had so far only involved things like covering church fêtes and the football reports from Alfreton Town.

What he wanted, though, was a big story, one that would get him noticed. He dreamed of a story that might even result in him becoming a crime reporter, chief crime reporter perhaps and eventually taking over as editor.

What would he do when he met Penny? Kiss her on the cheek? The last time he'd kissed her, it certainly wasn't on the cheek. Instead, they had partaken in some heavy snogging. Jonathon had wanted to go further. But Penny hadn't and the argument they'd had as a result had led to them breaking up. The thought of the things he'd said that night still caused him to cringe.

Jonathon sat on one of the benches opposite the cricket pitch and after a few minutes, he saw her approaching. She looked even lovelier than he remembered, no longer an innocent schoolgirl. She now looked more sophisticated and worldly wise. He almost couldn't believe she was the same girl who had refused his advances less than three years previously.

"Hi Jonathon," she said, taking the lead and kissing him on the cheek. "You've put on some weight since I last saw you."

Jonathon was somewhat crestfallen by her comment, although he tried not to show it.

"It's all those full English breakfasts in the staff canteen," he joked. "But look at you. You look stunning. I must have been mad to have finished with you."

"We were young, and I was hoping to go to university, whereas you wanted to stay here. It would never have lasted. We were right to split up when we did. I hear you're going out with Angela Brown these days."

"Yes, but it's not serious."

"Angela wouldn't know what the word serious meant," Penny replied. "Anyway, you said on the phone that you wanted to do an investigation into Alice's disappearance."

"Yes, it's one of the great unsolved mysteries of recent years."

"When you mentioned that you wanted to talk about Alice, I nearly refused to see you," added Penny. "After all, it was the most traumatic event in my life, and I didn't want you opening up old wounds. But then I thought about it and decided I needed to know the answers in order to bring about closure. She was my best friend, after all. Everybody who knew and loved her deserves to know the truth about what happened. You know the police at the time were absolutely useless. At first, they thought that I had something to do with her disappearance. We'd had a row the morning she disappeared. She wanted to go for a walk and I wanted to go to a nearby farm to feed some baby calves."

"Don't tell me. You were invited by Bung and Bonar," interrupted Jonathon.

"Yes, but how did you know that?"

"They were trying the same trick with a couple of South African girls when I was in the pub in Bleckley last Friday. I had a word with the publican, and he tells me they do it all the time. They invite some girls from the youth hostel back to see the animals. But what they really want to do is to roll around in the hay with them."

"It's a little bit more than just rolling around," said Penny. "I'm convinced Bung would have raped me if I'd have stayed. Then the bastards told the police that I hadn't been with them when Alice disappeared and that caused me no end of problems. I couldn't account for my movements, you see. The situation was made even worse by Merv the Perv."

"Who the hell is Merv the Perv?" asked Jonathon.

"That was the name we gave to Mervyn Baston, the youth hostel warden. He was a right slimy toerag. If you were a girl, he'd never look you in the eyes. His line of sight was always focused on your chest instead. He told the police that I'd returned that morning in an aggressive mood. They questioned me for hours and it was only when the lady from the pub said she'd seen Alice walking near Great Hucklow that they decided to let me go. Mind you, they'd wasted a lot of time by then and even though they got a tracker dog to see if they could locate her, it yielded nothing."

"You mean that the tracker dog couldn't pick up Alice's scent?"

"No, it picked it up all right. But then the trail just ended in Great Hucklow."

"Do you think she got into a car there?"

"Alice was too sensible to get into a car with someone she didn't know and anybody she did know wouldn't be driving around in thick fog miles from anywhere. Eventually, the police decided she had just run away and didn't want to be found. Being as though she was over eighteen, they said there was nothing more they could do. There was no evidence of foul play, you see. It was ridiculous, of course, and her parents were absolutely furious. They wrote numerous letters to the *Derbyshire Times* and to Eric Varley, the local MP, but it didn't do any good."

"Bung said she was carried off by the Beast of Bleckley and she was the latest in a long line of the beast's victims," commented Jonathon.

"That's a load of crap," replied Penny. "It's just a story he tells in order to frighten any girls he meets in the pub. He uses it as an excuse to walk them home and try it on with them at the same time."

"That's as maybe. But that doesn't explain why three other people have disappeared around Bleckley in the past ten years. Then there was the workman who was definitely killed by an animal."

"The police have explanations for all those disappearances, and someone was convicted over the workman's death. No, I think Alice is the only person where there's been no credible explanation for her disappearance."

"But don't forget that when Alice vanished into thin air, the police had an explanation for that as well. They thought she'd run away because of her argument with you and pressure from her parents regarding her A levels."

"They only said that so Alice's disappearance wouldn't show up in the crime statistics. If they'd have said she'd been abducted or murdered, they would have had to say it was an unsolved crime."

"And do you think she was abducted or murdered?"

Penny cleared her throat and tears appeared in her eyes. It was quite obviously a difficult subject for her to talk about.

"If I'm honest, I think she's dead and her body is somewhere on the moors near Bleckley. The worst of it is that she was right not to want to go to the farm with Bung and Bonar. If I had gone with her, she probably would still be alive today."

"Or you could well be missing just like she is," added Jonathon. "There's no point in blaming yourself, Penny. If Alice is dead, there's only one person responsible and that's the person who killed her."

"Do you have any theories about what happened to her then?" asked Penny.

"My prime suspect is Hugh Stanton, not because of anything to do with Alice, but because his name is the only one that keeps on cropping up regarding the other four. One of the people who disappeared was his wife and another was his son. The workman who was killed had been working on his land and the man whose dogs allegedly killed him was camping in his field. Also I strongly suspect that the potholer who disappeared might have been staying there as well."

"I met Hugh Stanton a couple of times on the day before Alice vanished. He was a nasty piece of work and a drunkard. But he couldn't have had anything to do with Alice's disappearance. She was last seen walking into the village of Great Hucklow, a mile and a half away from Bleckley, when she disappeared. That was according to the landlady of the Three Tuns anyway, who saw her as she was taking her daughter to school."

"I intend asking her about this sighting," added Jonathon. "I want to see if she's remembered anything else since."

"Don't forget there were a couple of men from the youth hostel who walked the first few yards with her until they turned off for Foolow."

"Ideally, I'd like to speak to them as well, but I guess I'll have little or no chance of tracking them down."

"That's not correct," said Penny. "Everybody who stays in the youth hostel has to sign the visitor book and write down their address and telephone number. There were only the two men and a couple of German girls staying there the night before Alice disappeared. It should be really easy to trace them"

"That's odd," replied Jonathon. "In all the newspaper reports I've read, none of them have ever mentioned any German girls."

"That's because they were a few days into an eight-week holiday and the police never tried to find them, despite the fact that their home addresses were in the youth hostel's register. The police could have easily contacted them after they had returned home. But they had already decided that Alice had run away by then. It was really sloppy police work. They contacted the two men because that was easy. But they ignored the two German girls because they were too difficult to track down and, by the time they'd returned to their homes in Germany, the police had already closed the case."

"Do you think the two German girls may lead me to the secret of Alice's disappearance?"

"I wouldn't get too excited about them if I were you. They were still in the youth hostel when Alice and I both left. I suppose the two of them were waiting for the fog to clear. Not that it did clear up. In fact, it hung around all day."

"And had they left by the time you got back?"

"Yes, I guess they must have got tired of waiting and decided to set off anyway."

"And they never got in touch with the police once Alice's disappearance had been splashed all over the newspapers?"

"They couldn't have done, otherwise it would have been in the papers. Of course, being foreigners, it's more than likely they wouldn't have watched TV or read the newspapers. They probably never even knew about Alice's disappearance. If the police had asked me, I could have told them they were moving on to Hathersage. But they didn't and I was in such a state, I didn't even think about it at the time."

"Well, I'll see if I can track them down. Who knows, they may be able to throw some light on Alice's disappearance. Is there anyone else you think I need to speak to?"

"You might try James Hargreaves who lives in the village. He's a bit of a recluse and he definitely has no time for Hugh Stanton. He had a fight with him after he accused Hugh of poisoning his dog. It nearly started again the last night we were in the pub. The only reason it didn't was because Matt, the landlord, intervened. There certainly was no love lost between the two of them. If there is one person in Bleckley who would help you to prove Hugh Stanton's involvement, it is James Hargreaves."

"Thanks for that, Penny," said Jonathon. "It's enough to get me started, at least. I'll let you know if I discover anything."

They kissed before the two of them walked off in different directions. Jonathon couldn't help but look over his shoulder as she walked away. She was a good-looking, intelligent girl and he rued the day he had blown his top and finished with her.

"If I can solve this mystery, not only will it be good for my career, but it might also just spark a romance with Penny again," he thought to himself as she disappeared around the corner.

Jonathon had decided that he really should stay in touch with her this time. He didn't know it then, but that fleeting glance of her disappearing towards the park gates would be the last time he would ever set eyes on her.

Chapter 18
Saturday evening, December 23rd, 1978

"You vicious cow, you caught me off guard," shouted Bung as he rubbed his eyes, which had turned red and were streaming. "You must be one of these man-hating lesbians. What you need is a real man to give you a fucking good fucking."

His anger seemed to be on the edge of boiling over as he took a step towards where Lydia was standing. He looked as if he was about to hit her. Mind you, it looked as if Lydia was ready for him. She still had the can of pepper spray in her hand.

"No, you don't," said Spencer who'd gone to intercept him.

He took up a position between Bung and Lydia and produced his warrant card.

"I'm DS Spooner and this is DI Rothwell," he continued. "If you don't want to be charged with affray, you will take your pint and sit down quietly in the corner."

"But what about her?" Bung replied. "She attacked me for no reason."

"Grabbing a piece of arse may be no reason where you come from," added Diane. "But where I'm from it's called sexual assault. Besides which, if you wanted me to take it further I can. In fact, I can already imagine the newspaper headline. Burly farmer is floored by eight-stone girl after he attacked her in Derbyshire pub."

Bung got the message and he and Bonar went and sat down near the fire. He was still muttering to himself about what had happened.

As soon as everything had died down, Lydia thanked Diane.

"I'll take that," said Diane, pointing at the canister. "You know that pepper spray is illegal in the UK, don't you? It's banned under section 5b of the 1968 Firearms Act."

"I didn't realise you were a police officer," said Lydia, at the same time handing over the can of pepper spray. "You aren't going to charge me, are you? I bought it in the States for personal protection. I never thought I'd need it in the Peak District. But with men like Bung and Bonar around I'm glad I brought it with me."

"Let's just forget about it, shall we?" replied Diane. "After all, if the weather doesn't improve, we could all be here together for some time. It's not really the time for arresting people. Anyway, you seem to know a lot about the locals. Have you been here before?"

"No, I haven't. But this place is only a small hamlet and Matt briefed me yesterday about the people who live here. That included warning me about the Law brothers over there. Bung, the one who pinched my arse, is the worst. Matt told me he's a sexual predator who tries it on with all the girls who come to the village. His brother Bonar isn't as bad. He's just weird."

"They both seem weird to me," replied Diane, "especially since their names are Bung and Bonar."

"They're only their nicknames," said Lydia. "Bung is short for Bungalow. He supposedly acquired his nickname because he's big downstairs and has nothing upstairs. Bonar's real name is Andrew Law and is called Bonar after Andrew Bonar Law, who was Prime Minister in the 1920s."

"Anyway, why are the two of you here?" she added.

"Spencer and I were here as part of a routine enquiry that's turned out to be anything but routine. If it doesn't stop snowing, we could well end up staying here until after Christmas."

"And what about the other two?" Lydia continued whilst looking over towards Cec and Robert.

"Oh, they are both draymen from the brewery. They'd just delivered beer to the pub when they got stuck in a snow drift and couldn't get out of the village."

Whilst they were talking, some of the locals started to arrive at the pub and Lydia told Diane and Spencer who they all were. She'd been introduced to them all the previous night.

The first people to arrive were the Hallsworths, all four of them. It didn't take Diane long to work out that one of their son's wasn't wired up correctly. Maybe it was when he came over to where they were standing and started barking like a dog and grunting like a pig.

"Take no notice of him, he's harmless," said Mr Hallsworth. "He likes to associate people with animals."

"He's got it bang on this time," shouted Bung. "A bitch and a couple of pigs."

Bung had a smug look on his face, which soon disappeared when a woman who'd just come into the pub addressed him.

"Language Brian, I didn't bring you up to speak to people in that manner."

Bung was surprised by the interruption. He hadn't spotted his parents entering the bar and, after being rebuked by his mother, he apologised to Diane, Spencer and Lydia. It seemed that Bung liked to play the big man. But only when his mother wasn't in the same room as him.

Bung and Bonar's parents sat down next to Cec and Robert. They hadn't seen Robert for quite some time, and they wanted to share the local gossip with him. At the same time, they teased him with stories about when he was little and used to walk up the hill from Foolow to play with Hugh Stanton's son. One of the stories was about the two of them playing matadors with Hugh's bull using an old red tablecloth. Hugh had rushed out of the house screaming and yelling. It wasn't because he was concerned that the boys would get hurt, but because he was worried his prize bull might injure himself.

Eventually, the friendship between the two boys had withered. It wasn't that they ever fell out, it was just that they were put into different classes when they went to senior school. They made new friends, and the final blow came when the two of them discovered girls.

"Those were happy, innocent days," said Mrs Law. "Who'd have thought Hugh would turn to drink and his whole family would desert him."

Robert just smiled and took another sip of his pint. It wasn't the past he was thinking of; it was the present and the fact that his wife and family were so close, yet tantalisingly out of reach.

The next person to walk in was James Hargreaves with his dog. Diane wouldn't have noticed him as he took his pint and blended into the background. But Mike Hallsworth nodded towards his neighbour and Lydia explained who he was.

A few minutes later, Mervyn Baston came in. He wasn't a frequent visitor to the pub. But there was nobody staying at the youth hostel over Christmas. So he'd come in search of some company.

Diane noticed that he was the only person other than Spencer, Matt and herself who was drinking Great Northern

Bitter. She made the comment that she was glad there was another person in the pub who had taste. Diane might have been drinking cask ale for the first time, but she was already turning into a real ale snob.

"I wouldn't be so keen to heap praise on him," commented Lydia. "Matt also warned me about him. He told me that he was a right pervert."

Mervyn took his pint and looked for somewhere to sit down. Diane, Spencer and Lydia were seated at a table for four, although it looked as if it was only the two girls sitting there as Spencer had gone to the toilet.

"I say," said Mervyn. "I never expected there to be two beautiful young ladies in the pub tonight. Do you mind if I join you?"

"He-llo," joked Diane with a suggestive intonation. "I didn't know that Leslie Phillips was in the pub tonight."

It was like water off a duck's back to Mervyn, who just winked and said, "Ding, dong."

He sat down, even though neither Diane nor Lydia had invited him to do so. At that moment, Spencer arrived back and sat down as well.

"I'm Mervyn Baston," said Mervyn, holding out his hand, "Warden of the youth hostel in the village."

"Spencer Spooner," replied Spencer.

"And which one of these lovely ladies is your wife?"

Diane kicked Spencer under the table, which he took to mean it was wind-up time.

"No, you've got the wrong end of the stick," said Spencer. "I'm not married to either of these two women. I'm a police officer and these two women are my prisoners."

Spencer took out his warrant card and showed it to Mervyn.

"I'm escorting them to Rampton high security mental hospital for the criminally insane. We've been trapped here by the snow and are looking for somewhere to stay. I don't suppose you have any beds at the youth hostel, do you? There's no need to worry. I'll handcuff them to their beds, so they won't escape."

"But aren't they dangerous?" asked Mervyn. "You just went to the toilet and left them by themselves. They could have killed someone."

"No, they couldn't," replied Spencer. "Neither of them has killed anybody recently. Besides which, I've given them both Valium in order to calm them down. Mind you, they were the last of my tablets, I'm afraid."

It was Lydia who cracked first. She'd been holding back the laughter for several seconds. In the end, she couldn't hide her shoulders from going up and down, even though she did have her hand in her mouth at the time and was biting it.

"You've been winding me up, haven't you?" said Mervyn pathetically.

"I'm afraid so," replied Diane. "I'm his boss and Lydia here is a PhD student. I'm sorry for the wind-up, but we need to do something to keep us amused whilst we're stuck here. Lydia's booked in for Christmas. But Spencer and I really are trapped here by the snow, as are Robert and Cec over there. We've got no change of clothes, no toothbrush and no deodorant. If we are still here by Tuesday, you'd better sit on the other side of the room from us."

"Hey, I can help you out with those things," said Mervyn. "We've always got people forgetting stuff like toothbrushes. That's why I keep a supply in the youth hostel."

"Mervyn, I could kiss you," said Diane. "I don't suppose you've got a supply of ladies nickers as well, have you?"

"I bet he's got a store full of them," whispered Lydia, "ones he's pinched from the women's dormitory."

"No, but I've got something even better," replied Mervyn. "Quite a few people who come to the youth hostel don't realise how cold it is up here. After all, we're really high up and exposed to high winds blowing over Bleckley Edge. That's why I have pairs of thermal underwear for sale. I can arrange for a private fitting if you like?"

"You were doing quite well up to that point," said Diane. "I didn't really mean it when I said I could kiss you, you know. So, I think it's best if we both just ignore your last comment."

Getting up she added, "Shall we go now?"

"Oh, I wouldn't do that if I were you," said Bung who'd overheard their conversation. "You don't want to go wandering around after dark around here. The beast might get you."

Chapter 19
Thursday morning, September 20th, 1973

Two days after his meeting with Penny, Jonathan set off for Bleckley on his Kawasaki S1. He'd bought the motorcycle shortly after joining the *Derbyshire Times* and considered it essential for getting to a breaking news story quickly. Not that he needed speed in order to go and see Alfreton Town play. Indeed, they probably would have delayed the kick-off if he was ever held up in traffic.

The first person Jonathon wanted to see was Helen Yates from the Three Tuns. He'd decided that his best approach was to come clean about his reason for visiting and to ask her to tell him precisely what she'd seen on the day Alice disappeared.

On this occasion, his strategy worked, and he was pleased to discover that Helen was a pleasant woman, only too keen to help solve this two-year-old mystery. She even got Lauren to break off from her cleaning duties and make them both a cup of tea.

"It was just as I told the police at the time," said Helen. "It was a quarter to nine and I went past her when I was taking the girls to school."

"Are you absolutely sure it was her?" asked Jonathon.

"On the way out I wasn't. It was very foggy, and she was wearing a grey anorak and had her back to me. I didn't see her until the last minute, and I nearly ran her over. But on my return,

I saw her face in my headlights. It was definitely her. I'd seen her in the pub on the previous two nights."

"And when you saw her for the second time, it was where precisely?" Jonathon continued.

"It was just after I left Great Hucklow," she replied. "Up by Hucklow Edge. She was walking towards the village."

"And do you remember anything else about her, Mrs Yates? For example, did she look anxious or distressed in anyway?"

"Sorry, love, I only caught a brief glimpse of her. I didn't have time to study her face."

Jonathon decided to ask Helen if she knew anything about any of the other cases.

The disappearance of Grant Cartwright, the potholer from Sheffield, had taken place in 1963, three years before she and her husband had taken over the Three Tuns. Consequently, she knew nothing other than local gossip about his disappearance.

The workman who'd been attacked and killed by dogs had died in 1968 though, two years after she and Matt had moved to the village. She remembered it well and was pretty scathing about Hugh Stanton and the type of people he allowed to camp on his field.

"We're a family pub," she told Jonathon. "We get lots of people here with kiddies, nice people who don't cause any trouble. There's only one person who regularly gets drunk and wants to fight with everybody and that's Hugh Stanton. I've spoken to Matt on numerous occasions about him. I've asked him to bar him, but oh no. Matt says that he spends too much in the pub and we need people like him in the wintertime when there are no tourists about. The problem is that other people have stopped coming here due to him. As soon as he comes in, most of the other customers simply get up and leave. Matt will see sense one of these days. I only hope it's before we go bankrupt rather than after."

It was obvious to Jonathon that Helen Yates had absolutely no time for Hugh Stanton.

"As for his campsite," she continued, "well, it wasn't really a proper site. It was just a couple of fields and a tap. What type of people want to stay on a site like that, where you've got to piss and crap in a bucket and then empty it behind a bush? Not families, I can tell you, but people who've got tattoos on their necks and own pit bulls. It's a pity really. If he'd bothered to put in decent facilities, he could have attracted decent people and that would have been good for us."

"So why didn't he?" asked Jonathon. "He could have made a small fortune if he'd done that."

"Hugh was far too tight-fisted to pay to have a toilet block built," Helen continued. "It was short-sighted of him really. As you say, he could have got more campers and charged them far more if he'd had proper facilities. But I think he was quite happy with the people he got as they were like him, nasty people who kept vicious dogs. Anyway, even these people eventually wanted a few more comforts and he attracted less and less campers as a result. That's why he closed the campsite in 1970. He felt he could make more money from selling silage. We breathed a sigh of relief when that happened, I can tell you."

"And after the incident with the workman, Mr Stanton's wife and son disappeared," said Jonathon.

"That's right, although there's nothing sinister regarding their disappearance. The son left first, shortly after the workman's body was discovered. He'd been arguing with his father for years and just had enough and upped and went. Old Hugh's drinking had always been bad, but it got worse after that and he made his poor wife's life hell. I pitied poor Mary. I'd see her wandering about the village with a black eye and blood on her collar where the bastard had hit her. No surprise then that she upped sticks and left him a year later. She's gone back to her sister's in Ireland, so I'm told. After she left, Hugh went even further downhill. Nowadays, he usually stays in bed until lunchtime and starts drinking as soon as he gets up."

"You don't know her sister's name, do you, or where she lives?" asked Jonathon

"I'm afraid not," Helen replied. "I didn't really know Mary Stanton. She never came in the pub, probably because her husband was always here."

Jonathon made a note to try and trace Mrs Stanton's sister, but not knowing her name or where she lived in Ireland, he didn't hold out much hope. Still, if he was able to track her down, at least she could confirm if Mary Stanton had moved in with her.

Helen had been pleasant enough but, in truth, she hadn't added anything to what Jonathon knew already. Next on his list of people to see was James Hargreaves. After asking Helen where he lived, Jonathon walked the few yards to his cottage.

"I'm not interested," was his response to Jonathon's request for an interview before he slammed the door in his face.

Following the warm welcome that Jonathon had received from Helen Yates, James Hargreaves's reaction came as a bit of a surprise. If anything, he'd expected a better reception from him than from anyone else in the village. After all, he was a fellow writer, albeit a writer of fiction. Although some people might argue that most of the stories in the *Derbyshire Times* were fiction as well. Then there was the fact that there was no love lost between James Hargreaves and Hugh Stanton, which

Jonathon had assumed would mean he would be amenable to dishing the dirt on him.

Not to worry though, because Jonathon still had the most important visit of the day to make. He was going to the youth hostel to see if he could find the addresses of the German girls who were there at the same time as Penny and Alice.

Jonathon had decided on a different approach this time. He presumed the warden wouldn't be too keen to show him the guest book if he told him the truth about why he was there. To avoid this possibility, he had decided to tell a white lie.

He entered the youth hostel and immediately came across Mervyn Baston who was in the small room that served as an office next to the front door. Mervyn didn't immediately see Jonathon come in, as he had his back to him. So the journalist cleared his throat.

"Hi," he said whilst holding up his press card. "My name is Jonathon Stoppard from the *Derbyshire Times*. YHA head office should have told you I was coming."

"No," said Mervyn whilst looking at his ID.

"Bloody hell, not another one," Jonathon continued. "You know, I've visited nine youth hostels in the past week and four of them didn't even know I was coming. You make five. Anyway, not to worry, let me tell you why I'm here. The Derbyshire Tourist Board is keen to promote Derbyshire as a destination for foreign tourists. So they've come up with a competition in conjunction with the *Derbyshire Times*. Part of the competition is aimed at all the youth hostels in the county. What I need to do is to note down how many foreign tourists you've had staying here over the past three years. We take the yearly average and divide it by the number of beds in each youth hostel. Then in a year's time, I come back and the warden of the youth hostel that has the biggest uplift wins a prize of £500 in Thomas Cook vouchers. You've got to be in it to win it. Therefore, is it alright if I do a headcount?"

Mervyn was completely taken in by Jonathon's story and even made him a cup of coffee, which he served with a plate of biscuits.

"Perhaps he thinks I'll reduce his starting number if he's nice to me," thought Jonathon.

The fictitious competition did mean Jonathon had to waste half an hour counting all the foreign tourists who had been to the youth hostel over the past three years. He was grateful that the building only had fourteen beds. Some of the larger youth hostels in the county had over ten times that number. If the youth hostel in Bleckley had been as big as that, he'd have been there all day.

Eventually, he came across the page for April 1971 and the address and telephone numbers for Claudia Zimmer and Hanna Schweinsteiger, both from Darmstadt in Germany. Their names were immediately below Penny and Alice's entries in the book. They, in turn, were below two men who Jonathon presumed were the two who walked with Alice as far as the Foolow turnoff.

Jonathon wrote down the details for all four of them and, having gotten what he'd come for, he decided it wasn't worth counting more visitors. After all, Mervyn would be happy if he missed a few foreign visitors off. Not that it would do him any good, being as though there wasn't actually a competition.

"Right, that's 309 in total, which means your target for the next twelve months is 103," said Jonathon. "Every foreign visitor above that will take you one step closer to the prize of £500. But don't forget that the incentive is actually worked out on a per bed basis. You've got as much chance of winning it as one of the bigger youth hostels."

"Great," said Mervyn. "I suppose you've only got another three youth hostels to go if you're doing all the ones in Derbyshire."

"That's right, I'm off to the one in Elton tomorrow."

With his job now completed, Jonathon thanked Mervyn and left. He didn't like lying to people. But in journalism, as in life, his mantra was that the end always justified the means. If he managed to solve Alice's disappearance and bring someone to justice over it, then it was worth telling Mervyn he was in a fictitious competition to win £500.

The first thing Jonathon did when he got back to Chesterfield was to read the story about Grant Cartwright, the potholer again. One point he hadn't picked up on was that he actually came from Totley just outside Sheffield. Fortunately, the office of the *Derbyshire Times* had copies of all the telephone directories for North Derbyshire, North Nottinghamshire and South Yorkshire. A quick look through all the Cartwrights in the Sheffield area revealed that three of them lived in Totley.

It only took two calls before Jonathon hit the jackpot when Grant Cartwright's mother answered the phone. She was able to tell him that her son had been only 24 when he disappeared, and he had still been living at home with her and his father.

"Grant loved the moors," she told him, "and with Totley being on the edge of the Peak District, he often went for long walks to places like Hathersage. He could get the train back home from there, you see. When he was sixteen, he became obsessed with caverns after a visit to Castleton. A year later, he joined the Sheffield caving association, where he was a real rising star. In 1962, he became the first person to break through to Cartwright's Chamber, a large previously unexplored pothole in the Castleton cavern system. They named it after him, you know."

Jonathon had never even heard of Cartwright's Chamber.

"I bet you were so proud," he said.

"Oh, I was," she replied. "But having a chamber named after him was only a start. Later that year, he heard the rumour that that there was a large cave complex below Bleckley Moor. Grant became obsessed with it and was determined to be the first person to discover and explore it."

"Can I ask when last you saw your son?" asked Jonathon.

"It was April 1963," she replied. "He'd been going to Bleckley most weekends during the summer of the previous year looking for this bloody cavern. But he had to stop once winter arrived. He was really disappointed about this as he'd spotted a narrow opening in an area that he hadn't explored yet on his last visit. He was confident that it was the entrance to the cavern system he'd been searching for. But the weather was terrible that day as it had been pelting it down with rain and there was a risk of flooding. Being caught underground due to rising floodwater is a potholer's worst nightmare. So Grant decided to delay any further exploration until the following spring, when the weather would be better. He left here on Friday afternoon on April 5th, and I haven't seen him since."

There was one question that Jonathon was dying to ask her.

"Mrs Cartwright, can you tell me if your son stayed locally when he went looking for this new cave system?"

"Yes, he stayed on a farmer's field," Mrs Cartwright replied. "He told me it was very basic, with no facilities. But it was near the area he was exploring. He seemed really happy the day he was going back, as he thought he was going to make a major discovery. He was a wonderful son, and my husband and I miss him so much. I don't like to think of him dying alone, trapped underground in a dark cave. The police searched every inch of Bleckley Moor but could find no trace of him."

Jonathon thanked Mrs Cartwright for her help and promised to let her know if he discovered anything. At least, she'd been able to confirm what he had suspected. Grant Cartwright had been camping on Hugh Stanton's field just before he had disappeared.

Jonathon's next call was to the two gentlemen who were staying at the youth hostel at the same time as Alice and Penny. They were also the ones who had walked with Alice as far as the Foolow turnoff on that fateful day.

He was lucky first time around. The man he'd phoned was called Graham Fletcher from Preston and he had recently taken early retirement from his job in local government. However, Mr Fletcher wasn't really able to add anything to what Jonathon already knew. He told him that he and his friend Jim had only walked with Alice for about 400 yards before they took the turning to Foolow, whilst she headed towards Great Hucklow. He also said that the fog was really thick that day. So thick, in fact, they almost decided to postpone their hike.

"The fog was less dense in Foolow, and you could see a little bit further," Graham added. "But, in truth, it didn't properly clear up at all that day. I told her that she shouldn't go walking by herself and asked her what had happened to her friend. She said that they had fallen out and she didn't want to talk about it. And that was about it. A few minutes later, we reached the turnoff and went our separate ways. I'm sorry I can't tell you more."

"No, that's been most useful, Mr Fletcher," Jonathon replied.

The last call he had to make was to Germany. He was a bit nervous. Jonathon couldn't speak German and he hoped whoever he spoke to could speak English.

Fortunately, he wasn't disappointed. Not only did Claudia Zimmer answer his call, but as luck would have it, her English was perfect.

"I remember the backpacking holiday that Hanna and I went on in 1971 very well," she said. "And yes, I do remember Alice and Penny, we shared a dormitory with them. But I didn't know that Alice had gone missing. In fact, I didn't know anything about her disappearance until just now, when you told me about it."

"So when was the last time you saw Alice?" he asked her.

"It must have been the last day we were at the youth hostel in Bleckley," she replied. "Hanna and I were moving on that day to the youth hostel in Hartington, but we delayed setting off as the fog was extremely thick. We thought that if we left it a bit, the weather might improve. I was surprised when Alice set off at about half past eight as the conditions were atrocious. Anyway, we left it for about an hour and, when the weather hadn't improved, we decided we ought to set off anyway. After all, we had a booking for the youth hostel in Hartington for that night. We'd only gone about 400 metres when we bumped into Alice walking back towards the youth hostel."

"Are you sure it was her?" asked Jonathon. "Because the last reported sighting of her was in Great Hucklow. If you saw her after that, it must mean she'd decided to turn around and head back to Bleckley."

"It was definitely her," replied Claudia. "We even had a conversation. 'Have you had a change of mind?' I asked her. 'Yes,' she replied. 'The fog is far too thick. I thought it was going to clear. But it wasn't getting any better by the time I reached Great Hucklow. So I decided to cut my losses and turn around.'"

Claudia went quiet for a moment. "I told her that we couldn't do that because we were booked in for the night in Hartington. 'Well, good luck,' she replied. 'I hope you don't get lost.' I never saw her again, but then I wasn't expecting to see her, was I? We were just two people from different countries who happened to be in the same dormitory for two nights. I never even thought about her until five minutes ago."

"Can you remember exactly where it was that you last saw Alice?"

"It was very foggy. You could barely see your hand in front of your face. It was very difficult to make out where we were, but I remember it was by a fork in the road. Hanna and I were going to take the left-hand fork and we'd bumped into Alice who was returning to Bleckley along the other road."

"Thank you very much," said Jonathon. "That really has been most helpful."

He put the phone down and thought about what he'd just discovered. He now knew why the tracker dogs had lost Alice's scent in Great Hucklow. She had turned around there and retraced her route. He also knew where Claudia and Hanna had bumped into Alice. It was right by the turnoff to Foolow. Alice had told Claudia she was heading back to the youth hostel, but she'd never made it. And what was between the Foolow turnoff and the youth hostel? Jonathon knew there were just the two fields owned by Hugh Stanton. They were the two he'd kept when he'd sold the rest of his farmland, the same fields, which he'd used as a campsite at one time. However, for the past three years, he'd used them for producing silage.

Jonathon knew what he had to do. If Hugh Stanton normally lay in bed until lunchtime, then he wouldn't be about early in the morning. Therefore, he intended going back to Bleckley first thing the next day armed with a metal detector. If there were bodies buried under those fields, they would probably have something metal on them. If that was the case, he intended to find them.

Chapter 20
Saturday evening, December 23rd, 1978

"What do you mean the beast might get me?" asked Diane.

"The Beast of Bleckley," replied Bung. "He lives on Bleckley Moor, only coming down to the village to kill sheep and for his favourite meal of human flesh."

"Really?" replied Diane with a sceptical look on her face.

"It's the truth," Bung added. "He's killed six people already and he's hungry for a seventh."

Diane didn't believe this rubbish for one minute. But the mention of six mysterious deaths did raise her curiosity. So she sat down again and asked him to tell her more.

"Let me tell you about it," said Frank Hallsworth, who brought his chair over to join the four of them. "That way you'll get the facts without any embellishment. I've heard Bung tell this story on many occasions over the years and every time he tells it, he exaggerates a little bit more."

"Rubbish," said Bung.

Frank just shook his head and continued.

"The first part of this story is definitely true, because it is well documented that, back in 1963, a wolf escaped after the lorry transporting it to the new zoo in Matlock crashed on the A623 near Foolow. An armed search team scoured the moors, but the wolf was never seen again. The theory was that the wolf had been injured in the crash and had disappeared into one of the caves under Bleckley Moor in order to die. Two months later, a potholer called Grant Cartwright disappeared whilst looking for the entrance to an undiscovered complex of caverns under Bleckley Moor. A search was mounted for the potholer. But he was never found. It was presumed he'd found what he'd been looking for and got stuck underground and perished."

"But hang on," said Diane. "Don't potholers normally go underground in groups, just in case that sort of thing happens?"

"That's right," replied Frank. "Only this potholer was a young hothead who wanted all the glory of finding this new cavern complex for himself. He'd already been up here on many previous occasions looking for the cavern's entrance. He used to camp on Hugh Stanton's field, which was a campsite back in those days. Anyway, at around the same time that all this was happening, there was a noticeable increase in attacks on sheep and this, combined with the disappearance of the potholer, led some people to believe it was the wolf."

"It was the wolf," shouted Bung. "You lost twelve sheep, didn't you dad?"

Mr Law nodded.

"A more credible explanation was that it was either foxes or dogs that were responsible for the attacks on the sheep," said Frank. "One local, who shall remain nameless, decided to take matters into his own hands and left out poisoned meat."

"What do you mean, shall remain nameless?" interrupted James Hargreaves who'd overheard the conversation. "We all know who it was. It was Hugh Stanton and the stupid drunken bastard poisoned my dog."

Ignoring the interruption, Frank continued.

"There were no more incidents for the next five years, until a council workman called Colin Loggenberg was killed. He'd been capping the old mine shaft on Hugh Stanton's land. The autopsy report said he was savaged to death by a dog. Two pit bulls belonging to a man who was staying on the campsite were held responsible, as they had escaped on the day he died. Both of them were subsequently put down. Of course, it is virtually impossible to tell from an autopsy report whether it was a dog or a wolf that had savaged him. That's because a wolf is really just a type of wild dog. Consequently, some people started saying it was the escaped wolf."

While he was speaking, Frank cast a glance at Bung and Bonar before continuing.

"A few days after the death of the workman, Hugh Stanton's son disappeared and a year after that his wife Mary left as well. But what you've got to understand was that Hugh was a drunkard and a bully. He used to beat the boy and his wife. That's why everybody believed they had run off in order to escape him. Well, everybody that is, apart from the Chuckle Brothers over there who say the wolf got them."

"He did get them," said Bung. "He killed them and dragged their bodies back to his lair."

"Believe that and you'll believe anything," said Frank. "Anyway, the next disappearance was in 1971 when a girl called Alice Barlow who was staying at the youth hostel vanished whilst going for a walk. She was just about to take her A levels and was coming under intense pressure from her parents to do well. In addition, she had just had a stand-up row with her friend Penny Foster. The theory at the time was that she'd run away to London or another large city. Unfortunately, she wouldn't be the first or last teenager to run away from home."

"That's true," added Spencer. "We deal with runaways all the time."

"The final disappearance happened five years ago. A young reporter called Jonathon Stoppard from the *Derbyshire Times* vanished the day after visiting the village. He went to the pub and to James's house. Finally he went to the youth hostel, where he examined the guest book. He was never seen again after that."

"But he didn't disappear around here," cut in Mervyn. "He told me he was going to Elton the next day, the day he vanished. I told all this to the police at the time and they did an intensive search of the route he would have taken. But they didn't find anything."

Diane looked around the room into the faces of the people who were in the bar. She was looking for any reaction from anyone present. But the only thing she noticed was that Lydia had a look of absolute horror on her face.

"Poor girl," thought Diane. "She didn't realise when she booked into this pub, she'd be stranded here over the Christmas holiday with a group of perverts, sexual predators and loonies. Not only that, but there may be a murderer here as well."

"Okay, you've got me interested," said Diane sitting down again. "But let's think about it logically, shall we? Firstly, we know that only one of these people is definitely dead and that's the council workman. As a result, we are talking about five people going missing and one death. Now, I am prepared to accept that all or some of these incidents are linked and that the police failed to investigate them properly. So let's look at the story about the wolf."

By this time, Diane had the entire pub hanging on her every word.

"I don't know how long wolves live for or how old it was when it escaped. But, if it disappeared in the winter of 1963, that is almost 16 years ago and it would be dead by now. Also, the fact that nobody's ever heard or seen it or noticed any trace of it in those sixteen years tells me it must have died shortly after it escaped."

"But I saw it," protested Bung.

"When did you see it?" asked Diane.

"Well, it was quite a few years ago now," replied Bung, "when I was about thirteen."

"And he's 28 now, which makes it about fifteen years ago," cut in Mr Law.

"That would be in 1963 then, shortly after it escaped," Diane continued. "Consequently, all the evidence points to the same conclusion that the police originally came to back then. In other words, the wolf probably discovered a safe place to hide and died shortly afterwards. Even if it didn't die immediately as a result of the injury it suffered in the crash, it probably died a few days later."

"But what about the missing sheep?" asked Bung.

"We've always had sheep killed by foxes and dogs," added his father. "But it was far worse than usual at the beginning of 1963. That was despite the fact that there were no townies taking their dogs for walks because of the snow. It didn't return to normal until the spring."

"So perhaps the wolf was able to survive for a few weeks rather than a few days. But the fact that the number of sheep deaths eventually returned to normal once more, tells me the wolf died sometime in the first few months of 1963."

Even Bung looked convinced by Diane's argument.

"Let's now look at the death of the workman in 1968. He was the only person who we know was killed for definite. As I've already said, this was different from the other five incidents, since all the other people disappeared without a trace. Furthermore, we know from the autopsy report that he was killed by a dog. Since we have ruled out the wolf, that only leaves one possibility, which is that the police at the time got it right. In other words, the dog responsible for killing him was one of the two pit bulls belonging to the man who was camping nearby."

"That seems logical to me," said Frank.

"Therefore, by discounting the council workman, it leaves us with five people who disappeared in this area. None of them have ever been seen again and it's this fact that leads me to believe that foul play was involved with all these incidents. As a result, I have to conclude that the culprit is far more dangerous than an escaped wolf. Instead, it's most probably someone who lives in this village."

At this point, everyone looked around the room at their fellow villagers. Most people's eyes ended up looking at James Hargreaves although some landed on Dave Hallsworth.

"That's right, let's blame the outsider, shall we?" said James.

"Hey, don't forget I'm also an outsider," commented Matt.

"Yes, from two miles down the road," added James. "I'm the only one in this village who's not from Derbyshire. That makes me different from the rest of you."

"Well, you certainly know how to look after yourself," said Bung. "You laid out Hugh Stanton with a single punch."

"So what? That doesn't mean that I'm a murderer."

"Nobody is accusing you, James," said Diane.

"Well, that's what it feels like. So okay. I know all about self-defence. I was in the army, for Christ's sake. But so were a lot of people."

"But not many of them were in the regiment you served with," said Frank. "I heard you were stationed in Hereford, and we all know who's based there, don't we?"

"Okay, if you must know, I did serve for a time in the SAS and, yes, I have killed a few men in my time, some of them with my bare hands. But that was over twenty years ago in Malaya where I saw things I never want to see again. But that's all in the past. I came here to get away from all that."

"And don't any of you go blaming Dave, just because he's a bit different," added Mike Hallsworth. "Everybody knows he wouldn't hurt a fly."

"If I can continue," said Diane. "Two names come to mind after discussing these five disappearances. They are Hugh Stanton and then there's you, Mervyn. That's because Alice Barlow was staying at your youth hostel and Jonathon Stoppard visited you the day before he vanished."

"They've got nothing to do with me," protested Mervyn. "Just because that girl stayed in the youth hostel doesn't mean I had anything to do with her disappearance. Anyway, Helen saw her last as she was driving the kids to school. Alice was virtually in Great Hucklow by then and you nearly ran her over, didn't you, Helen?"

He was looking at Helen Yates, hoping she would support him.

"She was wearing a grey anorak and it was extremely foggy," Helen added. "I didn't see her until the last minute."

Diane wanted to keep pressurising Mervyn though.

"You were also the last person to see Jonathon Stoppard before he disappeared," she continued.

"But that was a whole day before he went missing. I may have been the last person in this village to see him alive, but I bet other people saw him after I did. For a start, I think I read in the paper that he lived with his parents. They must have seen him after me. Jonathon Stoppard just came to the hostel to look through our guest book. He spun me a yarn about an incentive his paper was running in conjunction with the Derbyshire Tourist Board. He also spoke to Helen and James and he said he was going to Elton the next day. Back me up, Helen," he added, pleading with her.

"I'm afraid he didn't mention to me that he was going to Elton," Helen replied.

"Nor to me," added James Hargreaves. "Mind you, I only spoke to him for about twenty seconds."

"Well, you remain on my list of possible suspects," added Diane. "But from what I've been told so far, my main suspect is this Hugh Stanton fellow. It was his land the potholer was camping on before he disappeared and two of the other people who vanished were his wife and son. I think I ought to have a word with Mr Stanton."

"You'll have to dig him up first," Bung cut in. "He died three months ago and is buried in Eyam churchyard."

"That doesn't mean he wasn't responsible though," said Diane. "Can you tell me how he died?"

"Cirrhosis of the liver," replied Frank, "which came as no surprise to anybody around here."

"And what's happened to his property?" Diane asked.

"He lived at the back of the youth hostel and his house is empty whilst the solicitors work out who inherits," replied Matt. "I've got a key to his property behind the bar. I was given it in case anybody needs to gain access."

"Well, I suggest that Spencer and I go and have a look around tomorrow and see if we can discover anything."

"Are you going to come back to the youth hostel to pick up some things then?" asked Mervyn.

"I think I'll leave it until the morning, if that's alright," replied Diane.

"So you're not totally convinced that the story about the beast is made up then?" commented Bung.

Diane merely ignored him and said instead, "I think it's time for another pint and it must be your round, Spencer."

Chapter 21
Sunday morning, December 24th, 1978

"Avert your eyes, Spencer," said Diane as she got out of bed the following morning.

It was eight o'clock and Diane had decided that she and Spencer would go to the youth hostel before having breakfast. As she made her way to the bathroom, she stepped gingerly over Spencer who was still half asleep on his mattress.

She supressed a giggle. It wasn't every day that her forty-year-old, fifteen-stone sergeant slept under a pink Snoopy quilt.

"I can't wait to spill the beans about him the next time he makes a sarcastic comment about me at the station," she thought to herself. "It's a pity I didn't bring my camera."

Diane had a quick shower before rejoining Spencer who had gotten dressed in the meantime.

"It's still snowing but not nearly as badly as it was yesterday," he said before going into the bathroom for a wash.

Diane looked out of the window and noticed the sky was grey and snow was still falling, but only gently now. It wasn't the blizzard-like conditions of the previous day.

"Do you think we'll be able to get away today?" she asked Spencer as he came out of the bathroom.

"I bloody well hope so," he replied. "I don't want to spend Christmas Eve here. Father Christmas won't know where to deliver my presents."

Spencer looked rough. Normally, he shaved every day but, not having a razor, he looked unkempt with his stubble.

"Right, shall we go and see what Mervyn has for us?" suggested Diane.

The two of them put their coats on and walked downstairs into the bar where Cec and Robert were awake and chatting. It seemed that neither of them had been able to get a good night's sleep. The benches they'd slept on were not very comfortable. Not only that, but the pub's log fire had gone out during the night and Matt was busy remaking it.

"Bung and Bonar have been out with their tractor clearing the snow this morning," he told Diane as soon as he spotted her.

It appeared that the two brothers had a snowplough that they could attach to the front of their tractor. This had enabled them to clear the road between their farm and the pub. Normally, the council wouldn't allow them to clear the main road for fear they might damage the surface. But since there was nobody from the council to stop them, they had cleared the entire village anyway. Of course, this didn't make any difference to the fact that Bleckley was cut off. The road was still blocked by the dray in one direction and by the abandoned cars a mile away in the other. At least it made it easier for people to get around the village, for which Diane and Spencer were grateful.

It was a cold day even though the wind had subsided and, as a result, Diane and Spencer were thankful that the youth hostel was close by. They were also pleased to discover that Mervyn was already up and about.

He opened the door and was dressed in a thick jumper, a jacket, a bobble hat, and a pair of gloves. With all those layers on he looked twice as big as he did in the pub the previous night.

"Do come in," he said to them. "I'm afraid the heating's not on in the main building, being as though we've no guests. It's just on in my flat, which is as warm as toast."

Diane didn't want to spend any more time in the youth hostel than was absolutely necessary. So she and Spencer went straight to the office, which was where Mervyn kept the various toiletries he had for sale. Spencer was pleased to see that he had a packet of Bic razors and a can of shaving cream. He also had several toothbrushes and deodorants. Diane and Spencer bought one of each. They also bought a tube of toothpaste, which they agreed to share.

Finally, Mervyn produced his selection of thermal underwear, both long Johns and vests.

"If you don't know what size you want, you can always try them on," said Mervyn. "I promise I won't look."

"No, thank you, Mervyn," Diane replied. "It's so bloody cold in here, Spencer's balls have retreated up inside his body and are forming a trio with his Adam's apple."

Then she muttered under her breath, "And my nipples are sticking out like chapel hat pegs."

Diane hadn't thought Mervyn would hear her last comment, but unfortunately for her he had.

"Let me know if you want me to warm them up for you," he commented, which instantly made Diane regret her flippant comment.

Instead, she paid him and the two of them left.

"Ma'am, you need to be careful what you say when you're around Mervyn," said Spencer once they were heading back to the Three Tuns. "Remember, Lydia told you that he's a pervert and Matt has also warned you about him. Also, he's one of your suspects in a possible murder case."

"Thank you, Spencer," Diane replied. "But I'm more than capable of looking after myself. Also, I don't really believe he's got anything to do with these disappearances. I only said that last night to wind him up. No, I believe our prime suspect is the recently deceased Mr Hugh Stanton. That's why you and I are going to take a look around his farm later this morning.

They returned to the Three Tuns to the welcoming smell of bacon cooking. Lydia, Cec and Robert were already tucking into their full English breakfasts. Diane and Spencer joined them.

"For a second I thought it might be another turkey dinner," said Diane as Matt put her plate down in front of her.

"No, that's this evening and it's turkey sandwiches for lunch," he replied.

"Surely, we'll be out of here before then," Diane replied. "It has virtually stopped snowing now."

"That's true," commented Matt. "But I've just listened to the forecast and it's due to start again later this afternoon. It's the most snow we've had in the Peak District for fifteen years. Many roads are blocked, and the authorities are struggling to clear them. Bleckley is only a hamlet with a few inhabitants. We'll be at the back of the queue when it comes to clearing our road of stranded vehicles."

"Well, if it's going to start up again, I'm going to walk to Foolow before it does," cut in Robert.

"I'd really advise against that," said Diane. "I appreciate you want to be with your wife and family at Christmas. But we've already had over two feet of snow and it's far deeper where it's drifted. Foolow is a mile and a half away down a really steep road that was the first to be closed by the weather. You are far better off waiting here until the authorities reopen the road. Just think how upset your missus would be if anything happened to you."

But Robert was not at all happy about the advice he was being given.

"Fuck, fuck, fuck," he yelled in frustration. "There is no way I'm going to spend the night sleeping on that bloody bench again."

"You can always sleep in the youth hostel," said Spencer. "But I'd get Mervyn to put the heating on first if you do. We've just come from there and it's switched off in the main part of the building. It's absolutely freezing."

"Well, let's just see," added Cec. "Maybe we'll be lucky. The council might be able to clear the road after all."

Diane and Spencer finished their breakfast and returned to their room in order to brush their teeth and put their thermal underwear on.

"How do you think I look?" asked Spencer after he had put the blue long Johns and thermal vest on.

"Do you really want me to answer that, Spencer?" Diane replied. "To be honest, all you need is a blue pointed hat and people would start mistaking you for Poppa Smurf."

Spencer looked a bit crestfallen by Diane's comment and didn't say anything else whilst he put the rest of his clothes on.

"At least I'm now properly dressed for going outside," he said, once he'd finished.

Diane was soon finished as well and the two of them headed back to the bar where they bumped into Matt again, who was looking flustered.

"Would you believe it?" he said. "I've just phoned the BBC to complain about the lack of coverage on Look North regarding the snow in North Derbyshire. And do you know what they said?"

"Let me guess," Diane replied. "They didn't know they covered North Derbyshire?"

"Basically. They said they just covered Yorkshire and I needed to contact *East Midlands Today*."

Diane just nodded. She'd already had personal experience of the fact that most of the *Look North* reporters thought their region ended at the border between South Yorkshire and Derbyshire. Not that most of them knew where that border was. Many of them believed that Chesterfield must be in South Yorkshire because it had a Sheffield postcode.

"Right, we're off to look around Hugh Stanton's farm," she said, changing the subject. "Can we have the keys, please?"

Matt went to one of the drawers that were behind the bar, opened it and pulled out a set of keys, which he passed to Diane.

"I hope you discover something," he said as he handed the keys over. "If Hugh really is to blame, he's beyond justice now. But we need to solve these mysterious disappearances once and for all, for the relatives' sake if nothing else."

"We'll do our best," Diane replied before she and Spencer set off for Hugh Stanton's farm.

The farm itself was on the track that led off the main road. It was located between the youth hostel, which was on a corner plot, and the farm belonging to the Laws' family. It had stopped being a proper farm years ago when Hugh Stanton had sold off most of the land after his son had vanished. The only two fields he'd kept were alongside the main road, just after the youth hostel. In between them stood a large stone barn.

As they approached the farmhouse, the first thing they noticed was that someone had cleared a path to the front door.

"I wonder who's done that and why?" said Diane. "It's one thing to be neighbourly, but why go to the bother when there's nobody living here?"

It was a mystery, but Diane and Spencer were grateful to whoever had done it as it made their journey a lot easier.

The farmhouse itself was several hundred years old and built from Derbyshire stone with mullioned windows and a stone roof. It was not in a good state of repair and looked bleak and unloved. Diane wondered what would happen to it now that Hugh Stanton was dead.

"It will probably be bought by someone who'll commute to Sheffield or Manchester," she thought to herself. "They'll doubtless spend a fortune installing an Aga, a bespoke kitchen and Laura Ashley furnishings."

She took out the key and went to unlock the door. But much to her surprise the door wasn't locked.

"Either somebody has forgotten to lock it, or Bleckley's one of those places with no crime, where everyone leaves their front doors unlocked," she said as she opened the door.

"No crime apart from mass murder then," commented Spencer.

The farmhouse may have been destined for a gentrified future, but its present state was anything but. The kitchen they found themselves in was dirty and old-fashioned with an ancient stove, a Belfast sink covered in grime, a flagstone floor and a huge pitch pine cupboard.

One thing that surprised her, though, was that the farmhouse wasn't anywhere near as cold as the youth hostel had been. The reason for this soon became clear. The stove was lit.

"What the hell do you think you're doing?"

Diane and Spencer both spun round to discover a man brandishing a twelve-bore shotgun.

"We're the police, sir," said Diane calmly. "Now why don't you put that gun down?"

The man didn't seem too keen on that idea until they'd shown him their IDs.

Diane and Spencer both produced their warrant cards, and the man reluctantly lowered his weapon.

"It wasn't loaded, anyway," he told them.

"Thank you, sir," said Diane. "Now can we start by asking who you are?"

"I'm Hugh Stanton," he replied, "and this is my house."

Chapter 22
Sunday morning, December 24th, 1978

After a brief period of confusion, Diane and Spencer realised that Hugh Stanton had not, in fact, risen from his grave in Eyam and walked back to Bleckley. The Hugh Stanton they were talking to was in fact the son of the Hugh Stanton who had recently died.

"That clears up one of the mysteries," said Diane. "Would you mind telling me where you've been for the past ten years?"

"Sure, I've been down in Kent working on a farm near Maidstone."

"And you didn't think to tell anybody where you were?"

"That's not true, my mother had my address as did Mildred Brown at the post office in Eyam. When I first left home, I used to write to my mum care of the post office and Mum would collect my correspondence from there. I only wanted to keep my whereabouts secret from my father, not from anyone else."

"And why was that, Mr Stanton?"

"Because he was a drunk and a bully who used to beat both me and my mother."

"But with you leaving, wouldn't that have made things worse for your mother?"

"Yes, it would, Inspector, and that is why I pleaded with her to come with me. I also asked her to join me in Kent in all of my letters to her. Then one day her letters to me stopped coming. So I phoned up Mildred, who told me she had disappeared. I presumed she had run away as well. It wouldn't have surprised me."

"Some of the people in the village reckon she might have gone to live with her sister in Ireland."

"That is highly unlikely, Inspector. My aunt is a Benedictine nun living in a convent in County Wexford. Mother was not a religious person and would never have joined her."

"Where do you think your mother is then?" asked Diane.

"She often spoke of a former boyfriend who she went out with before she met my father. They stayed in touch, and he never married. I'd like to think she's with him. But wherever she is, I hope she's happy."

"I presume the reason why you've returned now is because your father has died."

"That's correct. I may have hated my father, but he never cut me out of his will. He's left everything to me, well, what's left of everything. I understand he sold off most of the farm after I left and pissed the proceeds up against the wall. There's just the house and two fields left. The solicitors took their time tracking me down and I arrived yesterday, just before the worst of the snow. It may not look like it, but I've been tidying the place up. If you think it's bad now you should have seen it yesterday."

"And do any of the other villagers know you're back yet?"

"I haven't had time to tell any of them as I've been too busy. But I intend going to the pub later. It is Christmas Eve after all. I guess I'll reacquaint myself with them all when I go there."

"It'll be a bit of a shock for some of them. A lot seem to believe that you were carried off by the Beast of Bleckley."

"The what?" he asked in astonishment.

It was obvious that Hugh had never heard of the legend.

"It's a wolf that escaped in 1963," she said.

"I remember," he replied. "But everyone thought that it had died shortly after escaping."

"Well, certain people in this community have been blaming it for a string of disappearances and deaths in the area, including your disappearance and that of your mother."

"Well, as you can see, I haven't been eaten by a wolf," said Hugh. "So who else has disappeared, then?"

"The first person who went missing was a potholer from Sheffield. That happened two months after the wolf escaped."

"I remember that," said Hugh. "Although I never connected the two events."

"Then there was a council worker called Colin Loggenberg, who was found savaged to death on your father's land, just before you disappeared."

"I can clear that one up for you right away," replied Hugh. "I know all about the death of Colin Loggenberg as it was his death that ultimately led me to leave the village. He wasn't killed by the beast or by the camper's pit bulls. He was killed by Spike and Thor, our two rottweilers."

There was a shocked silence before Diane managed to say, "Go on."

"Back in the summer of 1968, Colin Loggenberg was capping some of the old mine shafts in the area. We had a mine on our land, which was the final one he had to fill in with rubble and cap with concrete. Mr Loggenberg told my father that he would have some loose chippings and concrete left over and for a small sum, he could put the chippings on the driveway and lay the concrete in the yard."

"So Mr Loggenberg was effectively stealing from his employer," said Diane.

"You're absolutely right. It was a dodgy deal, as the materials belonged to the council. But the driveway and the yard did need resurfacing and the price Mr Loggenberg quoted was very cheap. Anyway, when my father came to pay him, Mr Loggenberg saw the size of his wallet and asked for more money. That was what my father told me anyway. Personally, I think it was far more likely that my father refused to pay him. But whatever the reason, my father and Mr Loggenberg had a fight, which is why Spike and Thor attacked him. It was to protect their master."

"So why did the pit bulls get the blame?"

"Because when he saw what our dogs had done, my father went over to the field where Stan Baxter was camping and untied his two dogs. But not before he'd shot Spike and Thor. He later buried them in the back garden. I was heartbroken as I loved those two dogs. But he said he had to put them down now they had tasted human blood. In reality though, it was because he wanted there to be no doubt that the pit bulls were to blame."

Hugh Junior had tears in his eyes by this stage as he recalled what had happened.

"You know that after all the physical abuse I'd suffered over the years, it was the fact he'd shot his two dogs, who were only defending him, that finally did it for me. Two days later, I packed my bags and left."

"But Mr Baxter could have gone to prison," said Diane. "You should have reported what you knew to the police."

"I realise that and please believe me when I say I would have done something if that had been the case. But the fact was that Mr Baxter didn't lose his liberty, he only received a suspended sentence. At the end of the day, I may have hated my father, but I guess there's some truth in the saying that blood is thicker than water. I wouldn't have dreamed of reporting him to anyone."

"What about Mrs Loggenberg? Didn't you think she deserved to know what happened to her husband?"

"What good would it have done if I'd come forward? The only thing I could tell her was that her husband was killed by two rottweilers rather than two pit bulls. Besides which, if I'd spoken up back then the whole dodgy deal between him and my father would have been revealed. At least, I spared her from all that."

"That's very noble of you, Mr Stanton," said Diane sarcastically.

Hugh didn't take any offence.

"So who were the other two people who disappeared?" he asked.

"One was an eighteen-year-old girl called Alice Barlow who was staying at the youth hostel," said Diane. "The other was a young reporter from the *Derbyshire Times* called Jonathon Stoppard."

"I don't know either of them, I'm afraid."

"There's no reason why you should," said Diane. "Neither of them had ever been to the village when you lived here. Anyway, what do you plan to do with your inheritance? Sell up and return to Kent, I suppose?"

"Good God no, I intend to stay. I was born in this house and I've always loved it here. It was only my father who drove me away. I intend to reopen the campsite, only this time I plan to do it properly and install a toilet block with modern facilities. Fortunately, there's already a building there, as I doubt that I would be able to get planning permission for a new one."

"Yes, I noticed the stone barn as we walked over," replied Diane.

"That's correct, it's located in exactly the right position, between the two fields just off the main road. But I have to correct you on one point, Inspector. It's not a barn. It's the old engine shed that used to house the steam engine for the mine shaft. The one Colin Loggenberg capped just before he was killed.

Chapter 23
Sunday morning, December 24th, 1978

Diane hadn't realised the old mine was so close to the village and immediately became interested in visiting it.

"Is it okay if we go over and take a look?" she asked Hugh.

"We can go straight away, if you like," he replied.

The three of them set off towards the old engine shed. Their progress was easy apart from the last ten yards, which was the only bit where the snow hadn't been cleared.

"Do you honestly believe your mother is alive and well?" Diane asked Hugh as they slowly made their way across the field through waist-high snow.

"Why not?" he replied. "If I can disappear for ten years, then why shouldn't she?"

"Hugh, I think there is every chance the reason she disappeared was because your father murdered her."

"Yes, but earlier today you thought I'd been eaten by a wolf and Colin Loggenberg had been killed by Stan Baxter's pit bulls. Let's not make any other assumptions, shall we?"

"He's got a point, ma'am," added Spencer.

Eventually, they reached the old engine house, which was surrounded by a barbed wire fence. The fence had been put up many years ago and was broken in lots of places. Nowadays, the only thing keeping people out was a sign, which said 'Danger, Old Mine Workings, Keep out'.

The sign was not a very effective deterrent, which was exemplified by the fact that there were footprints all around the old engine house.

"It looks as though someone's been here already today, ma'am," said Spencer. "They must have approached the shed on the other side of that drystone wall we've been following. That's why we didn't notice their footprints until now."

"Well, it wasn't me," added Hugh. "I haven't been here for ten years."

"It has to be somebody from the village, though, as nobody else could have got here," Diane replied. "Now, I wonder who it was and what they were looking for?"

The old door to the engine house wasn't locked and so they went inside. Once again, they were not the first visitors that morning, as the trail of footprints showed that the mysterious visitor had also been inside.

The interior of the engine shed gave no clue about its former use. All the old equipment had been removed over eighty years ago.

"Dad used it to store things in," Hugh explained.

The inside of the shed was a veritable Aladdin's cave of old farming equipment, everything from old milking stools to a 1920s Fordson tractor. However, there was absolutely nothing to connect it with the disappearance of any of the four missing persons.

Diane looked at the pile of old junk in amazement.

"Don't farmers ever throw anything away?" she asked. "A day barely goes by without somebody finding an old Bugatti or a 100-year-old traction engine in a farmer's barn somewhere."

"That's why they're so wealthy, ma'am," Spencer replied. "Most people just throw things away when they get worn out, but not farmers. They store them in a barn until they become valuable antiques."

The three of them went outside again and decided to walk around to the front of the building.

"What's that?" asked Diane, pointing at a mound covered in snow.

"Well, one thing I can tell you is it wasn't there when I was last here," Hugh replied. "That was where the old mine shaft used to be. If you look up there you can still see part of the mechanism that the steam engine used to raise and lower the cages."

Diane and Spencer looked up and could see a huge wooden beam sticking out from the upper floor of the building. Attached to its end were the remnants of an old metal wheel. When the mine had been operational, the miners and the ore they extracted were raised up the shaft by the steam engine. This was attached to a cage via a chain, which ran over the wheel at the end of the beam.

"Spencer, I noticed an old shovel back in the engine shed. Go and fetch it and let's see what's under all this snow."

Spencer did as he was told and was soon removing the snow in order to see what was buried underneath. But it soon became clear that the only thing hidden was a mound of earth.

"I wonder why anyone would anyone dump a load of earth over a sealed mine shaft?" asked Spencer.

"That's if it is really sealed," replied Diane. "Mr Stanton, you say you left Bleckley two days after your father shot the dogs, which therefore must have been two days after the mine shaft was sealed? Did you actually see it after it was capped?"

"Well, no, I was too upset and there was too much going on, what with Colin Loggenberg's death and all the commotion around that."

"So, you can't say for certain that it was actually capped?"

"No. I only know that Dad told me Mr Loggenberg had sealed the old mine shaft."

"And before it was sealed, did you ever go there?"

"When I was little, Dad wouldn't let me go there. He told me it was too dangerous, and I might fall down the shaft. In fact, he told me there was an old troll who lived in the engine shed who used to roast little boys and eat them for his Sunday lunch. It was only to frighten me and make sure I didn't go anywhere near the place. When I was older, he used to let me go there with him. We'd take things to store in the barn and even throw some things down the shaft. It was mainly rubbish and things like old fridges, which normally you'd have to pay the council to take away."

"But I thought the door on the shaft was padlocked?"

"It was, but my father cut the lock off with a pair of bolt cutters. He was never one to miss an opportunity to save money, was my old man. That was why he wouldn't let me go there when I was young. It was because he knew the entrance to the shaft wasn't locked."

"Thank you, Hugh, that's been most helpful," said Diane. "But I think that's about all we can do for now."

"No doubt I'll see you both in the Three Tuns at lunchtime then" he replied, before returning to the farmhouse.

Diane and Spencer went back to the pub. Once they were sitting down in the bar, they decided to go through everything they had discovered.

"Why cover up a sealed mine shaft?" said Diane. "It doesn't make sense. That's why I think we can safely assume that the shaft has not been capped. I believe there never was any excess gravel or cement and Colin Loggenberg used the material destined to seal the mine shaft for Hugh Stanton's driveway and yard instead. After all, the mine shaft was useful as a dumping ground for Hugh Stanton Senior. He probably did a deal with Colin Loggenberg to divert the materials and they fell out over the payment."

"I'll go along with that," replied Spencer.

"Colin Loggenberg was supposed to seal the mine shaft five years after Grant Cartwright, our maverick potholer, disappeared. Now if Hugh Stanton had killed him and dumped his body down the shaft, then surely it would have been in his interest to have the shaft sealed. After all, whilst it was still open, there was always the possibility that Mr Cartwright's body may be discovered. For that reason, I don't believe Grant Cartwright is down there. Also, there's the fact that Hugh Stanton Senior doesn't appear to have any motive for killing him."

"What if Grant Cartwright fell down the shaft and Hugh Stanton didn't know that his body was down there?" asked Spencer.

"That's a possibility, but unlikely. Don't forget that Grant Cartwright was an experienced caver. He was used to the dangers of being underground. He wasn't the type of person who would ignore a warning sign and fall down a mine shaft. No, it is far more likely that he met an accident whilst exploring a new cavern system. That was what the police thought at the time of his disappearance, and I've seen nothing that contradicts that theory."

"I'll go along with that," agreed Spencer.

"After Grant Cartwright, the next victim was Colin Loggenberg and, thanks to Hugh Stanton Junior, we now know what happened to him."

"Just one point, ma'am," interrupted Spencer. "Why did Hugh Stanton have to shoot his dogs? He could have just thrown Colin Loggenberg's body down the mine shaft and blamed his disappearance on the Beast of Bleckley."

"It was probably because Colin Loggenberg would have been listed as a missing person if he had thrown the body down the mine shaft. The ensuing search might have uncovered the mine shaft, which at this point should have been filled in. Then with all the material that should have been used to seal it spread all over Hugh Stanton's yard, it would have been obvious that he'd been up to no good. No, with a ready-made fall guy in the form of Stan Baxter and his pit bulls, it was far safer to let them take the blame. With regards to Stanton's two rottweilers, he needed to kill them so that there would be no question over which dogs had killed Colin Loggenberg. If the two pit bulls were the only dangerous dogs in the area, the police would have assumed that they were to blame. Especially if they had escaped at the time Colin Loggenberg was killed."

"But the police could still have found out about Hugh Stanton's rottweilers even though he had killed them and buried them in his garden," said Spencer. "Anyone in the village might have told them. Surely if that had happened, the mere fact that his dogs had disappeared would have thrown suspicion on him."

"That's very true, Spencer," added Diane. "Except that this is a close-knit community. Hugh Stanton might not have been the most popular person around here, but he was a local, whereas Stan Baxter was an outsider. The only person who might have reported Stanton was James Hargreaves and he wouldn't do that because he doesn't like to get involved."

"So what you're saying is that everyone in this village was prepared to let an innocent man go to prison, just to protect someone local whom nobody liked."

"It happens, Spencer," Diane replied. "Believe me. I'd like to think that someone would have said something if Stan Baxter had received a custodial sentence. But I'm by no means certain that they would have, despite everything that Hugh Stanton Junior said. Talking about him, he was our victim number three."

"Who we now know wasn't a victim at all," added Spencer.

"Exactly. He was living and working in Kent, as most rational people suspected all along. Then after him, it gets interesting. The fourth victim was Mary Stanton, Hugh Stanton's wife. She might merely have run away like her son. But I don't think so. We know that Hugh Stanton was abusive, and his abuse got worse after his son left. Therefore, I think he killed his wife. He may not have meant to. Perhaps he came home drunk one evening and hit her. She could have banged her head on the hearth or something like that. To be honest, it doesn't really matter, because whatever happened, I think he killed her and dumped her body down the mine shaft."

"But if that were the case, then wouldn't Hugh Stanton have been concerned that a search for his wife could have led to someone discovering that the mine shaft hadn't been capped?"

"That was probably why he put it about that his wife had returned to Ireland. It effectively stopped anyone from looking for her."

"Well, there's one way we can prove whether she's down there or not," added Spencer. "We need to remove that mound of earth and have a look to see what's underneath."

"My thoughts entirely," replied Diane. "That's the first thing I intend doing once the weather improves. Let's move on to Alice Barlow, our next victim. Her disappearance was intriguing as she was last seen approaching Great Hucklow over a mile away. Furthermore she was walking away from Bleckley. The question we have to answer is, did she turn around and come back again or is her disappearance not linked to the others? If it's the former, then why would Hugh Stanton kill her? He doesn't appear to have any motive. Also, with Alice's disappearance there was a very real risk that someone would discover that the mine shaft hadn't been capped, which makes me question whether she's down there. After all, Hugh Stanton wasn't to know that the police weren't going to pull out all the stops in order to find her. Which means, if it was him who killed her, he got lucky on this occasion. Once again, we'll know a lot more after we've removed that mound of earth and looked down the mine shaft.

"That then brings me to our final victim, Jonathon Stoppard. He was a reporter with the *Derbyshire Times* investigating the disappearances. I don't believe he was going to Elton on the day he disappeared. That was just something he said to Mervyn Baston as part of his story to gain access to the guest book at the youth hostel. No, I believe he discovered something that led him to the old mine and Hugh Stanton killed him there. He must have done it to prevent him from finding out what was at the bottom of the mine shaft. I think Hugh Stanton realised that he'd been lucky so far, which is why, after he had disposed of Jonathon Stoppard's body, he covered the mine shaft with a mound of earth. In other words, it was to stop anyone else from opening it up and shining a torch down it."

"So you're absolutely certain that all these people are dead?" asked Spencer.

"They have to be," replied Diane. "I'm also certain that it was Hugh Stanton who killed his wife and Jonathon Stoppard. I'm less certain about who killed Alice Barlow, although it probably was Hugh Stanton. The one I'm the least certain about is Grant Cartwright."

"How many bodies do you think are at the bottom of the mine shaft?"

"I'm not sure, Spencer. But Mary Stanton and Jonathon Stoppard are definitely down there, and there could well be three if Alice Barlow is there as well."

"Or possibly four if Grant Cartwright is also down there," added Spencer.

"I don't believe he is, though," replied Diane. "I think we'll find his body somewhere else."

"Don't forget that Hugh Stanton Junior warned us against making assumptions though, ma'am."

"I know he did, Spencer, which is why we need to look under that mound of earth as soon as this bloody snow melts. Until we've done that, all we can do is speculate, I'm afraid."

Chapter 24
Sunday lunchtime, December 24th, 1978

It was 12.30 and Diane was surprised how many of the locals were in the pub. She shouldn't have been. It was Christmas Eve after all, and there wasn't anything else to do. The four members of the Law family were already there, as were the four Hallsworths. In addition, Cec and Robert were sitting at a table, each with a pint of bitter and a turkey sandwich in front of them.

Suddenly, the calm was shattered when Hugh Stanton walked in.

"Bloody hell," shouted Bung, "I don't believe it, young Hugh's back from the dead."

"Yes, I heard you've been putting it about that I'd been eaten by a wolf, Bung."

"I should have known you were too tough for a wolf to chew on. He probably took one bite and spat you out again."

"I'm sorry I've ruined a good story, Bung," Hugh replied

"Bloody hell, Hugh, where have you been all this time?" asked Robert.

He had a look of total astonishment on his face. But, at the same time, he was obviously pleased to discover that his old pal wasn't dead.

"I've been working down in Kent for the past ten years, Robert. Anyway, what are you doing here? Shouldn't you be at home with your missus?"

"It's a missus and two little ones these days," he replied. "Cec and I got snowed in here yesterday and I've a good mind to walk back to Foolow if the snow holds off. It's only a mile and a half away and I have no desire to spend Christmas away from the kids."

"I'm afraid I have bad news for you, Robert. It started snowing again about ten minutes ago."

"You've got to be joking," said Robert and went over to the window only to discover that Hugh was telling the truth.

"What do you intend to do with the farm, Hugh?" asked Mike Hallsworth.

"I'm going to reopen the campsite. Only this time, I'm going to install a proper toilet block, one with showers, toilets and an Elsan disposal point. It's an absolute necessity these days if you're going to attract visitors. The old engine shed is the ideal building in which to put it. Mind you, it might cost me a bit more than I originally planned. Inspector Rothwell here thinks the old mine shaft there has never been capped.

"Good God," said Matt. "What makes you think that?"

"Because the materials that should have been used to seal it ended up on Hugh Stanton Senior's driveway," Diane replied. "Also, someone has dumped a mound of earth over the entrance to the mine shaft. Whoever did it probably wanted to stop people from noticing that the steel door was still intact."

"Bloody hell, you don't think you'll find any bodies down there, do you?" asked Helen.

"Let's not jump to conclusions, shall we?" said Diane. "All I'm saying is that, as soon as the snow has melted, I intend removing the earth and having a look to see what's underneath."

With that announcement, the whole room went quiet and then the murmuring started with everyone speculating about what may or may not be under the mound of earth. Was the mine shaft really capped? If not, then could the bodies of the missing people be down there?

Finally, it was Robert who spoke.

"I've had enough," he said standing up. "I really want to be with my family at Christmas. If I don't go now, the weather is going to get even worse, and it'll be dark."

"Don't be an idiot," interrupted Diane. "You've seen how deep the snow is. Besides which, it's blowing a blizzard outside. You are far better off staying here until we get rescued."

Robert was quite obviously unhappy with what Diane was telling him, but he sat down again and finished his pint.

"I'll phone Mervyn at the youth hostel for you," said Matt in an attempt to cheer up Robert. "I'll get him to put the heating on. You can spend the night in a warm room in a proper bed."

If Matt had thought this would lift Robert's spirits, he was sadly mistaken. Despite the fact that it meant the draymen wouldn't have to spend the night on one of the bench seats in the pub again, Robert looked downcast.

Matt went to make the phone call but returned a few moments later.

"Sorry guys, the phone's dead. The line must be down."

"That's no problem," said Cec. "The youth hostel is only a few yards away. We can go around and ask him to put the heating on and then come straight back to the pub again. We may be better off sleeping there rather than here, but I don't want to spend any more time in the youth hostel than is absolutely necessary. You've got beer and a log fire here, which Mervyn doesn't have at the hostel."

"Yes, and it's turkey with all the trimmings tonight," added Matt. "We've even got Christmas crackers."

"By the time we get out of here, I'm sure I will never want to see another turkey dinner as long as I live," whispered Diane as Cec and Robert set off for the youth hostel.

Diane didn't normally drink at lunchtime, but these were not normal times. She and Spencer were stranded in a pub high up in the Peak District. And it was Christmas Eve. She was supposed to be going to midnight mass at Nick's church that evening and then have dinner with him on Christmas Day. It was now looking highly likely that she wouldn't be able to make either of these. She was resigned to her fate, which was why she decided to have another drink.

"If Alice Barlow isn't at the bottom of that mine shaft, then where is she?" asked Spencer.

"I don't know," replied Diane. "The more I think about it, the more convinced I become that she's down there with Mary Stanton and Jonathon Stoppard. But since she was last seen walking towards Great Hucklow, that can only mean one of two things. Either she turned around and walked back again, or somebody brought her back in order to dump her body down the mine shaft."

"But that brings us back to the question of motive again," said Spencer. "Why would Hugh Stanton or anyone want to kill Alice Barlow?"

"That is the million-dollar question, Spencer."

A few minutes later, a flustered looking Cec burst into the bar.

"The complete idiot," he cried. "I couldn't stop him. Robert's decided to walk back to Foolow. The two of us got as far as the youth hostel and I went towards the door. But when I turned around, he wasn't there anymore. He must have carried straight on. We need to send out a search party to find him."

"That would not be a good idea," Diane replied. "The conditions outside are horrendous. If we went after him, there wouldn't be just one person missing, there would be several of us. Robert's a local. He knows the road between Bleckley and Foolow like the back of his hand. If anyone can make it to Foolow, he can."

"He knows the road in normal circumstances," said Hugh. "But it's been totally obliterated by the snow. I say that we should go and look for him."

"It's too dangerous, Hugh," said Diane. "You can barely see your hand in front of your face out there and don't forget there's a sheer drop over Bleckley Edge. I said that if anyone could make it then Robert would be that person and I meant it. But it would be utter madness for us to go after him. Let's phone the local police and tell them what's happened. They can contact his wife and see if he has made it home."

"Except the phone isn't working," added Matt.

"In which case it's a good job we've got a police radio in the car," replied Diane who immediately sent Spencer out in order to use it.

"Even if Robert does get lost, he can always build himself a snow hole," she said. "You sometimes hear of people surviving for days in a burrow under the snow. "

Spencer soon returned with the latest news.

"The situation is that most of the phone lines are down in the area," he announced. "As a result, they can't phone Robert's house. But the road into Foolow from the A623 is still open. In fact, a snowplough has just been through the village. So our colleagues at the station in Bakewell are going to send a police Land Rover over to his house. They will let us know if he's there. Now there's no way I am going to sit in the car freezing my balls off waiting for their call, which was why I said I would call them back at 3.30. That's about all we can do for now. Let's keep our fingers crossed."

"'I wouldn't hold out much hope for him," said Bung. "If he doesn't freeze to death, the beast will get him."

Chapter 25
Sunday afternoon, December 24th, 1978

"Bung, when will you get it into your thick skull that there is no beast?" said Diane.

"Hey, less of the insults. I'll have you know that I was the brightest boy in my class," Bung replied indignantly.

Quite clearly, he was starting to believe his own stories.

"In which case, I pity the rest of them," Diane added.

She was feeling hungry. But since the pub only had turkey sandwiches, she opted for a packet of cheese and onion crisps, some peanuts and a pickled egg instead. Mind you, her sandwich didn't go to waste as Spencer ate it in addition to his own.

"You know it's roast turkey for dinner again tonight," she said to him.

Spencer took another bite of his sandwich.

"And for lunch tomorrow," she continued.

Spencer nodded.

"You're going to end up looking like a turkey if you eat any more."

"Better to look like a turkey than a pig," said Bung.

"And you're going to look like a runt on a spit after I ram my truncheon up your arse," added Diane who was starting to get very annoyed with Bung.

Lydia entered the bar at this moment. She'd been up in her room working on her thesis all morning.

"Have I missed all the fun?" she asked.

Diane filled her in about the day's events and said, "Lydia, you're an expert on lead mining, do you know how deep the mine shaft on Hugh Stanton's farm would be?"

"I'm not an expert on the way that lead mining was carried out," she replied. "My field is the economic effect that lead mining had on the local community. I do know that most of the lead mines in this area were relatively small-scale operations, employing only a few men. Also most of the veins of lead were fairly close to the surface. Consequently, the mines were not as deep as the coalmines in the east of the county. Most of the shafts were less than ninety feet deep. In fact, those that were deeper than that would be arranged in what were known as turns. A turn is where one shaft of up to ninety feet was dug. It went down to a tunnel and then a second shaft was dug down from that level to a lower level below. It wouldn't matter how deep the vein was, the first shaft would never be more than ninety feet deep."

"That's interesting," said Diane. "Does it mean that, if there is anything at the bottom of the shaft, it shouldn't be too difficult to discover it?"

"No, but it won't be a pleasant job and, if there are any bodies down there, it won't be easy getting them out," added Spencer.

It was ten to three by this stage. Matt called for last orders as he rang the bell behind the bar, which didn't go down too well with Diane.

"Put a sock in it, Matt, will you?" she said. "Nobody's going to enforce the licensing laws today, and I for one could do with a pint."

"Whatever you say," replied Matt whilst pouring her another pint of Great Northern Bitter.

Forty minutes later, Spencer went out to Diane's car to see if there was any news about Robert. He returned after ten minutes.

"He's not at home," he announced. "I've spoken to Duncan Disorderly from Bakewell nick, and he tells me that a couple of PCs went around to Robert's house, but he wasn't there."

Duncan was the desk sergeant at Bakewell police station and his real surname was Dissington. However, everyone always referred to him as Duncan Disorderly. It was pretty apt, given that he was known to put away sixteen pints of Hanson's Bitter in the Peacock Inn most Saturday nights.

"They've informed Derbyshire mountain rescue," Spencer continued. "They've said they will start a search for him as soon as it's safe to do so."

That news cast a dampener on the atmosphere in the pub. Everybody realised something dreadful had probably befallen Robert and they were all helpless to do anything about it.

By then it was nearly four o'clock and, as it was Christmas Eve, the news on the BBC was at a different time than usual. The normal TV schedule had been abandoned in order to make way for the early evening film. This year it was the *Great Escape* starring Steve McQueen.

Matt put the TV on and caught the end of *Mary Poppins*, which had been showing that afternoon. It finished half an hour later and was followed by the main national news, which focused on the traffic chaos caused by the weather. There were long tailbacks on both the M1 and the M6 and the runway at Manchester Airport had been closed. It was not good news for people hoping to get away for Christmas.

However, there was a bit of good cheer in the form of the weather forecast. This said that Christmas Day was going to be cold and bright, as a ridge of high pressure was now going to be sitting over the UK. More importantly, it meant that it wasn't going to snow.

"Hopefully, that means they will be able to recover the cars that are blocking the Eyam road, and we will be able to go home," said Diane.

Look North followed the weather forecast. Everyone was hoping it would contain a report about Robert's disappearance and the fact that the village of Bleckley was about to spend its second night cut off from the outside world. It didn't. Instead, there was a report from the Lion at Blakey Ridge in the North York Moors about customers who'd been rescued just in time for Christmas after spending the previous night in the pub.

"What about us?" cried Matt. "It's alright for them. They've been rescued. We are still cut off after two days and there's no mention at all about poor Robert. It's absolutely sickening."

Nobody was going to disagree with him and so the TV was switched off in disgust.

"Right, who wants to eat?" asked Matt.

"I don't suppose you've got anything other than turkey, have you?" asked Diane.

"I'm afraid not and we've got fifty portions to get through by Boxing Day," replied Matt. "That's why I've invited the entire village to come to the pub for a meal tonight."

"Really, how on earth will you fit them all in?"

Diane was being sarcastic again.

Over the next hour, all the villagers started to arrive and even Emma and Lucy, Matt and Helen's two girls, were allowed into the bar. The two of them sat in a corner drinking Coca Cola through straws.

Last to arrive were the Hallsworth family, with Dave wearing a Father Christmas outfit.

"Ho, ho, ho," he kept saying as he wandered through the bar.

Everyone tolerated him. After all, most of them had known him all their lives and knew that his lift didn't go up to the top floor.

Suddenly, he approached Lydia and pointed at her chest.

"It's a good job I confiscated her pepper spray," thought Diane.

"P… P… Penny's p… p… puppies," stammered Dave.

Chapter 26
Sunday evening, December 24th, 1978

"It is you, isn't it?" said Frank.

"I thought I recognised you," added Bung. "Bloody prick-teasing mad bitch."

"Bloody hell," said Mervyn. "I can see now. You've cut your hair short and dyed it blonde, but it's definitely you."

"Right, that's enough questions from everybody," announced Diane. "If we can all stand back and let the girl explain what's been happening here."

There was no point in Penny pretending anymore. Daft Dave had well and truly blown her disguise. He'd recognised her, well, recognised a certain part of her to be precise.

"The only reason why I booked in under an assumed name was because I didn't want Bung or Mervyn to know I was here," said Penny.

"Why, what have I done wrong?" asked Mervyn.

"Apart from bursting in on poor Alice when she'd just come out of the shower, ogling my chest whenever you'd got the opportunity, and playing strip poker in the lounge of the youth hostel, nothing at all. Oh, and you can add being an all-round pervert to that list. But having said that, you can consider yourself to be a radical feminist when compared with you, Bung."

"What, me? I am just a normal red-blooded male," Bung replied.

"One who thinks when a girl says yes, she means yes and when she says no, she still means yes. You would have raped me if I hadn't struggled free."

"Bollocks, it was just a bit of high jinks," protested Bung.

"No, it wasn't, it was a sexual assault. I was still a virgin at the time and when I said no, I meant no."

"I bet you'll still be a virgin when you're a pensioner at the rate you're going," added Bung.

Diane decided it was time to jump in and change the subject.

"Why Lydia Lopokova?" asked Diane. "Why not Janet Smith or Sue Jones?"

"Lydia Lopokova was the name of John Maynard Keynes's wife. I was telling the truth about being a PhD student. I'm studying in the Economic History Department of the University of East Anglia."

"Who the hell is John Maynard Keynes?" asked Spencer.

"He's Milton Keynes's younger brother," joked Diane, unable to resist having a laugh at Spencer's expense.

"John Maynard Keynes is the most famous economist who ever lived," said Penny. "You might know him as the guy who said that, in the long term, we are all dead."

"That explains why I'd never heard of him then," replied Spencer, with a touch of irony in his voice.

"What I want to know is why come back here now, seven years after Alice disappeared?" asked Diane.

"I will try to explain," said Penny. "Back in October of 1971, I started my university course. It was six months after Alice had disappeared and I still wasn't properly over the shock of what had happened. Some people, including Alice's parents, blamed me. Alice and I had had a row just before she disappeared, and I wasn't with her when she went on her fateful walk."

Penny stopped to compose herself. After eight years, it was still difficult for her to talk about her friend's disappearance.

"I kept going over and over in my mind about what could have happened to her that day. But the more I tormented myself about it, the more confused I got. Well, time is a great healer and eventually I settled down to my studies. I really liked university life and the new friends I'd made there. Then, in September 1973, I got a phone call out of the blue from Jonathon Stoppard. He'd been one of my boyfriends when I was at school. and he was now a reporter for the *Derbyshire Times*."

"Bloody hell," said Bung. "Don't tell me she had a boyfriend. Now that's a surprise. I always thought she was just a man-hating prick teaser."

"Shut it, Bung," said Diane in a stern voice.

"Jonathon had been here to the Three Tuns," Penny continued. "He had heard the story about the Beast of Bleckley and wanted to do an article about the people who'd disappeared. Personally, I only thought it was Alice's disappearance which needed explaining. I believed the official version of what had happened to all the others. Anyway, Jonathon promised to let me know if he discovered anything and I went back to university again. I never heard from him after that."

"Didn't that raise your suspicions, though?" asked Diane.

"No, I took it to mean that he hadn't discovered anything and couldn't be arsed to let me know. After all, when he phoned me in 1973, it was the first time he'd bothered to contact me in nearly three years. Then when he disappeared, I was back in Norwich again, so I never realised he was missing. My parents don't get the *Derbyshire Times* and there couldn't have been anything about his disappearance on *Look North*. I am sure they would have let me know if there had been."

"No surprise there then," whispered Spencer.

"In 1974, I graduated and later that year, Carol, one of my friends from university, and I set off on a gap year, backpacking around the world. It was whilst we were in California that I bought the pepper spray. Two women travelling by themselves can be very vulnerable. So, we bought one each for our personal protection. I have to say it was the best $5 I've ever spent as I'd been waiting seven years to get my own back on Bung. At the time I bought it, I hoped I'd never have to use it. I never thought that when I did, it would give me so much pleasure."

"I know a way in which you could have had even more pleasure and it wouldn't have cost you a penny," Bung cut in.

"I thought I told you to shut it, Bung," said Diane.

"The gap year eventually turned into two," Penny continued. "We earned money doing things like fruit-picking and we even lived on a kibbutz in Israel for a bit. But all good things come to an end. In 1976, we returned to the UK, and I now had to make up my mind what to do next. I knew that my personal tutor from university had always been keen for me to go back and continue with my studies. So I contacted him again and he persuaded me to return. In October of that year, I went back as a PhD student."

"Where does your interest in lead mining come from?" Diane asked.

"My tutor knew I came from Derbyshire. He suggested that I base my thesis on the collapse of the lead mining industry in the county and the effect this had on local communities. He thought this would be of interest to me. It was, especially since my studies gave me access to several old maps, including those that indicated where the mines used to be located."

"So that was how you found out about Stanton Mine," said Diane.

"That's right. It was whilst carrying out my research that I discovered that Stanton Mine, which closed in 1892, was located here in Bleckley. Not only that, but the area surrounding the village was peppered with old mine shafts. My enquiries also revealed that many of these old mine workings hadn't been filled in when they had been abandoned. Sometime later, I discovered that there was a programme by Derbyshire County Council in 1968 to make all the remaining mines safe. This involved filling in and capping all those that had not been properly sealed. There were six of these around Bleckley and a man was sent out to complete the work. It was then that I realised that the man they'd sent was Colin Loggenberg, the council worker who'd been killed by dogs on Hugh Stanton's land. Up until that point, I hadn't made the connection."

Penny took a sip from her drink.

"I began to ask myself, what if Colin Loggenberg hadn't completed his task before he'd been killed? If that was the case, there'd be at least one mine still out there that hadn't been made safe. That's why I came here, to see for myself if any of the shafts were still open."

"So why did you come in disguise?" asked Diane.

"My appearance has changed quite a bit during the past seven years, anyway, which was nothing to do with coming back to Bleckley. I no longer have long hair and I've been dying it blonde for the past two years. Consequently, I thought nobody would recognise me. But to make sure, I decided to use a false name just in case it got out to Bung and Bonar that I was back in the village. I would have gotten away with it if Dave over there hadn't sussed me out. In fact, I think he recognised me yesterday, which is why he started barking at me."

"Dave might have his limitations, but he is very good at remembering faces," added Frank. "He even remembered a woman once who'd been to the stables as a little girl. He hadn't seen her for twenty years and, in the meantime, she'd grown up and had a couple of kids. But he still recognised her and remembered her name. It's a special skill he has. It kind of makes up for some of the other ones he lacks."

"That's great, Frank, but I don't think it was my face he recognised," Penny replied.

"What were you hoping to find when you got here?" asked Diane.

"Well, I've got a map with the six mines marked on it and it was my intention to visit all of them in order to discover if any of them hadn't been filled in. Unfortunately, the weather got in my way. I've so far only been able to visit the one in the village."

"So, it was your footprints we saw when we went their earlier today?" commented Diane.

"Yes, I went there this morning, first thing after breakfast," Penny replied. "Only I didn't discover anything. There was too much snow and soil on top of the old mine shaft."

"I'm pretty certain Colin Loggenberg never capped that shaft and the earth mound was put on top to disguise the fact," Diane explained. "I intend to excavate the site as soon as this snow melts. I dread to think what we may find down there."

"Do you think Alice might be down there?"

"I'm not certain about her, but I do think that Mary Stanton and Jonathon Stoppard are," Diane replied. "But tell me, Penny, did you not consider it dangerous to come to a place where four people have disappeared, one of whom was your best friend, and another was your old boyfriend?"

"It's back up to five now Robert's vanished," added Bung.

"But I didn't know Jonathon had disappeared," Penny explained. "I had no idea about what had happened to him until I heard you talking earlier."

"That was why you looked so shocked," said Diane.

"Also, as I said, I believed the official explanations of what had happened to all the others. I never thought foul play could be a factor in their disappearances. In fact, I didn't think it was a factor in Alice's disappearance either. I just thought she had fallen down a disused mine shaft. She wouldn't be the first person in the Peak District to meet their end that way."

"I'd be surprised if she fell down a disused mine shaft, Penny," Diane replied. "Every indication is that she was walking on the road. People tend not to walk across fields in the fog. It would be too easy to get lost."

"Anyway, the only danger I thought I was likely to encounter here was from Bung's one-eyed trouser snake."

"The real Beast of Bleckley," added Bung who looked quite pleased with himself for thinking that one up.

"In which case, your classmates should have called you Bellend Brian rather than Bung," added Diane.

Diane felt she was close to solving this mystery. But she was frustrated that there was nothing she could do until the weather lifted and she could excavate the area around the old mine shaft.

The atmosphere in the pub that night was pretty muted for Christmas Eve. Robert's disappearance had ensured that that was the case. Diane didn't really enjoy her turkey dinner and couldn't help thinking about the fact that she should have been going to midnight mass with Nick that evening.

Still, at least she'd now discovered real ale and, if she could solve the mystery of four disappearances, it was bound to boost her reputation with her superiors.

Chapter 27
Monday morning, December 25th, 1978

"Bugger, Father Christmas has forgotten us this year," said Spencer after opening one eye.

Diane was already up and awake and looking out of the window.

"A merry Christmas to you too, Spencer," she replied sarcastically. "And by the way, he hasn't forgotten us, he's brought us the best present ever. It has finally stopped snowing. Hopefully that means we will be able to get away today."

Outside the sky was blue and the snow was glistening in the sun. Under normal circumstances, the scene would be picture perfect. But at that precise moment in time, all Diane wished for was a rapid thaw.

Bung and Bonar had been out with their snowplough again. But this time, they had ploughed as far as the abandoned cars that were blocking the road to Eyam. It was in anticipation of the fact that they would probably be recovered later that day, thereby ending Bleckley's isolation.

As she looked out of the window, a police helicopter flew overhead.

"They'll be looking for Robert," said Diane. "The chopper will be doing the spotting for the mountain rescue team."

"It's a pity they can't just land and pick up the two of us," replied Spencer.

Ian Walker

"Hopefully, there will be no need for that as I'm sure the road will be cleared later on today," added Diane.

Spencer had a quick shower. The two of them went downstairs for breakfast where they were soon joined by Cec and Penny. Cec had decided not to sleep in the youth hostel, as he didn't want to be alone in one of the dormitories. Consequently, he'd spent another uncomfortable night sleeping in the bar on one of the benches.

"I reckon they'll clear the road today," said Diane. "What are you going to do, Penny, go back to Norwich?"

"No, I think I'll go and spend a bit of time with my parents in Chesterfield. I'll return to the university in early January," she replied. "Will you keep me informed about what you find when you excavate the mine?"

Diane promised she would let her know one way or another as soon as she'd had the earth mound removed.

"And I suppose you'll be going home to Monyash, Cec?"

"Too bloody right I will. I don't want to stay here one minute longer than I have to. No offence, Matt, but I can't wait to sleep in my own bed. I don't think I could take another night on that bench."

"None taken," replied Matt, before turning to Diane and saying, "what do you think the chances are of them finding Robert alive? I didn't dare even think what Ellen, his wife, must be going through. It's a bad enough thing to happen at any time of the year. But it's Christmas. There'll be all his unopened presents and an empty chair at the dinner table. It's bloody awful."

"That depends on a whole host of factors, Matt. If he merely got lost and dug himself a snow hole, he's got every chance of being found alive. If, however, he stumbled over a cliff edge

220

then the chances aren't that great. Anyway, we need to remain optimistic."

"Why don't I put the TV on?" said Matt. "You never know, there might be some news."

So Matt switched it on. BBC1 were showing Tom and Jerry in '*Twas the night before Christmas*, which had always been one of Diane's favourite cartoons when she was little. But she'd barely had time to even look at the TV, when it went off again, as did the lights. About two seconds after that, the fire alarm started bleeping.

"Bloody hell," said Matt. "Now the electricity has gone off. Is there anything else that can go wrong?"

"Does that mean you won't be able to cook lunch?" asked Spencer who was always one to put his stomach first.

"Fortunately, we've got a gas cooker," Matt replied. "We don't have mains gas up here, but we do have a bloody great propane gas tank out the back. There's no need to worry about going hungry. We've got at least nine months' supply."

In the end, they didn't need nine months' worth of gas though, as six hours later they were finally rescued. Mind you, those last few hours seemed to drag on forever, especially with no electricity and no phone. It was half past four and starting to go dark before the council snow plough arrived, signalling that the road had been cleared. The electricity was still not on, which had forced Helen to cook Christmas lunch by candlelight, as there wasn't a window in the pub's kitchen.

Penny had decided to remain at the Three Tuns for another night and then to move on to her parents' house in the morning. But there was no way that Diane and Spencer were going to delay returning home even for a minute. They were off virtually as soon as they saw the lights of the snowplough outside the pub. The two of them offered to run Cec back to Monyash, being as though he didn't have any transport. It was quite a long way out of their way and, as a result, it was nearly six o'clock before they finally arrived back in Chesterfield.

Both of them were amazed as they entered the town. There was no evidence of the chaos that existed just up the road. Chesterfield had escaped the blizzard and there was virtually no snow to be seen anywhere.

Diane headed back to the police station in Beetwell Street, which was where Spencer's car was still parked. However, just before they got there, they received a call from Bakewell station with the news they had both been dreading. Robert Hancock's body had been found. He appeared to have fallen over Bleckley Edge and had plunged to his death.

Chapter 28
Monday evening, December 25th, 1978

"Don't let it spoil your evening, Diane," said Spencer.

Spencer never called Diane by her first name. The fact that he'd done so now reflected how rotten the two of them both felt about Robert and his poor family. Both of them could envisage his Christmas presents remaining unopened under the tree.

Diane dropped Spencer off and decided to go straight over to see Nick. It was half past six by then, two and a half hours later than she had agreed to be there. But since she'd already had three turkey dinners in the last three days, she wasn't really bothered about missing the food. All she wanted was to cuddle up in a nice warm bed with her favourite vicar.

Diane didn't look her best. She was wearing her work clothes, the same twin set she'd worn for the past three days. Underneath it she was wearing her long Johns and thermal vest. She didn't have any makeup on, and her hair was a complete mess.

"He'll just have to accept me as I am," she thought to herself as she pulled up outside the vicarage.

Diane went and knocked on the door.

"Bloody hell," she thought. "I haven't even got him a card, let alone a present. I do hope he hasn't got me anything. Otherwise, I will really be embarrassed."

Nick opened the door. He'd got a wine glass in his hand and a smile on his face. But his smile soon vanished when he saw Diane.

"Diane, I didn't think you were coming," he said.

"I've been stranded in a pub in the Peak District for three days, Nick. We were snowed in. That was why I didn't come to midnight mass last night."

"But all the snow's been up in Yorkshire according to the news. There's been nothing about any in Derbyshire on the TV, and look, there's been hardly any snow here."

"There might have been none in Chesterfield, but there was three feet of it up in Bleckley where I was stuck. I cannot describe how bad the conditions were."

"But why didn't you phone me?" asked Nick.

"Because all the phone lines were down," replied Diane who was becoming irritated by now, especially since she was still standing in the freezing cold on the doorstep of the vicarage.

"Nicky darling," a woman called from inside the vicarage.

It was an embarrassing moment and Nick was looking flustered.

"Diane," he said.

"Oh, I see," she interrupted him. "I'm stranded in the middle of nowhere and rather than trying to find out what's happened to me, you find another woman to share your bed."

"I'm sorry, Diane. I thought you'd blown me out and I didn't want to be alone on Christmas Day."

"So you immediately went and warmed up the substitute. Is she wearing a shirt with number twelve on her back?"

"Not quite, Annie is my organist from church. She's been very kind to me."

"I bet she has," added Diane cuttingly. "Someone should have told her that it's the church organ she should be playing.

She doesn't have to play with yours as well. Never mind though, the two of you were obviously meant for each other. Nick the Dick and Annie the Fanny, a perfect fit for each other. I hope you are both very happy."

Diane turned and left. She didn't want Nick to see that she had tears in her eyes.

A few minutes later, she arrived back at her small house in Brampton. It was dark and cold and there was no beer or wine in the fridge. She hadn't had any time to stock up before she'd become stranded in the Three Tuns.

The only thing she had was a bottle of Cyprus sherry, which she opened and poured herself a glass. She sat down in her armchair and put the TV on. It was the *Morecambe and Wise Christmas Special*.

"Good grief," she said to herself. "This must be my worst Christmas ever. I never thought I'd hear myself say this, but I really wish I'd gone down to Guildford to spend it with Mum and Dad."

Chapter 29
Tuesday morning, December 26th, 1978

Diane went into the station early on Boxing Day. She'd given Spencer the day off. It was the very least she could do, bearing in mind he hadn't been able to spend most of the Christmas period with his family.

Colin and Nigel were also on holiday, which meant the only two members of her team who were due in that day were Alan and Claire.

It was Alan who arrived first, looking extremely pleased with himself.

"You're looking very happy with yourself, Alan," said Diane. "You must have had your annual Christmas shag."

"Very funny, guv. No, I was just thinking that you and Spencer ought to go away more often. Whilst you were away, the rest of the team and I have solved six crimes."

"Go on, fill me in then," Diane replied. "And by the way, it's either Diane or ma'am, not guv."

"Sorry, ma'am," he replied. "Anyway, you remember the car that was blocking the road to the pub you were stuck in?"

"How could I ever forget it?"

"Well, it turned out the car involved was an orange Ford Escort. I put two and two together and took the photofit of our suspect down to the hospital where the driver was being treated and, bingo, it was our man. I cautioned him and told him we were going to put him into an identity parade. But in the end that wasn't necessary. He's confessed. It seems he used to be a clerk in Northern United's finance department. He'd lost his job when the Sheffield site closed and most of the finance jobs moved to Manchester."

"I always thought that someone from the brewery was behind this," added Diane.

"Not only that, but his girlfriend is the company's load planner responsible for matching up the orders with the drays. She's the person who decides the order in which the deliveries are made. Or rather that was what she used to do until the brewery went over to fixed runs. Her main job now is to ensure that none of the lorries go out over their weight limit. The only time she needs to plan deliveries these days is during the run-up to Christmas. The implementation of fixed runs was quite a comedown for her, and her job was downgraded as a result. As well as that, she now has a far longer commute to work, being as though the depot is in Staveley and she lives in Sheffield."

"So basically, we had two unhappy bunnies who wanted to hurt Northern United and, at the same time, line their own pockets," said Diane.

"Precisely," Alan replied. "Anyway, both of them have been charged and they are due to appear in court on Friday."

"You know," said Diane, "it never ceases to amaze me how stupid and how greedy some people can be. It was obvious that it was somebody from the brewery who was tipping the thief off and it was only a matter of time before we found out who that person was. And what did they get away with, less than £1,500? Now they'll both have a criminal record, a huge fine and face the prospect of going to prison."

"Still, it's a good job that most criminals are stupid," added Alan. "It makes them a lot easier to catch."

"Easy or not, you've still done a good job, Alan," added Diane.

"Thank you, ma'am," he replied. "What did you and Spencer do whilst you were snowed in? Did you try to drink the pub dry?"

"If only that was all we had to do. No, Spencer and I found ourselves in the middle of a mystery going back over fifteen years. The mystery involved five people vanishing and, while we were there, one of them miraculously turned up out of the blue. But, as well as that, there was a miscarriage of justice, an escaped wolf and a suspicious death, all in a small hamlet with only fifteen inhabitants."

"It sounds intriguing, ma'am."

"It's a long story. So you'd better go and fetch Claire. It's bad enough that I'm going to have to brief Colin and Nigel separately. I may as well brief you two at the same time."

It took Diane nearly an hour to tell Alan and Claire what she and Spencer had discovered in Bleckley. When she was finished, Alan summed up the situation.

"So the most likely explanation is that the mine was never capped, that Hugh Stanton Senior murdered all or some of the four missing people, and that he dumped their bodies down the shaft."

"That's right. The person I think is the least likely to be down there is Grant Cartwright, the potholer. He disappeared before the mine was supposed to be filled in. If Hugh Stanton had dumped his body there, then he would surely have wanted it covered up with a few tons of gravel and concrete."

"But if his body isn't at the bottom of the mine, then where is it?" asked Claire.

"I still think the original explanation for his disappearance is the correct one," replied Diane. "In other words, he was trapped underground and perished whilst looking for the new cavern complex. The other person I'm not totally certain about is Alice Barlow, as she was last seen walking towards Great Hucklow a mile and a half away. But if she isn't down there, then I don't know where she could be. She might have turned around and headed back towards Bleckley or somebody could have killed her and brought her body back. If either of those two possibilities are correct, her body might be at the bottom of that mine shaft. Either way, we won't know what's happened until we remove the mound of earth. I want a mechanical digger at the scene first thing in the morning. The latest weather forecast is that it's going to be ten degrees and raining today. Therefore, the snow will be melting fast."

"What about the death of Robert Hancock, ma'am?" asked Alan. "You said that you thought it was suspicious. Surely, he was just disorientated. He must have lost his sense of direction and fallen over the cliff. After all, most of the landmarks that were familiar to him would have been covered in a blanket of snow."

"It's possible, but I doubt it. Robert was a local lad from Foolow. He'd have been acutely aware of the danger posed by Bleckley Edge. That's why I'm not convinced it was an accident. Get hold of Dr Thompson, I know it's Boxing Day, but I need him to do an autopsy this afternoon. In the meantime, Claire and I will take a trip out to Bleckley Edge to see the place where Robert Hancock fell to his death."

Chapter 30
Tuesday afternoon, December 26th, 1978

One hour later, Diane and Claire were heading back towards Bleckley. If Diane had any fears about getting trapped again, they were soon dispelled. It may have been less than 24 hours since she and Spencer had been freed, but already the landscape had changed dramatically.

The warm front from the southwest had pushed back overnight, bringing rain with it. The snow was melting fast, and flooding had replaced blizzards as the major hazard.

But flooding was not an issue where they were going. Bleckley Edge was 1,300 feet above sea level, high up in the hills of the Peak District.

Initially, police from the station in Bakewell had treated Robert's death as an accident. But following an intervention from Diane, the scene was now subject to a police cordon. In fact, there were two areas roped off, one was the place where Robert had fallen from and the other was where he'd landed.

They first went to the scene of his fall. It was opposite the entrance to the youth hostel and there was supposed to be a uniformed officer guarding it. But when they arrived, he was nowhere to be seen. Shortly afterwards he appeared, approaching them from the direction of the Three Tuns.

"Where have you been, constable?" Diane asked him. "You're supposed to be guarding my crime scene, not drinking in the pub. What if somebody had crossed the tape and interfered with it?"

"I wasn't drinking, ma'am," said the young recruit who was probably no older than twenty. "I was sheltering from the rain and I could see the crime scene from the pub window."

"Jesus Christ, you've got a coat, haven't you?"

"Yes ma'am," replied the PC whilst looking sheepish.

Diane and Claire went to take a look at the cliff edge where Robert had fallen, but there wasn't anything to see. Snow and rain had obliterated any footprints and the whole area was now covered in something resembling a brown Slush Puppy.

The cliff edge itself was about fifty feet away from the road, with a sheer drop down to the valley below. It was an area very popular with rock climbers and mountaineers in the summertime. But it was also very dangerous, with numerous signs in the area warning ramblers not to venture too close.

"One thing, ma'am," said Claire, "if Robert Hancock was intending to go home to Foolow, why did he head in this direction? Surely, even in a blizzard, he would have known that he needed to carry on past the youth hostel rather than head towards the cliff edge."

"That's what I thought," Diane replied. "But the more I think about it, the less convinced I am. The conditions were absolutely horrendous that day. Plus, he was extremely emotional about getting home to his family for Christmas. He just wasn't thinking straight."

Mind you, even as she said it, Diane wasn't convinced. The brewery dray had become trapped in the snowdrift only a few yards further down the road and was still there when Robert had wandered off. Surely, he would have known that he had to walk past it if he wanted to take the road to Foolow.

At that moment, the forensic team arrived. They were due to carry out their investigation of the scene of Robert's fall.

"Right," said Diane. "Now that they're here, let's go and look at where he landed."

Paul, the young PC, went with them. He'd been one of the first people to visit the site after the mountain rescue team had discovered the body. Diane wanted him to describe what he had found.

He wasn't a bad lad, as Diane was to discover while talking to him. He lived in the section house over in Bakewell and, since he wasn't married, he had volunteered to work over the Christmas period. Just like Diane, he'd decided to let his colleagues with children take Christmas off instead.

"Didn't you want to spend Christmas with your parents then?" asked Diane once they were back in the car.

"They live in Leeds," Paul replied. "Mum and Dad never really wanted me to join the police. They wanted me to train as a doctor or an accountant. I really didn't want the hassle of them badgering me over the Christmas period."

The story was not dissimilar to Diane's own, and she began to feel some sympathy with the young constable. She'd obviously been too quick to criticise him earlier.

The brewery dray had been removed earlier that day and they were now able to take the road to Foolow. Halfway down the hill, Paul told Diane to stop and the three of them got out.

A brief walk along a footpath at the bottom of the cliff face brought them to another area that was surrounded by police tape.

"This is where he ended up then?" Diane asked Paul.

"That's right, ma'am. If you look up, you will see the cliff above where we've just been standing. When he fell, he landed approximately here. He dragged himself a few yards up this slope. He presumably did this to try and get out of the blizzard.”

“The fall didn’t kill him straight away then?” Diane asked. “That’s surprising being as though it’s such a big drop. It’s got to be at least 300 feet onto solid rock.”

“That’s right, but if you’d seen it yesterday, you’d see why he wasn’t killed outright. There were three feet of snow on the ground and that broke his fall. He was obviously badly injured, which makes it all the more amazing that he was able to drag himself up here. It didn’t offer him very much protection from the elements, as it’s just an overhanging rock. It didn’t do him any good either. He was dead when the mountain rescue team found him the next day.”

“Okay, I’ve seen enough,” said Diane.

The three of them returned to the car and drove back to Bleckley, where they dropped off Paul.

“Before we drive back to Chesterfield, I want to go to the youth hostel,” Diane told Claire.

The two officers got out and walked to the building with its familiar green triangular logo fastened to the outside wall. There was still nobody staying there, and the door was locked. Diane rang the bell and a few seconds later Mervyn answered it.

He smiled at the two officers.

“Ding, dong,” he said whilst looking at Claire.

It reminded Diane of the first time they’d met, which was something she’d rather forget.

“Diane, I must compliment you,” he continued. “Your current partner is far better looking than your last one.”

Claire could feel her face colouring up.

“Cut the crap, will you, Mervyn?” said Diane as she brushed past him into the hostel’s lounge.

"I want to look at your guest book," she continued.

"Very well," said Mervyn who disappeared into the office to fetch it.

He returned a few minutes later.

"What are you looking for? I might be able to help you."

"I want the names and contact details of all the people who were in the hostel at the same time as Alice Barlow and Penny Foster. We need to speak to them, because if Alice's body is really at the bottom of that mine shaft, we still won't know how she got there, and one of them might be able to help us."

Claire took down the names, addresses and telephone numbers of the six boys, two men and two German girls, all of whom had stayed in the youth hostel in April 1971. Once that was done, the two officers set off back to Chesterfield.

"What do you think happened then?" she asked when they were back in the car.

"What? To Alice Barlow or to Robert Hancock," replied Diane.

"Both of them," said Claire.

"Regarding Alice Barlow, I'll let you know as soon as we've dug the earth from that mine shaft tomorrow. Where Robert Hancock is concerned, I'll let you know what my feelings are about him once I've spoken to the pathologist, and that's the first thing I intend doing when we get back to Chesterfield."

Thirty minutes later, they were back heading down Chatsworth Road towards the town centre where the Royal Hospital was located.

The mortuary was at the back of the hospital in a separate block well away from the main hospital building. It was as if the hospital didn't want to advertise to the sick patients on the wards where they would end up if their treatment failed.

Richard Thompson, the pathologist, was busy hosing away the blood from the top of his stainless-steel autopsy table when Diane and Claire entered the room.

"DI Rothwell, I've got a bone to pick with you," he said as soon as he noticed Diane. "I had tickets for Chesterfield's game against Sheffield Wednesday today and you've made me miss a six-goal thriller."

"Never mind, doc, I'm sure you'd rather be cutting up dead bodies," Diane replied. "Anyway, what did you discover?"

"Our victim was a well-nourished man in his mid-30s," he told her. "He appeared to be a picture of health, apart from some hardening of the liver caused by too much alcohol. He died of hypothermia."

"He didn't die as a result of his fall, then?"

"No, despite the fact that he had suffered a fractured pelvis, a broken left arm, dislocated right wrist and a fractured skull, it wasn't the fall that killed him. In fact, he may well have recovered if he'd been found earlier. He froze to death, Inspector."

Diane started to feal pangs of guilt over Robert's death. After all, she had insisted that they shouldn't send out a search party to look for him. If they had, they would perhaps have found him before he froze to death. But then again, Robert was at the bottom of a cliff face and there was no way they could have got to him in a blizzard. No, her decision had been the right one. She was convinced of it.

"Is that all?" she asked. "Isn't there anything else you can tell me?

"Oh yes, Inspector, I have a little mystery for you to solve. Despite being very badly injured and being in terrible pain, our victim dragged himself out of the snow to a place where an overhanging rock offered him a bit of protection from the elements. Once he was there, he placed these six stones in his pocket."

He showed Diane a plastic bag containing the stones he'd removed from Robert's pocket.

"What? Are you absolutely sure that he did it after he had fallen?"

"Without a shadow of a doubt, Inspector. You see, he placed six stones in the front right pocket of his trousers. His keys were also in the same pocket and they left an impression on the top of his leg where he landed on them. But there were no such marks from the stones. That's why he must have placed them there after he fell."

"But how could he do that with his injuries?"

"It's amazing what the human body can do when someone puts their mind to it. He must have been in absolute agony but was utterly determined to do it."

"But why?" asked Diane.

"I presume it was because he wanted to send a message to you, Inspector," Dr Thompson replied. "Now all you have to do is to work out what that message was."

Chapter 31
Wednesday morning, December 27th, 1978

"You know that I said I would let you know what had happened to Robert Hancock once I'd spoken to the pathologist," said Diane to Claire the next morning. "Well, just ignore me if I ever say that again, will you? Because, in truth, I still haven't got a clue."

Diane's team was back up to full strength again as Spencer, Nigel and Colin had all returned from their Christmas break.

Spencer was briefing Nigel and Colin about the Beast of Bleckley case as they had decided to call it. That was in spite of the fact that nobody believed that an escaped wolf was responsible for any of the disappearances.

Eventually, the three of them went and joined Diane, Claire and Alan in the incident room.

"Now that everybody is fully up to speed, let's look at what we are going to do today," said Diane. "Alan, you can start by telling the team what you've organised."

"I've arranged for a digger and a mobile winch to go to Stanton Farm in Bleckley," he said. "If, as we think, the mine shaft hasn't been filled in, we intend opening it up and lowering Dr Thompson down in a basket. We expect to find at least two bodies at the bottom if the shaft has not been sealed. In which case, it's not going to be a pleasant or an easy task to recover any human remains we may find down there."

"Thanks, Alan," said Diane. "Spencer, Alan and Colin, I want you to come with me to Bleckley. Meanwhile, Nigel and Claire, you must remain here and track down the ten people who were at the youth hostel at the same time as Alice Barlow. Now, if that's all clear, do we have any questions?"

"Yes," said Spencer. "Are we treating Robert Hancock's death as an accident, murder, or suicide?"

"We are keeping an open mind on that one for now, Spencer. You all know that Dr Thompson discovered six stones in the right front pocket of Robert Hancock's trousers. Does anyone have any ideas about why they were there or what they might mean?"

The room went quiet, indicating that nobody had a clue. So Diane called the meeting to a halt.

"Right, let's get on with it then," she announced.

"Did you hear what they said on the TV yesterday about the snow?" said Spencer once he and Diane were in the car.

"No, did they say it heralded the start of a new ice age?"

"No, they said that it wasn't a white Christmas this year. To be classified as a white Christmas, a single snowflake has to fall on the roof of the London weather centre on Christmas Day. They didn't get any snow in London. So this year's Christmas isn't classed as white."

"Bloody hell, Spencer. That means we must have imagined all that white stuff that kept us trapped in Bleckley for three days."

"You do know that sarcasm is the lowest form of wit, ma'am?" Spencer replied.

Forty minutes later, the two of them arrived in Bleckley with Bateman and Wallace arriving shortly afterwards. Dr Thompson, his assistant and several forensic scientists were already there, and they had erected an evidence tent next to the mine shaft. It was also there to act as a makeshift mortuary ready to receive any bodies they may recover.

In addition, there were several workmen next to a mechanical digger. A large A-frame with a pulley attached to it was standing alongside the mound of earth. It was waiting to be moved into place over the shaft once the earth had been removed.

Diane started to feel nervous.

"Good God, I hope I'm right about all of this," she thought to herself. "I'm going to look like a right idiot if all they discover is a concrete cap underneath all that earth."

Diane's worries turned out to be unnecessary as fifteen minutes into removing the mound, the workmen discovered a metal trapdoor.

"That's the original door they put over the entrance to the mine when it closed," said Spencer. "You were right, ma'am. This shaft has never been capped. Furthermore, it isn't locked. If it wasn't for the earth that's been put on top of it, anyone could have opened it."

The trapdoor was old and heavy, but the workmen soon had it open.

Dr Thompson lay down on his stomach and shone his torch down the shaft.

"I can see a motorbike down there and a load of rubbish and, what's that? Hello? I think congratulations are in order, Inspector, I can see at least one body as well."

It took the workmen another hour to erect the A-frame with the pulley attached to it and then to connect the winch and the basket. As a result, it was nearly lunchtime before the team were ready to lower Dr Thompson into the mine.

"Rather him than me," muttered Spencer as the pathologist descended into the old mine shaft.

Dr Thompson intended to make a preliminary inspection of the base of the mine shaft before the team decided what to do next.

In total, he was down there for forty minutes before he was eventually pulled out again.

"Well," said Diane, "what did you find?"

"It's difficult to be precise because there's so much rubbish down there. But so far, I've discovered five bodies.

Chapter 32
Wednesday afternoon, December 27th, 1978

"That's three human bodies and two animals," Dr Thompson clarified.

"So what's next?" asked Diane.

"Firstly, we are going to remove the bodies one by one whilst trying to preserve as much of the evidence as possible. It is not going to be easy as conditions are pretty cramped down there. Once they are all out, we will take them back to Chesterfield in order to carry out autopsies, which hopefully will establish the cause of death of each of them. Then the forensic team will begin the painstaking task of removing and examining all the rubbish down there. It's going to be a long job. So we'd better get on with it."

Diane decided to leave Alan and Colin at the scene whilst she and Spencer went to break the news to Hugh Stanton Junior. After all, one of the bodies discovered by Dr Thompson was almost certainly that of his mother. In addition, it was highly probable that his father was the man responsible for all three of them being there in the first place.

When they arrived at the Stantons' farmhouse, the first thing they noticed was several black bin liners filled with rubbish. They were stacked by the dustbins and were waiting to be collected. Hugh had obviously been sorting out his father's rubbish.

Diane knocked on the door and Hugh opened it.

"Hi," he said. 'I saw all the work going on at the old mine this morning. Have you discovered anything?"

"Can we come in please, Mr Stanton?" Diane replied.

He ushered the two officers into the farmhouse kitchen. It was still pretty gloomy but was looking much cleaner than when she and Spencer had last been in it.

"Hugh, I've come to inform you that our forensics team have discovered that the mine shaft on your land was never capped. Furthermore, when they opened it up, they discovered three bodies at the bottom of the shaft. We shan't know for certain until we get the bodies back to the lab, but since four people have gone missing in this area, we believe that the bodies we've discovered will be three of those four people. In which case, one of them is almost certainly your mother."

"I should have stayed," said Hugh. "I was a coward. I should have stood up to him instead of running away. I should have protected my mother."

"We don't know for certain that your father was responsible for all three deaths. But I have to tell you that this house is now a crime scene. We need to get our forensics team to go through all your father's belongings, including those you've already put out to be disposed of. I presume that it's his stuff in those black bin liners out there?"

Hugh nodded. "I've been clearing out his old clothes," he added.

"Unfortunately, I'm going to have to ask you to move out whilst we carry out our search," explained Diane. "Is there anywhere you can stay?"

"I'll take a room in the pub until you've finished. Is it okay if I go and pack a bag?"

"That's fine, Hugh," Diane replied. "Just be careful not to touch anything that might be of use to us as evidence."

Ten minutes later the three of them walked out of the farmhouse and Spencer placed crime scene tape over the door.

"Right," said Diane once she and Spencer got back in the car. "There's nothing more we can do here, Spencer. Let's get back to the station and see if Nigel and Claire have discovered anything."

Diane started up the flying ashtray and they headed back to Chesterfield.

"You think that the three bodies are those of Mary Stanton, Alice Barlow and Jonathon Stoppard, don't you?" said Spencer once they were back on the A623.

"I'd be astounded if they weren't," Diane replied.

"And Hugh Stanton killed them all and disposed of all their bodies in the mine shaft?"

"That's correct," said Diane.

"I can see why he murdered his wife, after all, what man wouldn't want to do that?"

"From where I'm sitting, I think Rachel is far more likely to murder you than the other way around," Diane replied. "By the way, I never asked you if she liked the food mixer."

"Not exactly," he replied. "I think she would have preferred some perfume."

"I told you that the food mixer was a mistake," said Diane. "You should consult me in future before buying her anything. I'll point you in the right direction."

"Thank you very much, Ma'am," Spencer replied. "Just getting back to the bodies in the mine shaft for a minute. I can also see why he would have murdered Jonathon Stoppard. It must have been to stop him from discovering his wife's body.

But why murder Alice Barlow? He doesn't appear to have a motive, or the opportunity come to that, being as though she was at least a mile and a half away when she was last seen."

"I have absolutely no idea how or why he murdered Alice Barlow. That is something I intend to find out."

Twenty minutes later, they arrived back at the station where Diane went straight to the incident room in order to speak to Nigel and Claire.

"I've managed to track down four out of the six boys who were staying in the youth hostel at the same time as Alice Barlow," Nigel told her. "They were all living with their parents back in 1971 and it was their parents' addresses and telephone numbers that were in the hostel's register. In the intervening seven and a half years, they've all moved out, apart from one of them. So I had to get their new contact details from their parents."

"And what did they say?"

"The ones I've spoken to so far couldn't throw any light on the disappearance of Alice Barlow. It seems that they had moved on to Castleton the day before she disappeared. Three out of the four couldn't even remember her. They might have done if she'd been three or four years younger but, at eighteen, she was out of their league. In fact, she didn't even register with most of them. The fourth guy, however, did remember both her and her friend. He looked as if he was the oldest one in the group, and he tried unsuccessfully to get served in the Three Tuns, whilst his mates waited outside. He said that both girls were in the pub that night. Out of the two of them, it was Penny who stood out, as she wasn't wearing a bra. He also said that he noticed the two of them again at breakfast the next day, but unfortunately Penny now had a bra on. They all left a little later for the youth hostel in Castleton. As a result, I don't believe that these lads can really help us with our enquiry."

"Okay, and what about the other people who were there?" asked Diane.

"It was easier to track down the two older men who were staying there as they both live at the same addresses as they did back in 1971," replied Nigel. "Both of them remember Alice and Penny, probably because they were young and pretty."

"That's not surprising," said Diane. "It's a well-known fact that women get more and more invisible with age."

"On the day she disappeared, they walked with Alice as far as the fork in the road," Nigel continued. "That was where they turned off towards Foolow, whilst she headed straight on towards Great Hucklow. They both described her mood as unhappy, which they put down to the fact that she'd just had an argument with her friend."

"And Penny confirms that they had had a row," Diane cut in.

"Graham Fletcher, one of the two men, told me that he'd received a phone call from Jonathon Stoppard two years after Alice had disappeared. He was asking very similar questions to the ones I wanted him to answer now. We know he was investigating Alice's disappearance and it seems he contacted Mr Fletcher as part of that investigation. Anyway, that was all I've been able to discover. It's not much, I know, but Claire has found something of far more significance. I'll let her explain."

"I made the mistake of telling Nigel I'd got an O level in German," said Claire. "Consequently, he suggested that I would be the best person to try and track down the two German girls. Believe me, it was not an easy task, being as though both of them now live at different addresses than those they lived at back in 1971. Furthermore, both of them are now married and have different surnames. Also, I haven't spoken German for six years and all I can remember from my O level is how to count to ten and how to order sausage and chips in a restaurant. Anyway, most of the people I spoke to were far more proficient in English than I was in German. As a result, I was able to track down the two of them."

"So what did they say?" asked Diane.

"They both remembered Alice and Penny and were able to recall what happened on the day Alice went missing. They told me that they had delayed setting out on that morning due to thick fog. Eventually at about 9.30 they set off, even though the fog hadn't cleared. Then as soon as they had reached the Foolow turnoff, they bumped into Alice, who was walking back towards Bleckley. She told them she had decided to abandon her walk due to the weather and she was going back to the youth hostel."

"That's interesting," added Diane. "What that tells us is that Alice did retrace her steps that morning and it puts Hugh Stanton back in the frame for murdering her. In addition, the Foolow turnoff is very close to where we discovered the three bodies."

"Claudia Zimmer, or Claudia Walbrecht as she is now called, was also able to tell me that, two years after that, Jonathon Stoppard phoned her. He was obviously following up the same leads as us, asking the same people very similar questions, which was why he'd phoned both Graham Fletcher and Claudia Walbrecht. Anyway, Claudia confirmed to me that she had told him about seeing Alice heading back to Bleckley. Therefore, I believe that one of the bodies we've discovered is his. I think that on the day he disappeared, he had decided to go and look at where Alice had last been seen. But someone must have noticed what he was doing, murdered him and dumped his body down the mine shaft."

"Well done you two," said Diane. "I agree that one on the bodies will probably be that of Jonathon Stoppard, as we know he drove a motorbike and one was discovered at the bottom of the shaft. We also now know that Alice Barlow was near to Hugh Stanton's farm when she disappeared and, consequently, he would have had the opportunity to kill her. Therefore, I believe that the three bodies will turn out to be those of Alice Barlow, Jonathon Stoppard, and Mary Stanton. The only missing piece of this jigsaw is why Hugh Stanton should murder Alice Barlow. So all we need to discover is why he killed her, and we've got this case solved."

However, Spencer added a note of caution to the proceedings

"Apart from discovering what happened to the fourth missing person and why, Robert Hancock was found at the bottom of a cliff with six stones in his pocket," he added.

Chapter 33
Thursday morning, December 28th, 1978

Diane had a case review meeting with her boss, Superintendent Jeff Barker, at 10 o'clock the following morning. Normally, she didn't look forward to these meetings, but on this occasion, she was positively relishing it.

"Good morning, sir, did you have nice Christmas?" she said on entering his office.

Unlike Diane, Superintendent Barker had been able to take five days off over the Christmas period. It was one of the privileges associated with his rank.

"Excellent, thank you, Diane," he replied. "And I hear you have been busy whilst I've been off and that congratulations are in order. I believe you've solved three murders?"

"Yes, we've recovered three bodies from a mine shaft in Bleckley and we are pretty certain about their identities and who killed them. We will know a bit more once Dr Thompson has completed the autopsies later today."

"And I understand the person who is most likely responsible for all this is now deceased?"

"That's correct sir, our chief suspect is Hugh Stanton Senior who died of cirrhosis of the liver back in September. It is likely that one of the victims was his wife and another is a reporter from the *Derbyshire Times* who was investigating the disappearances in the area. We are working on the theory that the reporter discovered the mine hadn't been filled in and that there were bodies in it."

"So Stanton killed him in order to keep him quiet?"

"That's right, sir. We believe the third body was that of Alice Barlow who disappeared in April of 1971. At the time, the last sighting of her was in Great Hucklow and we believed she was heading away from Bleckley. Now, however, new evidence has come to light to say that she turned around and headed back towards Bleckley. She was last seen near Hugh Stanton's farm. The only thing we don't know yet is why Stanton should kill her."

"Well, that's great, Diane. However, I wouldn't waste much more time on this case. After all, it will never go to court, being as though Stanton is dead. Consequently, you don't have to prove beyond a reasonable doubt that he did it. We can just release a statement to the press, and you can bask in the glory of having solved three murders. Are any of Hugh Stanton's relatives likely to challenge your version of events?"

"No, sir. His only living relative is a son, also called Hugh Stanton, and he believes that his father is guilty just as we do."

"Excellent, Diane, that's that then. We can wrap up this enquiry after the autopsy. After all, we don't want to overspend our overtime budget, do we?"

"No, sir, we don't," Diane replied.

"And it's not just the three murders that have been cleared up. I believe you've also solved the case of our mystery closing time thief."

Closing time thief was the name dreamt up by the *Sheffield Star* when they ran a report on the arrest of the man responsible for the six robberies.

"It's DS Bateman who needs to take the credit for that one, sir. I was trapped by the snow in Bleckley when that particular crime was solved."

"You are too modest, Diane. DS Bateman is part of your team. He's a good officer, but he couldn't have done what he did without the groundwork you put in first."

"If you say so, sir," replied Diane.

"It was definitely one of my better decisions when I decided to put you in charge of our licensed trade crime team. You'll go far, believe me. The ACC is overjoyed by what you are doing. I think I'll have to go on holiday more often if this is the result, what with nine crimes being solved in the space of five days. Please convey my congratulations to everybody in your team, will you? And remember, no more overtime."

"I will, sir," Diane replied, before leaving his office to rejoin her team.

"Well?" said Spencer.

"Twice," replied Diane.

"You're joking, he must be in a good mood. My betting was on him mentioning it at least three times."

He was referring to the word 'overtime' and the team's sweepstake betting on the number of times Superintendent Barker would mention it during his meeting with Diane. It was a running joke amongst Diane's team that it was the only thing he was really interested in.

Following her meeting, Diane decided that she and Spencer should go and get an update from Dr Thompson. So the two of them drove over to his pathology laboratory.

Dr Thompson's team had worked through the night to recover the three bodies from the mine. It was not an easy job to extract them from the bottom of the mine shaft, being as though they were badly decomposed and were lying in a confined space. In addition, the fact that a motorbike had been thrown down on top of them hadn't exactly helped either.

Eventually though, all three had been removed and transferred to Dr Thompson's laboratory in Chesterfield. Once this task had been completed, Dr Thompson's team, the SOCOs, and Bateman and Wallace had all gone home for some well-deserved rest. The SOCOs were due to return that afternoon in order to look for further evidence at the bottom of the mine shaft. This time, Nigel and Claire were going to go with them as there were now two crime scenes that needed investigating.

His team might have gone home, but Dr Thompson hadn't. He had remained in order to start doing the autopsies. It was as if the man didn't need any sleep, a fact that Diane was eternally grateful for.

"Ah, Diane, Spencer," he said as they entered the room. "I've already got some news for you."

"Great, let's hear it then, Richard," Diane replied.

"Firstly, I understand that the motorbike we discovered was a Kawasaki S, registration number TRB 365 K. The SOCOs have told me that it was registered to Jonathon Stoppard."

"That follows," said Spencer.

"Then there were the autopsies I carried out on the two animals that were found."

"Bloody hell, doc, I didn't think you were going to do autopsies on them as well."

"I'm nothing if not efficient, Diane," he replied. "They were both dogs and large dogs at that. Probably a breed like a rottweiler. Both of them were killed by a shotgun wound to the head. There are still traces of the pellets. Also, I think you should know that the bodies of the dogs were discovered underneath the three human remains."

"Which proves that Hugh Stanton was lying when he said that he'd buried his dogs in the garden. That's actually good news, doc, since we know Hugh Stanton killed the dogs. Therefore, we can prove he had already thrown the bodies of the dogs down the mine shaft before any of the human remains were dumped there. That also means that one of the bodies can't be that of Grant Cartwright, our missing potholer, as he disappeared in 1963, five years before Stanton shot his dogs."

"Which takes me nicely onto my next discovery. I obtained the dental records of all four possible victims before commencing the autopsy. There's nothing like good preparation and planning to speed an investigation along. On this occasion, it paid off as I have already identified our three bodies as being Mary Stanton, Alice Barlow and Jonathon Stoppard."

"Yes," said Diane punching the air. "I knew it."

"That was the easy bit though," Dr Thompson continued. "Far more difficult was identifying the cause of death of each of them. After so much time, it is very difficult to identify which injuries were post-mortem and which were ante-mortem. Especially after all three bodies had been thrown down a mine shaft and had a motorbike dumped on top of them. However, I have done my best."

"I wouldn't expect anything less, doc," said Diane.

"Both Mary Stanton and Jonathon Stoppard have depressed fractures to the skull suggesting they were hit over the head with our old friend, the blunt instrument. It could have been a hammer or something similar. Alice Barlow has no such head wound. But what she does have, is far more damage to the lower part of her body, including various crush injuries. They are similar injuries to what you might find in a road traffic accident."

"Are you suggesting she was run over?"

"I would say it's highly likely. But given the severity of her injuries, I would hazard a guess that it wasn't a car. It's more likely to be something like a lorry or a large van. It could have been a car if it had been travelling at speed. But given that all the roads in the area are narrow with many tight bends, that is highly unlikely. Consequently, it is far more likely to have been a commercial vehicle."

"How about a tractor?" asked Spencer.

"Quite possibly," replied Dr Thompson.

"Please go on, doc," Diane encouraged. "You always manage to throw in a little nugget at the end, something you've discovered, that you can't quite explain."

"Well, far be it for me to disappoint you, Inspector," replied Dr Thompson. "The surprising thing about these three bodies is that Alice Barlow's had a gold St Christopher around her neck, a watch on her wrist and a couple of silver rings on her fingers."

"What's surprising about that? It's normal jewellery that you'd expect a teenage girl to wear," commented Spencer.

"Ah, but that's not the mystery here," Dr Thomson replied. "The mystery is that neither of the other two bodies had any items of jewellery on them at all. Now Mary Stanton was a married woman. Wouldn't she have been wearing a wedding ring? Also, when did you last see a journalist not wearing a watch?"

"So the murderer removed these items before disposing of their bodies," said Diane.

"In which case," announced Dr Thompson, "the real mystery is why should he remove jewellery from his first and third victims, but not from his second?"

Chapter 34
Thursday afternoon, December 28th, 1978

"Perhaps Alice Barlow's jewellery wasn't worth very much," suggested Spencer once they'd left the pathology lab. "She was a teenage girl after all, her stuff wouldn't have been all that valuable."

But Diane wasn't listening to him. She was deep in thought.

"Did you notice there was a tractor on Hugh Stanton's farm when we went there yesterday? I'm not talking about the old Fordson we discovered in the engine shed. No, this one was relatively new. It was in one of the barns and the barn doors had been left open. It reminded me of my childhood. Whenever I left a door open, my mother would always ask me if I was born in a barn."

"I can't say that I noticed it, ma'am," said Spencer.

"Well, that's just you being unobservant," Diane continued. "Farmers are notorious for not throwing things away when they no longer need them. What's the betting he merely put it in one of his barns when he sold his land off? Then a few years later, he would have needed it when he turned his two remaining fields over to make silage. So he got it out again. I think that on the morning of Alice's disappearance he was driving from his farmhouse to his fields. It was foggy and he didn't see her until it was too late. She also didn't see him and before either of them realised what had happened, he'd hit her. He'd killed her and he decided to dump her body where he'd previously dumped the body of his wife."

"But if what you're saying is true, the death of Alice Barlow must have been a tragic accident," said Spencer. "In which case, why didn't he admit it? After all, it was death by misadventure, not murder or manslaughter."

"Because he was Hugh Stanton," Diane replied. "He was a heavy drinker and he'd almost certainly been over the drink-drive limit at that time of the morning. Consequently, nobody would have believed that it was an accident. They'd have believed that the reason why he ran her over was because his faculties were still impaired from the previous evening. In all probability, he'd have been found guilty of manslaughter and sent to prison. Then with him not there anymore, what was to stop anybody from finding out the mine shaft wasn't capped? If that happened, it would almost certainly have led to the body of his wife being discovered."

"It makes sense to me, ma'am," Spencer replied.

"We've solved this one, Spencer. There's no point in continuing our enquiry. You can call the team back and tell them that we'll all be going out for a drink this evening to celebrate. But before we do that, you and I still have a few jobs to do. We have to go and break the bad news to Alice and Jonathon's parents and to Penny Foster."

Alice's parents lived on Whitecotes Lane in a semi-detached property, which had backed onto open fields prior to the new council estate being built four years ago. If she returned home today, Alice would never have recognised the place, not that Alice was ever going to come home.

Diane and Spencer walked up to the front door and Diane rang the bell. A few seconds later, it was opened by Alice's mother. The two officers produced their warrant cards.

"It's about Alice, isn't it?" she asked them. "For seven years, I've been dreading this moment. I know you've got bad news."

"Can we come in please, Mrs Barlow?"

Mrs Barlow showed the officers into the living room where they were joined by her husband.

"Why don't the two of you sit down?" said Diane.

A few seconds later, Diane started to tell them what they'd found out so far.

"Yesterday, we discovered the remains of three people at the bottom of a disused mine shaft in the village of Bleckley. One of the bodies has since been identified as that of your daughter, Alice. I'm very sorry."

Mrs Barlow immediately burst into tears and her husband tried to console her.

"How did she die?" he asked them.

"We think she was killed in a road traffic accident and her body was placed in the mine shaft."

"Placed?" said Mr Barlow. "What you really mean is thrown down the shaft like a sack full of rubbish."

Diane could hardly disagree with him. She was just trying to choose her words carefully in order to cause minimal distress.

"Why would anyone do such a thing?" sobbed Mrs Barlow.

"We think it was because the person who did this was drunk at the time. He drove into her, and he decided to dispose of her body because he knew he was over the drink-drive limit."

"Well, I hope you're going to throw the book at him," said Mr Barlow.

"We can't, I'm afraid. He died earlier this year."

"Typical," he replied. "Why wasn't her body discovered until now? This mine couldn't have been very far from where she was staying if it was in Bleckley."

"It was about 400 yards away. The problem was that according to all the records the mine shaft had been sealed with gravel and cement back in the 1960s. However, we've now discovered that this never happened."

"You said that you've discovered three bodies," said Mrs Barlow. "Can I ask who the other two were?"

"One of them was the wife of the man we think is responsible for all of this. We've identified who the other victim was, but we aren't releasing his name until his next of kin have been informed. But what I can tell you is that both the other victims were bludgeoned to death."

"But you don't believe that happened to Alice," said Mr Barlow.

"No, the pathologist is convinced that your daughter was killed by crush injuries caused by her being hit by a large motor vehicle."

Alice's parents were a typical middle-class couple in their late fifties, polite and respectful of the law. In many ways, they reminded Diane of her own mum and dad. They even offered Diane and Spencer a cup of coffee, which they accepted. The two officers felt that Mr and Mrs Barlow needed a coffee far more than they wanted any refreshments.

Diane discovered that Alice had been an only child and that her parents had kept her bedroom exactly as she'd left it on the day she set off for Bleckley. It was in the vain hope that someday she'd return home. Deep down, though, they always suspected she was dead.

"She was such a lovely girl," said her mother. "She was a perfect daughter and she'd got her whole life ahead of her. She'd set her heart on going to university and we were so proud when she was offered a place to study French in York."

Neither of her parents had ever held with the explanation that she'd run away from home. They were deeply hurt by the implication that they were somehow to blame for her disappearance. That by putting too much pressure on her to do well in her exams, she'd finally cracked and ran away. Now that they knew what had happened it still didn't bring closure, though. Diane fully realised that the fact the culprit was now dead himself was a totally unsatisfactory outcome for them. It meant there would never be a court case and they would never see him receive a life sentence.

When the two officers finally left, Diane consoled herself that at least Alice's parents now had some answers. They could have a funeral and would no longer have the constant question about what had happened to their daughter hanging over their heads. But despite this, Diane couldn't help thinking that the news they had just given them had condemned them to a future without hope.

"You mustn't think that way, ma'am," said Spencer when they were back in the car. "It's Hugh Stanton who is responsible for their suffering. Not you."

"But we, the police, are partially responsible," she added. "We shouldn't have taken the easy way out by suggesting that she'd run away due to pressure at home. If only we had carried out a proper investigation at the time and followed up all the leads. Then at least, her parents wouldn't have been wondering what had happened to their daughter for the past seven years. They wouldn't have been subject to wild speculation by the local gossips."

Diane and Spencer's next port of call was the home of Jonathon Stoppard's parents, a large four-bedroomed detached property on the west side of town. As they approached the front door, they could hear laughter coming from inside, laughter that would soon be turning into tears. Unlike Alice, Jonathon had two siblings, a younger sister and brother, both of whom still lived at home. The whole family were playing a game of jenga, totally unaware of the bombshell that was about to hit them.

Diane knocked on the door and Mr Stoppard opened it.

"Mr Stoppard," she said. "I'm DI Rothwell and this is DS Spooner from Derbyshire Constabulary. Can we come in, please?"

"Oh no, it's about Jonathon, isn't it?" he said.

The Stoppards lived in another middle-class home. People like them, just like the Barlows, weren't used to getting visits from the police. That was why both families knew precisely why Diane and Spencer were there as soon as they introduced themselves. And they also knew that they weren't very likely to be bringing good news. After all, it was highly improbable that their son had been discovered on a desert island suffering from amnesia. No, the only possible reason for them coming to their house was to tell them they'd discovered his body.

"Would he have suffered?" asked Mr Stoppard after Diane had confirmed their worst fears.

"Absolutely not," she replied. "Your son was struck a severe blow on the back of his head. He would have been killed instantly. He never would have known what had happened."

There was no way Diane could have known that. Secretly, she hoped it was true and that he hadn't been tipped down the mine whilst he'd still been alive.

Diane and Spencer stayed with them for about half an hour answering their questions to the best of their abilities. It was a thankless task. They could do nothing to relieve their suffering.

"I hate this part of the job," Diane said to Spencer once they were back in the car again. "I feel like the grim reaper bringing misery wherever I go."

As she was speaking, Nigel came through on the radio.

"Ma'am, I just thought I'd update you on the search of Hugh Stanton's house. SOCOs have discovered some of Mary Stanton's jewellery including her wedding and engagement rings. They've shown them to her son, and he says they were definitely his mother's. Furthermore, he told them that she would never have taken them off. He reckons his father probably removed them before disposing of her body. He says his old man was really tight-fisted and would never throw anything away, especially if it was valuable. But far more damming is that the SOCOs have discovered a gold men's watch. You'll never guess what the inscription on the back says?"

"Go on, surprise me," Diane replied.

"It says, To Jonathon on his eighteenth birthday, with love from Mum and Dad."

"If Mary Stanton would never have removed her rings and they were found in Hugh Stanton's house, it follows that he must have killed her," replied Diane. "The fact that Jonathon's watch was also found there proves he must have killed him as well. That's all the proof we need. Hugh Stanton is definitely our murderer. All we need to do is to show the watch to Jonathon Stoppard's parents and get them to confirm that it belonged to their son. Once we've done that, we will have this case wrapped up."

Diane thanked Nigel before she and Spencer set off for their last visit of the day. This was to see Penny Foster, who was staying with her parents in Newbold.

Her father answered the door and showed the two officers into the living room where Penny was sitting reading a book. Penny wasn't related to any of the victims, of course. That said, one of them had been her best friend and the other had been a former boyfriend. Also, Diane had promised to keep her informed of any progress. Therefore, she felt duty-bound to visit her and tell her about what they had discovered.

"As you know, Penny, we went back to Bleckley this week in order to remove the earth from the top of the mine shaft," said Diane. "We wanted to see what we might find underneath. Well, what we discovered was that the mine shaft had not been capped. Our subsequent investigation revealed that three bodies had been dumped down the shaft. We have now identified those bodies, and I have to inform you they are those of Mary Stanton, Alice Barlow and Jonathon Stoppard."

Penny was close to tears. Diane wasn't sure if they were tears of sorrow or tears of relief. She finally had discovered some answers to the questions that had been troubling her for years.

"Do you know what the last thing was that I ever said to Alice?" she sobbed. "I said she'd probably end up in a ditch. What a cruel bitch I was. How was I to know she would end up in a mine shaft?"

That was a question that didn't need an answer. But there was another big one that did.

"Do you know what happened to Alice and Jonathon?" she asked.

"We think Hugh Stanton murdered his wife and then murdered Jonathon in order to stop him from discovering the truth about the mine. But we don't believe he murdered Alice. We believe he killed her accidently, probably by running her over in his tractor. Then he disposed of her body down the mine shaft in the same way as he'd done with his wife."

"No, you've got it wrong, Inspector," said Penny much to the surprise of Diane and Spencer. "Hugh Stanton couldn't have killed Alice. That was what Jonathon thought. He said as much to me the last time I saw him. I told him Hugh Stanton couldn't have done it, because Alice was last seen in Great Hucklow."

"Yes, but we've now traced the two German girls," said Diane. "They've confirmed that Alice turned around in Great Hucklow and returned to Bleckley. They last saw her close to the mine shaft where her body was discovered."

"That's as maybe," Penny continued. "But what I was going to say was that after Jonathon had left, I remembered there was another reason why Hugh Stanton couldn't have killed Alice. He wasn't in the village when she disappeared. He was locked up in the cells at Chesterfield police station."

Chapter 35
Thursday afternoon, December 28th, 1978

"Let me explain," said Penny. "The night before Alice disappeared, we were all in the pub. Hugh Stanton was in there as well. He'd been drinking heavily all day, firstly at Flagg races and then in the Three Tuns. He was very drunk. So drunk, in fact, that he knocked a table full of glasses over and fell on the floor cutting himself badly on some broken glass. Matt had to phone for an ambulance for him. Well, I thought nothing of it until the police were interviewing me two days later. They were accusing me of somehow being involved in Alice's disappearance and I told them that they should be interviewing Hugh Stanton instead of me. They said that the one person who definitely had a cast-iron alibi for Alice's disappearance was Hugh Stanton. They'd arrested him the night before she'd disappeared, and they hadn't released him until 4pm on the day she'd vanished."

"Shit," thought Diane to herself. "Why wasn't I told that? Talk about making us look incompetent."

"What had happened was that he was taken to accident and emergency at Chesterfield Royal Hospital," Penny continued. "If his accident had happened during the daytime, then the minor injuries unit in Bakewell could have seen to him. But at that time of night, the only option was to go to the hospital in Chesterfield. Hugh was extremely drunk and, whilst he was there, he tried to punch the doctor who was treating him. The hospital called the police, and they handcuffed him to the bed, in order to stitch him up. As soon as he had been treated, he was carted off to the police station and put in one of the cells. I understand he was a complete arsehole whilst he was there, screaming and yelling and pissing on the floor. So the police weren't exactly quick to release him the following day. In fact, they didn't let him go until four o'clock in the afternoon. Even then he had to get the bus back to Eyam and from there it's a one and a half hour walk up the hill to Bleckley. He wouldn't have gotten home until after half past six that evening."

"By which time, Alice had already been missing for several hours," Diane added.

"Exactly. So you see, Inspector, Hugh Stanton couldn't have killed Alice with his tractor. He was in Chesterfield when she went missing."

"Thanks for telling us that, Penny," said Diane. "Even though it has put us back to square one again in our quest to discover Alice's killer."

Diane was stunned by Penny's revelation. She had been so sure that Hugh Stanton had been responsible for all three deaths. It was with a heavy heart that she and Spencer returned to the station, where the first thing they did was to check the custody record for April 13th, 1971. It confirmed everything Penny had told them. Hugh Stanton had not been released until 3.56 in the afternoon.

"Argh," shouted Diane once they were back in the incident room. She'd thought this case was going to be simple.

Spencer was frustrated as well. But his frustration was for a different reason. This latest revelation meant that the team wouldn't be going to the pub after work in order to celebrate.

"Well, this new development can only mean one thing," Diane announced. "Somebody else must have killed Alice Barlow and dumped her body down the mine shaft."

"Let me get this right, ma'am," said Spencer. "You are saying that in a small hamlet with a population of fifteen, two of whom are children, we have two murderers?"

"No, Spencer," Diane replied. "We have one murderer and that's Hugh Stanton. Alice Barlow wasn't murdered. She was accidentally run over, and her body was dumped. Anyone in that village could have done it. They all knew about the mine shaft."

"Yes, but most of them thought it'd been filled in back in 1968, don't forget."

"Well, one of them must have known that it hadn't been."

"Okay," said Spencer. "If she was killed accidentally, then why dump her body? If it had been Hugh Stanton who'd killed her, fair enough, he'd still have been over the limit from the night before. But why would anyone else want to hide what they'd done?"

"I don't know, Spencer. I really don't know. Let's go through the sequence of events and see if we can make any headway. We know that Mary Stanton was the first person who was murdered, and we're pretty certain that it was her husband who killed her. We know this because we discovered her wedding and engagement rings in his house, which he presumably removed before disposing of her body. In addition, we know he used to beat her. So he probably killed her during a beating that went too far."

"Technically, Mrs Stanton wasn't the first, ma'am," added Spencer. "Hugh Stanton killed his dogs before he killed his wife."

"I stand corrected, Spencer, and it was precisely because nobody discovered his dogs' remains that made him decided to dispose of his wife's body in the same way. By this stage, we have his dogs and his wife at the bottom of the mine shaft. Next, it's Alice Barlow and we know that she was knocked down and killed by a person or persons unknown. What we do know is that it couldn't have been Hugh Stanton because he was in custody at the time. Whoever killed her dumped her body in the mine shaft. Now that person probably didn't know Mary Stanton's body was already down there. After all, Hugh Stanton wasn't likely to have told anyone, was he? But what they must have known was that the mine hadn't been capped."

"But so far we've not come across a single person who knew that, other than Colin Loggenberg and Hugh Stanton, both of whom are dead."

"Perhaps one of them told someone."

"It's not very likely to be Colin Loggenberg, though, being as he was killed shortly after he'd failed to cap the mine shaft. As for Hugh Stanton, why would he tell anyone? He'd got every incentive not to."

"I don't know, Spencer. Just bear with me for a moment, will you? Another thing we are certain about is that Hugh Stanton killed Jonathon Stoppard. He almost certainly caught him snooping about on his land, probably after discovering the old mine had never been filled in. Hugh Stanton had to kill him once he'd found that out. After all, Stanton knew that a search of the mine shaft would reveal his wife's body at the bottom. That was why he murdered him, dumped his body and his motorbike down the shaft, and covered the entrance to the mine with a mound of earth."

"If what you're saying is correct, it means we've got two people responsible for these three deaths," said Spencer. "Both of them dumped their victims down the mine shaft and neither of them knew about the other."

"That's correct," Diane replied. "We know Hugh Stanton killed his wife and Jonathon Stoppard. All we've got to do now is to discover who ran over and killed Alice Barlow. Whoever killed her must be local in order to know about the mine shaft and would have had to be in the area on the day she was killed. We need to get back to Bleckley as we've got twelve adults in that village who were living there in 1971 and one of them has to be our killer. Furthermore, if Alice was killed by a heavy vehicle, that means we can narrow our search down still further. It must be either a member of the Law family, as they own a tractor, or one of the Hallsworths, because they own a horse transporter and a coal waggon."

The phone started ringing again and Spencer answered it. It was Nigel who was now with the SOCOs at the mine shaft.

The call only lasted a few minutes. When it was over, Spencer turned to Diane and said, "You're right that we've got to go back to Bleckley, ma'am, but not to interview the villagers. The team at the mine have just discovered something that points us in a completely different direction."

Chapter 36

Thursday, early evening, December 28th, 1978

Diane and Spencer were driving back to Bleckley on the A619, and Diane was mulling over what she'd just been told.

"It makes sense," she said to Spencer.

She was referring to the fact that the SOCOs had discovered a work glove in the mine that had the initials RH written in biro on it.

"The pub's normal delivery day is a Wednesday, and their time window is between nine and ten. As a result, the brewery dray would have been in the right place when she went missing. It was a foggy day and Robert probably didn't see her until it was too late. Don't forget, Robert was a local lad and used to play with Hugh Stanton Junior when he was little. What's the betting that he knew about the mine? Then when he got older, Robert made new friends and stopped going to Bleckley. I guess he never knew the shaft was supposed to have been capped. After all, he was local, but not that local. He lived one and a half miles away in Foolow."

"So you're saying that Robert Hancock killed Alice Barlow?" asked Spencer. "And then covered it up by dumping her body down the mine shaft."

"Yes. He must be the person responsible for dumping Alice's body, and, whilst he was doing it, one of his gloves must have fallen into the mine. When he realised that we were going

268

to open up the old mine, he knew we'd discover it and he'd be implicated. That's why he committed suicide."

"So you think he killed Alice Barlow and then, when he realised that we were about to discover what he'd done, he killed himself?" added Spencer.

"You've got to admit it fits the facts," Diane replied.

"Most of them," Spencer replied. "But why should he dump her body. Why not just report it if it was an accident?"

"Perhaps he was worried about losing his job. After all, he loved working for the brewery. He told me that much himself and, since he had a wife and two kids to support, he would have been terrified about being sacked."

"Okay. So why, if he did commit suicide, did he choose to do it by throwing himself off a cliff in the middle of a blizzard in the pitch dark? We weren't going to be able to open up that mine for a few days. He could have gone home, seen his family one last time, and then taken a mixture of alcohol and painkillers."

"I don't know, Spencer. He was drunk, emotional and confused, I suppose."

"So given that he'd just tried to commit suicide, why should he then haul his broken body up a slope and put six stones into his pocket?"

"I don't know the answer to that one either. However, the person who will be able to help us with some of these questions is Cec Stenen. After all, if Robert Hancock did kill Alice Barlow, then Cec Stenen would have been sitting right next to him when he did it. Which unfortunately poses yet more questions. He must surely have helped Robert to dispose of the body. Why would he do that and why has he remained quiet for all these years?"

The plan was to go straight to the mine and examine the work glove and then to go to Cec Stenen's home in Monyash. Mind you, being as though he was potentially facing some serious charges, they didn't intend interviewing him at his house. Monyash was only a short drive away from Bakewell and they decided to cross-examine him at the police station in the town centre.

It was dark when the two officers arrived in Bleckley. Well, it would have been dark if it hadn't been for the floodlights that illuminated the entire village. There were the ones being used by the SOCOs to light up the area around the old mine, as well as the ones belonging to the various TV crews that had assembled in the village. The discovery of a mass grave down an old lead mine was big news, so big that it was sure to make the national news programmes on both the BBC and ITV.

"Matt Yates is going to have a busy night tonight," said Diane. "What with all these journalists around, it's bound to be good for his business. I just hope he doesn't run out of whisky."

The reporters wanted to interview Diane, of course. But she didn't have time for that. She got out of her car and, ignoring their questions, she walked over to where Paul, the young PC she'd met two days previously, was guarding the crime scene.

"You haven't been here for two days without a break, have you, Constable?" she asked him as he lifted the police tape to let her and Spencer through.

"No, ma'am, they even let me take yesterday off," he replied.

Diane and Spencer walked over to the tent that had been erected next to the mine shaft, where they found Nigel waiting for them inside. His colleague Claire Adcock was no longer with him. She had gone to phone Alan Fisher in order to ask him about the type of work gloves used by the draymen at Northern United.

"There you are, ma'am," he said whilst passing a plastic evidence bag over to her.

In the bag was a workman's glove made of cloth and leather. It wasn't in the best of conditions after being at the bottom of a mine shaft for nearly eight years. But what was still quite clear was the initials RH written on it.

"Thanks, Nigel," said Diane before turning to her sergeant and adding, "right, Spencer let's go and pick up Cec Stenen."

The two officers made their way back to the car, running the gauntlet of the waiting reporters once more.

"I still can't see why Cec Stenen would help Robert Hancock dispose of a body," said Spencer as they were heading towards Monyash. "Just think about it. If you knocked down and killed somebody, I wouldn't help you to dispose of the body. Why would I? After all, I wouldn't have done anything wrong. But as soon as I helped you get rid of the body, I'd be guilty of assisting an offender and preventing a lawful burial. Both of those offences carry a maximum jail sentence of ten years."

"Maybe Robert Hancock had some kind of hold over Cec Stenen? Maybe it was just because they were colleagues, and they had a strong bond with each other. Anyway, we'll be able to ask him in a few minutes, won't we?"

Cec Stenen's cottage was located in Church Street not far from the Bulls Head pub. Derbyshire wasn't renowned for the variety of its pub names. Most were named after animals with bulls being a particular favourite. Diane knocked on the door and it was opened by Mrs Stenen, a lady in her late 30s who'd gone prematurely grey and hadn't dyed her hair.

Diane and Spencer both held up their warrant cards and asked if they could come in. Once inside, they spotted Cec who was sitting in an armchair watching the six o'clock news.

"Diane, Spencer," he said in a rather hesitant voice. "This a pleasant surprise. What are you doing here?"

"Cec, there's been some developments regarding the mine shaft in Bleckley," said Diane.

"Yes, I've just seen it on the news. You've discovered three bodies there, I see."

"That's correct, Cec, and I'm afraid we are going to have to ask you to accompany us to Bakewell police station. We've got some questions we want to ask you."

"Why?" asked Cec. "It said on the news that you know who's responsible. It was Hugh Stanton."

"You don't want to believe everything you hear on TV, Cec," said Diane, at the same time wondering who had leaked that information to the press.

Of course, it could have been anyone, one of the bereaved relatives or even Hugh Stanton Junior. She just hoped it wasn't one of her team who'd let it slip.

Cec went to fetch his coat and the three of them got into the car. It only took ten minutes to get to Bakewell, but all the way to the station Cec was asking them questions.

"Have I been arrested?" he asked.

"No, you're just helping us with our enquiries," Diane replied.

"Why do you want to speak to me?"

"Because you are a key witness."

"A key witness to what?"

"You were with Robert when he wandered off."

"But I didn't see which direction he went in. I just presumed he was heading towards Foolow."

"Just wait until we get to the station, and all will become clear," replied Diane.

"So was what they said on TV not entirely accurate? Why?"

"Wait until we get to the station, please, Cec."

Diane wasn't going to answer any more of his questions in the car. As a result, the conversation went on to resemble a typical police interview in reverse. The police ask the questions and the suspect replies, 'no comment'.

Bakewell was not a large station, but it had a couple of interview rooms and Diane and Spencer had been allocated interview room number two. The three of them took their seats.

"Are you sure I'm not under arrest?" Cec asked them.

"I've already told you that you're not, Cec," Diane replied. "You are just helping us with our enquiries.

"Only, if I was under arrest, I would want a solicitor present."

"How many more times do you want me to tell you that you are not under arrest, Cec?" said Diane. "So it's not really necessary for you to have a solicitor present. But you're more than welcome to have access to one. Would you like me to arrange for the duty solicitor to be present?"

"No, it's okay. I was just checking."

The interview started.

"Cec, can you tell us what your movements were on Wednesday, April 13th, 1971?" Diane asked him.

"Jesus, that's nearly eight years ago," Cec replied. "I can barely remember what I did yesterday."

"But I thought you worked a fixed run system? In fact, you and Robert were the pioneers of fixed runs. You must know which outlets you visited that day?"

"Well, I guess I must have visited my usual drops, but I can't remember April 13th specifically."

"And what are your usual drops on a Wednesday?" Diane continued.

"The Castle Inn Bakewell, Bakewell Workingmen's Club, the Monsal Head Hotel, the Bull at Foolow, the Three Tuns at Bleckley, the…"

"Okay, you can stop there," Diane cut in. "And what time do you normally arrive at the Three Tuns?"

"Their time window is between nine and ten in the morning."

"So that's the time you would have been there?"

"Normally yes, although sometimes we may get delayed due to traffic. You can always check on the delivery note. It would have the time we delivered written on it. Mind you, the tax man only insists you keep records for six years and that was seven and a half years ago. The brewery's copy would definitely have been destroyed by now and the licensee's copy probably would have been as well."

"The reason I'm asking you this question is because Wednesday, April 13th, 1971, was the day Alice Barlow disappeared at around 9.30 in the morning. That puts you and Robert in your lorry heading towards Bleckley at the same time as she vanished."

"But hold on," replied Cec. "I thought she was last seen in Great Hucklow?"

"That was what we thought originally," Diane replied. "But we now have new evidence that she was last seen heading into Bleckley at half past nine."

"That's as maybe, but I never saw her. Also, we might not even have been in the village at 9.30. We could have arrived at 9am and have left by then. Or we could have arrived at 10 o'clock in which case we wouldn't have been there when she was last seen."

"Do you recognise this?" said Diane as she pushed the plastic evidence bag containing the glove in front of Cec.

"It's an industrial glove, the type used by builders."

"Isn't it also the type used by draymen?"

"It is. But loads of people use them. They are in common use."

"If you look at the front of the glove, you can just see two initials written in biro. Would you mind reading them out to me."

"RH," Cec replied.

"And did this glove once belong to Robert Hancock?"

"Possibly. It's also possible that it belonged to Rolf Harris."

"Cec, I have to tell you that, earlier today, one of my officers contacted Alan Fisher. He told her that it is common practice for draymen to write either their names or their initials on their gloves. It stops other draymen from stealing them. Of course, it was only you and Robert Hancock working from the Bakewell satellite depot. So you didn't really need to do that. Only you had come originally from the main depot in Sheffield, and you'd been indoctrinated into all the company practices and procedures. In fact, that was something that counted in your favour when you were appointed. The company didn't have to train up two draymen, because they expected you to pass your knowledge on to your colleague. Alan Fisher told me as much himself."

"Okay, I told Robert he had to write his initials on the gloves. Sorry, I don't know where all this is going."

"Where it is going, Cec, is that we discovered this glove at the bottom of the mine shaft in Bleckley, next to where Alice Barlow's body was found. Furthermore, when my officer asked Alan Fisher to look at the company accident report book, he told her that your dray had some damage to it on April 13th, and Robert had reported that it was because he had hit a deer."

"I know he's hit several wild animals over the years," Cec replied. "But I can't remember the specific dates of those incidents."

"How convenient," Diane added. "Do you want to hear what I think happened?"

"Not really," Cec replied. "Why would I want to hear your wild guesses?"

"Well, that's too bad," Diane continued. "Because I'm going to tell you anyway. On April 13th, 1971, you and Robert were heading towards the Three Tuns. There was heavy fog and Robert didn't see Alice Barlow walking down the road. She was wearing a grey anorak. We know Helen Yates had almost hit her as she was driving her kids to school. Anyway, Robert wasn't so lucky, and he ran into her. She wouldn't have stood a chance, bearing in mind he was driving a ten ton lorry fully loaded with beer. Anyway, luckily for him, you were right by the old mine shaft. Robert remembered it from his childhood when he came to play with Hugh Stanton's son. Robert and Hugh Stanton's friendship had lapsed many years previously and, as a result, he never got to hear that the mine had been supposedly filled in. He just knew there was no lock on the metal door that covered the opening. Consequently, you and he picked up Alice's body and dumped it down the mine shaft. But, unfortunately for Robert, his glove fell down the shaft as he was doing it. All I want to know is why the two of you should dump her body and why you should help Robert in the first place? After all, you are now looking at quite a long stretch in prison."

Cec sighed, his head in his hands.

Eventually he said, "Okay, I'll come clean with you. But you've got it all wrong. It wasn't like you say it was. I wasn't even with Robert on April 13th."

Chapter 37
Thursday evening, December 28th, 1978

Cec started his story while Diane and Spencer sat back and listened.

"April 12th, 1971, was the day of Flagg races and both Robert and I went along."

"But hold on," said Diane. "Flagg races take place on Easter Tuesday. That isn't a Bank Holiday. How come the brewery allowed you both to have the day off?"

"It may not be a bank holiday, but the brewery expects us to work on Good Friday. That's why we get Easter Tuesday off. You see, customers who have their deliveries on a Monday or a Tuesday receive their telesales call before the weekend, which makes those delivery days unpopular. Most pubs sell the majority of their beer on Saturday and Sunday. Therefore, it's a lot easier to estimate what you need for your next delivery if you can place your order at the start of the week, rather than on a Thursday or a Friday. And so we have far fewer drops at the beginning of the week than we do on Wednesday, Thursday, and Friday. It's also why it makes sense for us to take the Tuesday after Easter off rather than Good Friday and explains why we were able to go to Flagg races. Anyway, we both ended up winning. Also the weather was really miserable that day."

"Your point being?"

"Well, the two of us spent most of the day in the beer tent. It was far better in there than it was outside. We drank quite a lot, celebrating our winnings. Afterwards, we both went back to the Bulls Head in Foolow and continued drinking there. This was before I bought the house in Monyash. Back then, I was renting in Foolow. Robert had told me about a cottage that was up for rent in his village, and I took it."

"You've never mentioned this before," said Diane.

"I never thought it was relevant. You can check it if you like."

"Don't worry, Cec. We will."

"Anyway, the two of us got completely hammered and I was throwing up half the night. I had a really bad hangover the next morning. Robert was feeling it as well, but not as much as I was. That's why he let me go home to bed. There's nobody at the Bakewell satellite to check up on us. It's not like it is at Sheffield or at the Staveley depot that's replaced it. Of course, we are not supposed to go out single-handed due to health and safety legislation. But that's not to say it can't be done."

"You're telling me that Robert made the deliveries by himself that day?"

"That's correct. Robert and I used to do it occasionally and we'd cover for each other when we did it. It wasn't very often, just for things like our kiddies' birthday parties or when our wives were sick. The company would have sacked us if they found out about what we were doing. We have to sign in and sign out each day. So we were falsifying company records, which is a disciplinary offence. That's why I didn't want to say anything. You see, Inspector, I know absolutely nothing about the death of Alice Barlow. This whole thing has come as a complete shock to me."

"And can anybody back up your story?" asked Diane.

"Well, the people Robert delivered to that day should be able to confirm I wasn't with him. Mind you, it was seven and a half years ago. So the best person to speak to would be Matt at the Three Tuns. After all, it wasn't a normal day for him, was it? I mean, it will stand out being as it was the same day Alice Barlow disappeared. He might remember that Robert was by himself."

Diane had no further questions and she ended the interview and arranged for Cec Stenen to be taken home in a police car.

"You won't tell anyone at the brewery about what I just said?" asked Cec as he was leaving the interview room.

"Not unless we need to," replied Diane.

Once he'd left, Diane and Spencer grabbed a coffee and went back to the interview room in order to discuss what Cec had just told them.

"What do you think?" asked Diane.

"I don't know, it fits the facts," Spencer replied. "Also, it explains why Robert wouldn't want to report the death. Firstly, he'd have been fired if the brewery had discovered he was delivering by himself. Secondly, if he'd been drinking all day the previous day, then the chances are he'd be over the limit the morning after."

"It is more than just covering for a colleague we are talking about here," added Diane. "They were defrauding the brewery as they were being paid when they weren't at work. It's not like skiving off school, you know. I wonder how many times they did it? I suspect it's more often than he's admitting. Also, don't forget that Robert had been an HGV driver since he was a young man. It was all he knew. To lose his job and his driver's license was probably more than he could bear. That's why he disposed of Alice Barlow's body. It also explains why he committed suicide. He knew he'd be rumbled as soon as we found that glove."

"So do you believe Stenen's story, then, ma'am?"

"Do I buggery, Spencer. My gut tells me there's something not quite right about it."

"You want to get your gut seen to, ma'am. It sounds as if you've got irritable bowel syndrome to me."

But Diane was not in a joking mood.

"We'll get the team together tomorrow," she said. "We need to go over everything we know and see if we can wrap this whole thing up once and for all."

Chapter 38
Friday morning, December 29th, 1978

The following morning saw the whole team assembled in the incident room with Diane briefing them on the latest developments in the case.

"It sounds like we've pretty well wrapped this one up," announced Nigel. "If we interview all the customers on Hancock and Stenen's Wednesday run, surely one of them would remember whether there were two draymen or one delivering."

"I wouldn't be so sure," Alan added. "After all, it was nearly eight years ago. There's been a hell of a lot of water under the bridge since then."

"The only way we are going to find out is to speak to them all," Diane replied. "Alan and Colin, I want you to go to Staveley and see Alan Fisher. I need you to pick up details of all the customers that Hancock and Stenen would have delivered to on April 13th, 1971. Also, whilst you are there, I want you to show him the glove we recovered from the mine and get him to confirm that it's one of theirs. Finally, I want you to ask him what their procedure is for checking on the crew at the Bakewell satellite depot. Somebody must go down there occasionally, mustn't they? Ask him if it's feasible for one of the draymen to fail to turn up for work without the company knowing about it."

"We'll get straight on it," replied Alan.

"Once you've done that, I want you to visit all the licensed premises that Robert and Cec would have gone to that day, except for the Three Tuns and the Bulls Head in Foolow, which Spencer and I will visit. We need to discover if any of those customers remember anything about the day that Alice Barlow disappeared. In particular, I want to know if there was one or two draymen making the delivery. But I also want to know if anything stands out as being different about the delivery they received that day. Also, whilst you are seeing Alan Fisher, show him the glove we recovered from the mine and get him to confirm it's one of theirs."

Diane suddenly stopped in her tracks.

"Shit, I've just realised what's been bothering me," she said. "Spencer, out of Hancock and Stenen, which one is the driver, and which one is the mate?"

"Robert Hancock's the driver," Spencer replied. "He was driving when we were following him in our attempt to get away from the Three Tuns in the blizzard the other day. He was definitely the driver."

"But when we interviewed Cec Stenen yesterday, he said that he and Hancock sometimes covered for each other. In order for them to do that, both of them must have HGV licenses. If that's the case, then either of them could have been driving the lorry on the day Alice Barlow disappeared."

"Right," she said looking at Alan and Colin. "I also want you to ask Alan Fisher if both Stenen and Hancock have HGV licenses."

Then she added, "Or does anybody else have any better ideas?"

"What about the two men who were staying in the youth hostel at the same time as Alice Barlow?" suggested Claire.

"Weren't they heading towards Foolow? Perhaps they noticed something."

"Except we know they left Alice at 8.30 and it would have taken them about forty minutes to walk to Foolow. We also know that the dray must have collided with Alice at about half past nine. Consequently, I doubt if they were around at the right time. However, it was a good idea and I still think someone ought to speak to them."

"Well, what about the two German girls then?" Claire replied. "The dray must have collided with Alice Barlow very shortly after they'd walked past her. They were heading towards Hartington. Which road would they have taken, the one towards Foolow or the one towards Great Hucklow?"

"Hartington is south of Bleckley," replied Nigel. "As a result, they would definitely have taken the Foolow road."

"In which case, the dray must have gone past them as well, just before it hit Alice," said Spencer.

"Okay, team," announced Diane. "Alan and Colin already have their jobs for the day. Nigel and Claire, I want you to contact all four people who were staying in the youth hostel on the night of April 12th, 1971, again. I need you to ask them if they remember a brewery dray passing them the following morning. I know it's a long shot, but can you also ask them if they remember seeing one or two people in the cab? I want you to find out anything you can about Cec Stenen and Robert Hancock. I want to know what kind of people they are, what their backgrounds are, what they eat for breakfast, when they last had a crap, absolutely everything."

Turning to Alan and Colin again, she added, "In fact, can you two also collect their personnel files whilst you are at the Northern United depot in Staveley?"

"Will do, guv," replied Alan.

Diane scowled at him.

"Whilst you four are busy doing all that," she continued, "Spencer and I will go back to Bleckley in order to see Matt Yates and Hugh Stanton Junior. After that, we'll go to Foolow in order to visit the Bulls Head and to see Robert Hancock's wife. So let's get busy."

The team set about their various tasks with Diane and Spencer preparing to set off for Bleckley. However, before they were able to depart, Superintendent Barker summoned Diane into his office.

"What's going on, Diane?" he asked. "I thought this case was all wrapped up. I even told Howard Hill of the *Derbyshire Times* that you'd discovered three bodies and knew who'd killed all three victims. You're going to look pretty stupid if that's not the case."

"You shouldn't have done that, sir," said Diane in frustration. "Hugh Stanton couldn't have killed Alice Barlow. He was in the cells here at the time she disappeared and, with respect, sir, it isn't me who's going to look stupid, is it?"

"We're all one big team here, Diane. You'd do well to remember that. If one of us is made to look foolish, we all look foolish. Remember, there's no i in team."

"Quite right, sir," replied Diane.

Superintendent Barker's latest outburst reminded her that he'd been on a team building course the previous month. Ever since then he'd been using phrases such as 'remember, no man is an island' and 'when i is replaced by we, even illness becomes wellness'. She was tempted to reply, 'there may be no i in team but there is in superintendent'. But she'd learnt some time ago it would be counterproductive.

Instead, she said, "Hugh Stanton did kill both his wife and Jonathon Stoppard and disposed of their bodies in the mine that was on his land. Furthermore, it was his dogs that killed Colin Loggenberg, the council workman, and he then let Stan Baxter's pit bulls take the blame. However, he couldn't have killed Alice Barlow, because he was locked in the cells when she died. I believe she was run over and killed by accident. The person who did it knew about the mine shaft, and he disposed of her body in it without knowing that the body of Mary Stanton was already down there. We are very close to finally solving this case and I am confident we will be making an arrest once we have completed our investigations today."

"Very good, Diane," replied Superintendent Barker. "Don't forget to keep me in the loop and also, please remember that I don't want to see any more overtime from your team."

Chapter 39
Friday morning, December 29th, 1978

Diane and Spencer arrived at the Three Tuns just before eleven and Lauren was busy cleaning the pub.

"Can you get Matt for us, Lauren?" asked Diane. "There's something that he needs to clear up for us."

Lauren duly disappeared upstairs, and a few minutes later she reappeared followed by Matt. He'd been having a late breakfast. Like so many publicans, the pub's opening hours prevented him from eating at normal times. That was why he usually had his first meal at 10.30 in the morning, his second at 4.30 before the evening shift started, and then had a snack after he'd closed up at night.

"Diane, this is becoming a habit," he said. "What can I do for you?"

"Before I get to that, I need to tell you that we've caught our closing time thief. He was coming here on the Saturday before Christmas, but he skidded off the road in the snow. In fact, this crash caused the road to be blocked between here and Eyam."

"That's good news," replied Matt. "Was he connected to the brewery?"

"Yes," Diane replied. "He used to work in the finance department but was made redundant when it was centralised in Manchester. His girlfriend still works for the company in load planning. Well, she did until we arrested her."

Diane moved on to the more important things she wanted to discuss.

"Matt, I know you wouldn't want to drop Cec in it, but he's told us that he and Robert sometimes used to do their deliveries single-handedly. Is that correct?"

"Well, I think I speak for all Robert and Cec's customers when I say that they were extremely popular with everyone they delivered to. They never gave us any problems, you see, always turned up on time and never tried it on. Also, they'd go the extra mile. In fact, you saw it for yourself when you were here before Christmas. Most delivery drivers wouldn't even have tried to deliver to us that day. The vast majority would have just turned around and gone back to the depot. But not Robert and Cec. They knew it was my last delivery before Christmas and I wouldn't be able to open if I didn't receive it. That's why they tried so hard to get through to me. What if one of them occasionally needed to take a day off? It wasn't as if they did it very often and none of their customers would ever have dreamt of reporting them to the brewery."

"So if Cec occasionally delivered by himself, that must mean he's got an HGV license as well as Robert?"

"That's correct. Robert and Cec weren't like the crews based in Staveley. Those crews have a driver who's effectively in charge and a mate who helps him. That wouldn't work in Bakewell, where there's only one lorry. When one of them is on holiday or off sick, it wouldn't be very easy to get an HGV driver from a temp agency in a place like Bakewell. But if both of them are qualified drivers and they plan their holidays to ensure they are never off at the same time, the brewery only need to get a labourer in to cover for the one that's off. That's why the company recruited two drivers."

"Of course, that only applied when one of them was officially off work," replied Diane. "When they were unofficially off, the other one just used to cover for him."

"That's correct. But like I said, it really wasn't that often."

"Which one of them usually drove?" asked Diane.

"As far as I could see, they shared the driving. Sometimes it would be Robert and sometimes it would be Cec."

"Now, Matt, I want you to consider this question very carefully. Do you remember who was driving on Wednesday 13th, April 1971, the day Alice Barlow went missing?"

Matt thought about it for a few seconds before he answered.

"That was the day following Flagg races, wasn't it? The day after I had to call the ambulance for Hugh Stanton, and they had to handcuff him to the hospital bed?"

"That's correct," replied Diane, who could tell Matt was struggling to recall that particular delivery. "Cec Stenen has told us he wasn't there that day as he had a bad hangover. Can you remember if that is correct?"

"The delivery was late that day. It didn't arrive until 10.15. I remember pulling Robert's leg about it. He wasn't in a good mood, and I put that down to the fact he was on his own. It also explained why he wasn't on time, as it would take him longer to deliver by himself. So yes, Robert was definitely by himself that day. Why the interest?"

"Because we are pretty sure that Alice Barlow was killed when she was hit by the brewery dray. If Cec Stenen wasn't there that day, it must mean Robert Hancock killed her and then committed suicide when he realised he was going to be found out."

"I'm sorry but I don't believe it, Diane. I've known Robert for most of his life. He was a careful driver. Even if he did knock that girl down, he would do the right thing. Also he would never have committed suicide, he loved Ellen and the girls too much."

"Well, I'm afraid that's what it looks like at the moment," Diane replied. "But we've still got other people to interview. We'll see what they've got to say before we jump to any conclusions."

Matt may not have liked the idea of Robert killing Alice Barlow, but he had just backed up Cec's story.

"What's your gut telling you now, ma'am?" asked Spencer once they were outside.

"It's confused, Spencer," Diane replied. "Just when I was beginning to think it was Cec Stenen who was driving and that he also murdered Robert Hancock, it now seems he wasn't even in the dray that day. Therefore, it must have been Robert who was driving. In which case, he must have committed suicide."

Diane and Spencer decided to walk to Hugh Stanton's house as it was only about 100 yards away. The SOCO team had finished their search of the premises and Hugh had been able to move back in. He was clearing out his father's junk once more when the two officers arrived.

When Diane knocked on the door, he stopped what he was doing and let them in. Once they had sat down in the lounge, Diane explained why they were there.

"Hugh, I wanted to update you on the progress of the investigation so far. The last time I spoke to you, I told you we had discovered three bodies in the old mine. I said that one of them was probably your mother. I'm afraid that I have to tell you that I can now confirm that she was one of the victims. We identified her from dental records."

There was a sharp intake of breath from Hugh and Diane thought he was going to burst into tears. But he managed to hold it together. So she continued.

"We also discovered the bodies of two dogs in the mine and we believe they are the two rottweilers your father shot. We don't believe he buried them in your back garden like he told you."

"It doesn't surprise me," Hugh replied.

"One of the other two bodies is that of Jonathon Stoppard, a reporter with the *Derbyshire Times*. We believe your father killed both him and your mother. Furthermore, as you know, we discovered Jonathon Stoppard's watch and your mother's rings in this house, which further incriminates him. We believe your father caught Jonathon Stoppard searching his land and killed him because he'd discovered there were bodies at the bottom of the mine shaft."

Hugh merely nodded indicating that he accepted what Diane was telling him.

"The third body is that of Alice Barlow who disappeared in April 1971 whilst going for a walk from the youth hostel. However, your father could not have killed Alice as he was in the cells at Chesterfield police station at the time she disappeared. Consequently, we are working on the theory that she was run over by the brewery dray driven by Robert Hancock, and it was him who dumped her body down the mine shaft. After realising that he was going to be discovered, Robert committed suicide."

"Not Robert," said Hugh. "He would never try to cover up a thing like that."

"With the greatest respect, Hugh, you hadn't seen Robert for ten years until the other night. In fact, you hadn't really been friends with him for over twenty years. People change over time."

"I still can't believe that of Robert though," replied Hugh. "What does the other drayman say about it? After all, he must have been with him when Robert allegedly did this."

"He says that Robert was delivering by himself that day."

"Which is most convenient being as though Robert isn't here to confirm or deny it."

"Yes, but Cec's claim that he wasn't there that day has been backed up by Matt from the pub. He's confirmed that Robert was delivering by himself that day."

"I still find it difficult to believe. People don't change that much."

"That's as maybe. But what I need to ask you is on the occasions when you and Robert used to play together when you were young, did you ever play by the old mine shaft?"

"Absolutely not," Hugh replied. "My father had terrified the life out of me with his stories about the troll. As a result, I always gave the old mine and the engine shed a wide berth."

"So you never went to the mine with Robert as a boy?"

"Definitely not," replied Hugh.

"Well, did you ever discuss the old mine with him?"

"Inspector, my father told me he would feed me to the troll if I ever discussed the mine with anybody. I was scared stiff."

"What about later then?" Diane continued. "Once you'd grown up and knew he'd removed the lock, did you ever discuss it with Robert when you were teenagers or young men?"

"Robert and I weren't really friends by that stage. It wasn't that we ever fell out. It was just that when we went to senior school, we were put in different classes and made new friends."

Instead of helping Diane, Hugh had muddied the water. If Cec wasn't in the lorry and Robert didn't know about the mine, then who had dumped Alice Barlow's body down the shaft?

Chapter 40
Friday afternoon, December 29th, 1978

"Could somebody else have told Robert Hancock about the mine?" said Spencer as they were walking back to the car. "After all, he visited the Three Tuns every week and someone could have mentioned it to him when he was there."

"Yes, I know he went to Bleckley every week. But he always went in the morning. There were no customers in the pub when he visited it. The only person who might have mentioned it was Matt and, for the past ten years, he thought the mine had been sealed."

"Perhaps somebody told him about it elsewhere then. It is possible, you know."

"I know it's possible, Spencer. Let's go and ask his wife if he mentioned it to her."

The two of them got into Diane's car and drove the one and a half miles to the village of Foolow.

Foolow was very different from Bleckley. For a start, it was about ten times bigger. Not that it was a large village, it was just that Bleckley was so small. Also, Bleckley was perched high up on Bleckley Edge, where it was exposed to the winds that battered it from the southwest. Foolow, however, was down in the lush valley below and looked as if it had stepped right out of *Derbyshire Life Magazine*. Its immaculate cottages and pub were arranged around its duck pond and village green.

Yet, for all its beauty, the village had an air of despondency hanging over it. One of its sons had died and it was as if the very fabric of the village was in mourning.

It didn't take Diane long to discover Robert Hancock's house and she couldn't help but notice the sign outside that said, 'Father Christmas please stop here'. Robert had probably put it up for his daughters a few days before Christmas. It was only a few days ago, but it was another time, another world.

Diane knocked on the door and Robert's wife answered. Her eyes were all puffy from crying.

"This is not going to be easy," Diane thought to herself as they followed Ellen Hancock into the lounge.

"Mrs Hancock," Diane started. "I'm very sorry for your loss. DS Spooner and I were trapped in the Three Tuns with your husband. In fact, we were with him on the night he died. All the time we were stranded there, the only thing he kept saying was that he wanted to get back to you and the girls."

Ellen began crying again and so Diane didn't continue until her sobs had subsided.

"Mrs Hancock, I'm sorry to have to tell you this, but we think Robert was involved with the death of a girl called Alice Barlow back in 1971. We are fairly sure she was run over by his dray and we found a glove with his initials on it next to her body."

"Good God, he's only been dead for less than a week and you are already accusing him of things," sobbed Ellen. "My husband is not here to defend himself, Inspector. He was a loving husband and a good father. He wasn't a murderer. How dare you even suggest it?"

"We are not saying he was a murderer, Mrs Hancock. We believe Alice Barlow was killed by accident. Also, we are not sure whether your husband was driving on that day or whether it was Cec Stenen. However, Cec Stenen says he wasn't with your husband on the day Alice Barlow went missing. Furthermore, Matt Yates from the Three Tuns is backing up his story. As a consequence, I have to ask you if you remember anything at all about that day. It was Wednesday, April 13th, 1971, the day after Flagg races. If it helps, it was the year when Cec Stenen was living in the village."

"Cec Stenen used to lead my husband astray, Inspector. Robert never used to drink that much before he met him. Okay, he'd always liked a few pints in the pub, but he would never drink to excess until he met Cec. If I'm honest, I was really glad when he eventually bought the house in Monyash and moved away from here. I was worried that Robert would become an alcoholic if he'd stayed."

"What about April 13th, 1971 then, Mrs Hancock?" said Diane in an attempt to bring her back on track again.

"I remember that they'd both got horrendously drunk at Flagg races on the previous day. Robert was absolutely paralytic when he came in and I had to put him to bed."

"And was he alright to go to work the next morning?" Diane interrupted her. "I presume he'd have to get up at about 6am."

"That's correct. That was precisely the time he used to get up in the morning. But Robert had remarkable powers of recovery. If ever he'd had a skinful, you could never tell the morning after. As far as I know he was fine."

"So he went to work as usual, did he?"

"Robert went to work as usual every morning."

"When he returned in the evening did you notice anything different about him? Or did he say anything about the day he'd just had?"

"It was seven and a half years ago and one day just blends into another. How am I supposed to remember things like that?"

"That's okay, Mrs Hancock," replied Diane. "My next question is very important. Did Robert ever say anything to you about an old mine shaft on Hugh Stanton's land in Bleckley?"

"No," she replied. "Why would he?"

"You're absolutely certain about that, Mrs Hancock? Please just think about it for a minute."

"I am completely certain, Inspector. My husband never mentioned an old mine shaft."

"Thank you, Mrs Hancock. We won't take up any more of your time. But I have to tell you that, if your husband did knock down and kill Alice Barlow, it is highly likely he committed suicide. That's because he would have known that he was going to be exposed."

"Inspector, my husband did not kill that girl and he definitely did not commit suicide. We are both Catholics and he would never kill himself. Suicide is a mortal sin. He just wouldn't do it."

Chapter 41
Friday afternoon, December 29th, 1978

"I don't believe the bit about how he'd never commit suicide because he was a Catholic," said Diane once they were back outside again. "Hitler was a Catholic, but it didn't stop him from blowing his own brains out. Also, she was his wife. So she's hardly likely to think badly of her late husband."

"Oh, I don't know," replied Spencer. "Being married has never stopped our Rachel from thinking badly of me."

"Yes, but I can understand that in Rachel's case. However, the fact is that she wasn't the only one who said Robert wouldn't have done it. Matt Yates and Hugh Stanton both said exactly the same thing. Having said that, all the evidence points to him being the guilty party."

Diane and Spencer had only one more person to visit and that was Reg Greatorex, the licensee of the Bulls Head in Foolow. Fortunately, he had also been the licensee back in 1971, which reflected the fact that pubs rarely changed hands in the Peak District. Those that did come on the market were usually snapped up straight away, and once they'd taken over, the new licensees tended to stay put for many years.

The Bulls Head was a fine looking pub, located in the centre of the village close to the duck pond. Diane parked her car and the two officers went inside. After producing their warrant cards, they sat down with Mr Greatorex at one of the tables in the bar.

Fortunately for Diane and Spencer, Reg Greatorex had a good memory and knew both Robert and Cec well. For not only did they deliver his beer every week, but Robert lived in the village and Cec had briefly done so as well. In fact, the two officers were doubly fortunate that afternoon because Reg provided coffee and biscuits for them.

"Can you talk me through the evening of Tuesday April 12th, 1971, the day of Flagg races?" asked Diane. "Then can you also talk me through your delivery the following day?"

"Well, we were really busy that evening. We always are the night after Flagg races. Robert and Cec arrived here at about 6.30 in the evening and they'd obviously been drinking heavily after spending most of the day in the beer tent at Flagg."

"Do you know how they got home from Flagg? Did they get a lift or was one of them driving?" cut in Diane.

"Sorry, Inspector, I didn't ask them."

"Never mind," added Diane.

"Anyway, they stayed until closing time and must have had at least another six pints each, plus a couple of whisky chasers before they left. They were as pissed as farts, but they weren't causing any trouble."

Diane thought about reminding Mr Greatorex that it was illegal to serve someone who was drunk but decided it would be counterproductive. Instead, she asked, "They didn't go home for something to eat then?"

"No, I'm pretty certain they'd eaten at the races."

"Can you talk me through your delivery the next day?" added Diane.

"Well, they arrived at about 8.45."

"Hold on," interrupted Diane. "So both of them were working the next day?"

"Yes, it was like any other day, there were the two of them as usual. Why?"

"Because Cec Stenen says Robert Hancock let him go home that day because he had a bad hangover. And Matt Yates of the Three Tuns says Cec wasn't on the lorry when they delivered to him."

"That's perfectly feasible, being as though Cec was living just down the road at the time. Robert could have dropped him off between here and Bleckley. He had a hangover, I can confirm that, as had Robert. In fact, they both had a hair of the dog whilst they were here in order to make them feel better."

"Is there anybody else who can back up the fact that Cec was on the lorry on that day?"

"Well, June, my wife, would have been in the kitchen, which means she'll be of no help. But I think I can do better than that as I've probably still got the delivery note. Let me go and see if I can find it."

He went off to the office and returned a few minutes later carrying a box file with 'Delivery notes 1971/2' written on it.

"You're in luck," he said. "If the delivery had been a couple of weeks earlier it would have taken place during the previous tax year, and I would have thrown it away by now. As it is, I should have binned these back in April, but I haven't gotten around to it yet."

It didn't take him long to find the delivery note for April 13th as it was only the second delivery that had been made in that particular financial year.

"There you are," said Reg. "See, I told you he was here. Look, he signed the delivery note."

"And if I'm not wrong, it's the driver who always signs the delivery note."

"Well, hang on, Inspector," replied Reg. "That might be the case in Staveley where there's one driver and he's in charge. But not in Bakewell where both crew members are HGV drivers. They have equal status. So either of them can sign it."

"I don't suppose you remember who was driving on that particular day, do you?"

"Sorry, Inspector," he replied. "My memory's good, but not that good."

Diane looked down at the delivery note and saw that the time the crew had left was 9.25. It would only have taken them five minutes to get to Bleckley. That left 45 minutes unaccounted for, which left plenty of time to knock Alice Barlow down and dispose of her body. It also left plenty of time to drop Cec Stenen off at his house.

Reg had confirmed that Cec was with Robert when he'd delivered to him, and Matt had confirmed he was absent when he'd had his delivery. Therefore, the question that now needed to be answered was whether he was dropped off before or after Alice Barlow was run over? If it was the latter who was driving?

Suddenly, something caught Diane's eye. She'd noticed something odd about Cec's signature on the delivery note.

"What's Cec's Christian name?" she asked Reg. "That initial doesn't look like a C to me. It looks more like a Z."

"That's right, Inspector. Most people think that Cec is a shortened version of Cecil, but not in Cec's case. He's proud of his Dutch heritage and I believe Cec is an anglicised version of a Dutch name."

Chapter 42
Friday afternoon, December 29th, 1978

"Let's discuss what we've discovered," said Diane once she and Spencer were heading back towards Chesterfield.

"We know both Robert and Cec are HGV drivers and either of them could have been driving the lorry. We are also pretty confident that Alice Barlow was killed by the brewery dray. That's why Robert reported he'd hit a deer on the day she went missing. It also explains the missing 45 minutes between the delivery to the Bulls Head and the Three Tuns. We know that both draymen made the delivery to the Bulls Head, but only Robert Hancock was present when the delivery was made to the Three Tuns. Finally, we also know it was Robert Hancock's glove we discovered in the mine shaft, which suggests that he was present when her body was disposed of."

Diane went quiet whilst she thought for a bit.

"You know, Spencer," she continued. "There are only three possibilities here. Firstly, it happened just as Cec said it did. In other words, Robert was driving, and he dropped Cec off at his house before continuing on to Bleckley. On his way there, he knocks down and kills Alice Barlow and disposes of her body before continuing with his deliveries. The second scenario is exactly the same as the first, but Robert didn't drop Cec off until after he'd knocked down and killed Alice. In which case, Cec must have helped Robert to dispose of the body. Then there's the third scenario. This is the one where Cec was driving rather than Robert. He knocks down and kills Alice, and it's Robert who helps him dispose of the body. Then they switch over and Robert drives him back to his house before continuing with his deliveries."

"So why would he do that?" asked Spencer.

"I don't know," Diane replied. "Perhaps Cec was in shock."

"Okay, I'll buy that," Spencer continued. "So what was the reason behind Robert's death then?"

"Well, the one thing I don't believe was that it was death by misadventure. Robert would never have stumbled over Bleckley Edge in error. He was a local lad, and he wouldn't have made that mistake even in a blizzard. Which means it was either suicide or Cec murdered him. I think it was murder."

"That's not your gut telling you that again, is it, ma'am?"

"No, Spencer, this time it's down to logic. If Robert had committed suicide, then why would he drag his shattered body up a bank and put six stones in his pocket?"

"So have you worked out what Robert was trying to tell us when he did that?" asked Spencer.

"No," Diane replied. "But in one way, it's irrelevant. The mere fact that he did it tells me that he didn't commit suicide. If that's the case, it means we can rule out scenarios one and two. Why would Cec kill Robert if it had been Robert who'd killed Alice? No, it had to be Cec who was driving that lorry and who killed Alice. He then went on to kill Robert when he realised that we'd discover Robert's glove after opening up the mine shaft. Robert would have been forced to tell us what had really happened that day and Cec would have faced the prospect of a long spell in jail. By killing him, he prevented him from spilling the beans and, at the same time, it enabled him to let

Robert take the blame for everything. It's the one scenario which explains everything that's happened."

"Which one of them do you think knew about the mine and the fact it hadn't been filled in?" asked Spencer.

"That had to be Robert," replied Diane. "Hugh Stanton might not have told him. But he was local, so someone must have. It couldn't have been Cec because he came from Sheffield. He didn't arrive in the area until 1970, two years after everybody thought the mine had been capped."

A few minutes later, the two of them arrived back at Chesterfield police station where the rest of the team were already waiting for them in the incident room. Diane brought them up to speed about what she and Spencer had discovered on their visit to Bleckley and Foolow. Once that was done, Alan Bateman was next to take the floor.

"The first thing we did was to go to the Northern United depot in Staveley in order to see Alan Fisher. We also picked up Hancock and Stenen's personnel files, which I have here."

"Right, before we go any further, please look inside Cec Stenen's file and tell me what his Christian name is," Diane cut in.

Alan opened the file.

"It's Zes," he announced.

"That's a peculiar name," said Diane. "I don't think I've ever heard anyone called Zes before, not even a Dutchman. How about you, Spencer?"

"The only Dutchmen I know are members of the Dutch world cup squad," he replied. "There's a Wim and a Pim, a Jan and a Johan. But to the best of my knowledge, there's no Zes."

"Well, never mind, I don't suppose it's important," said Diane before she instructed Alan to continue.

"I asked Alan Fisher how often anyone from Staveley goes to the Bakewell satellite. He told me one of his managers goes down once a quarter on the first Monday of the month. He went on to say that somebody might go down at other times if they ever got a complaint. But that had never happened in the eight years they'd been operating the satellite. He really rated Hancock and Stenen as a crew, saying their customer satisfaction results were way better than any of the crews at Staveley."

"Which means Zes Stenen was telling the truth when he said they just left them alone to get on with it," said Diane.

"Then I asked him if Hancock and Stenen were both HGV drivers and he told me that they were. He said that drivers are paid substantially more than drivers' mates. That's why there's only one qualified HGV driver in each crew at the Staveley depot. Cover for the drivers is provided by the warehouse staff, some of whom are HGV drivers waiting for a driver vacancy to occur. But they couldn't operate the same system at Bakewell. That's why they decided to hire two qualified drivers. This meant that the driver would always be one of their employees, even when the other one was on holiday or off sick."

"Which confirms what we already knew," added Diane.

"I also asked him to confirm that it was company policy for the driver to sign the delivery note. He told me it was, but because Stenen and Hancock were both drivers either of them could sign it."

"And that backs up what Reg Greatorex told us," said Diane.

"Finally, I asked him if it was possible for one of the drivers at Bakewell not to turn up, have the other driver cover for him and no one at Staveley know about it. He reluctantly admitted it was possible but said they would be taking a massive risk if they did that. It would only take one phone call from an angry customer to reveal what they'd been doing."

"But we know that all the customers loved Hancock and Stenen," Diane replied. "So that wasn't very likely to happen."

"I put that very point to Alan Fisher, ma'am, and he eventually agreed that it was indeed the case."

"Right, all this merely confirms what we'd worked out already, but it doesn't really move the investigation forward," said Diane. "Did you get details of their deliveries for that Wednesday?"

"Yes, there were fourteen of them in total," Alan replied. "Obviously, they cover a country area. So the average size of each order is relatively small and the distance between the outlets is large. In fact, it's the complete opposite of the way it is in urban areas. That's one of the reasons why they can operate the satellite system. It's because one run takes them all day whereas in South Yorkshire and North East Derbyshire the crews usually do two runs per day. Obviously, you can't do two runs from the satellite, because the only stock they've got is the stock on the lorry that was transported there during the night."

"That's all very interesting, Alan," said Diane. "But it's not really relevant to the matter in hand."

"Yes, sorry guv," he replied. "Anyway, we visited all the outlets that they delivered to on April 13th, 1971, with the exception of the two that you and Spencer visited. Three of them were clubs and two of them had different stewards to the ones that were there in 1971. The other nine were pubs, three of which had since changed hands."

"As a result, we had no joy in any of those outlets where the person in charge had changed," added Colin.

"That made seven outlets where the same person was running the outlet as they were in 1971," Alan continued.

"None of these seven people could remember that specific delivery. I mean, why should they? After all, it was just one delivery amongst many identical deliveries. There was nothing that stood out for them, unlike the two pubs you visited where a girl had disappeared or the two people making the delivery had got roaring drunk in the bar the previous night. In that regard, we didn't make any headway. However, two of them still had the delivery notes from that day and we examined both of them. These were the deliveries to Bakewell Workingmen's Club, which was signed by Z Stenen at 7.43 and the Rose and Crown, Eyam which was signed by R Hancock at 11.16."

"Okay, we know Stenen was in the dray when he and Robert Hancock delivered to the Three Tuns," said Diane reflecting on what Alan had told her. "The Rose & Crown's order was delivered after the Three Tuns and that's why Robert Hancock signed the delivery note."

"Ma'am, you said that Stenen had worked in Sheffield before he transferred to Bakewell," commented DC Adcock, "and he was fully up to speed with their policies and procedures. That was the reason why he told Robert Hancock to write his initials on his gloves, even though that wasn't really necessary. Well, what if the same thing applied to the signing of delivery notes? Stenen would have known it was the driver who always signed them. Don't you think he would have followed the same rule at Bakewell, even though they were both qualified drivers?"

"You are probably correct, Claire," replied Diane. "But it would be a very difficult thing to prove. After all, Alan Fisher has told us that either of them could sign the delivery note. Also, Stenen could well have been driving until they reached the Bulls Head, and Hancock could have taken over after that so Stenen could go home."

Diane reflected on what she'd just been told before Alan told her that was all that he and Colin had been able to uncover.

Next, it was the turn of Claire and Nigel. They had been tasked with contacting the four people from the youth hostel again and Hancock and Stenen's families. It was Claire who spoke first.

"I contacted the two men who were staying in the youth hostel at the same time as Alice Barlow in 1971. It was the first time I'd spoken to them, as it was Nigel who spoke to them the other day. Anyway, they both confirmed that they arrived in Foolow at about 9 o'clock. Neither of them could remember seeing a brewery dray on that particular day. That wasn't surprising, being as though it was so foggy. Also the dray was probably in the car park of the Bulls Head when they went through Foolow. We know that Hancock and Stenen left at 9.25 after making their delivery and having a beer. I guess they must have been parked there for at least thirty minutes."

"That seems logical," added Diane.

"I had more luck with the two German girls, as both of them remembered a lorry going past them on the road between Bleckley and Foolow. The reason it stuck in their memory was because it was so foggy that day and they were being extremely careful to avoid any oncoming traffic. In any case, this particular lorry stood out because it was the only vehicle that went past them that morning. Furthermore, it went past them three times. Once near the fork in the road, then twice more, close to the village of Foolow."

"Are they absolutely certain about that?" asked Diane.

"They both said exactly the same thing, ma'am. I also asked them if they noticed if there were one or two men in the cab but, unfortunately, neither of them could remember. In reality, it was probably too foggy for them to notice something like that."

"Well, it was a long shot anyway," added Diane. "But the fact that the lorry went past these girls on three occasions tells us quite a lot. For a start, it means we can now say for definite that Zes Stenen was in the cab when the lorry hit Alice Barlow. What other explanation can there be? Otherwise, why did the dray go past the German girls three times? The first time must have been when it was heading to the Three Tuns and hit Alice Barlow. The second time would have been when Robert was driving Zes back to Foolow and the third time must have been when he was heading back to Bleckley again."

"We still don't know for definite that he was driving when the lorry hit Alice Barlow, though," said Spencer. "Robert Hancock could have been driving all along."

"No, but we've probably got enough evidence to charge him with preventing the lawful burial of a body," added Diane. "However, I also want to be able to charge him with the manslaughter of Alice Barlow and the murder of Robert Hancock. So let's continue."

"That's all I've got, ma'am," said Claire. "It was Nigel who contacted the relatives."

"If I start with Robert Hancock," said Nigel. "He comes from a small family. The only relatives that I could trace other than his wife and daughters were his mother and a brother. However, they weren't able to provide any useful information. They just said Robert was a wonderful son and brother and that they didn't believe he would have killed anyone."

"No surprises there, then," added Spencer.

"Zes Stenen, though, comes from a very large family. In fact, he is the youngest out of a family of six children. He's got three brothers and two sisters, and both his parents are still alive. All his relatives live in Sheffield, and I contacted every one of them. I'll not bore you with all the details. Suffice it to say that what they said about him was virtually identical to the way Robert Hancock's family described him."

"You've got to love families, haven't you?" added Spencer.

"The only thing of interest came from what one of his brothers, Piet Stenen, told me. He said he wasn't surprised when Zes decided to move to the Peak District. He'd always loved the countryside as a young boy when their parents used to take them camping in Bleckley. When I pressed him on that point, he said they used to go every weekend during the summer and stay on Hugh Stanton's field. Furthermore, he told me that they'd discovered the old mine shaft and used to drop rocks down it and count the number of seconds it took to reach the bottom."

"So it was Stenen, not Hancock who knew about the old mine. It also explains why Robert had never heard that it had supposedly been filled in. After all, he wouldn't know about that. He hadn't been near it since he was a boy."

"It reinforces the fact that he was there when Alice Barlow's body was disposed of, but that's all it proves," added Spencer. "It doesn't help us to prove he was driving on that day, or that he murdered Robert Hancock."

"No, but it does provide us with sufficient evidence to interview him under caution," Diane replied, "which is precisely what I intend to do tomorrow. But before I do that, I need to speak to Julie van de Kerkhof and to Robert's wife again."

"Who the hell is Julie van de Kerkhof when she's at home?" asked Spencer.

"She's a friend of mine from university. She married a Dutchman, and she lives in Alkmaar."

Chapter 43
Saturday morning, December 30th, 1978

The interview with Zes Stenen took place at 10am at Chesterfield police station the following morning. Zes had his solicitor with him, as he was being interviewed under caution. Diane was leading the interview, with Spencer sitting next to her.

"Okay, Cec, or should I say Zes since we now know now that's your real name. Tell me again what happened on Wednesday, April 13th, 1971, the day after Flagg races?"

"I've never tried to hide my name," said Zes. "It's just that all my English colleagues started calling me Cec, because they'd never heard of anyone called Zes before.

"Just answer the question, please."

"As I've already told you, I had a bad hangover that morning and Robert let me go home in order to get over it."

"Yes, but when did he let you go home, before you set off for work, after lunch, when?"

Zes hesitated. It was obvious to Diane he was trying very hard not to incriminate himself.

"You've got to remember it was seven and a half years ago," he said eventually. "I'm not entirely sure."

"Well, let's see if this might help you to remember. Reg Greatorex at the Bulls Head in Foolow definitely remembers you making a delivery to him that day. He says you had a hair of the dog after you'd delivered his beer."

"That's correct, I remember now. We both had really bad hangovers that morning and we decided to have a hair of the dog in the Bulls Head. It perked Robert up, but I felt even worse. That was why Robert agreed to drop me off at my house on the way to Bleckley. I lived in Foolow then, you remember."

"So you were never in the dray when it went up the hill towards Bleckley. You weren't there when the dray hit Alice Barlow and you didn't help Robert Hancock dispose of her body?"

"I had no knowledge about any of those things. As I've already told you, I wasn't there."

"Robert reported having hit a deer on that particular day. Can you tell me anything about that?"

"He didn't hit one whilst I was in the cab. I can only assume it happened after I'd left."

"Zes, can you tell me who, according to company procedure, should sign a delivery note?" asked Spencer.

"Well, the customer, obviously, and a member of the crew."

"Any specific member of the crew?"

"Yes, it's supposed to be the most senior member. A drayman who's on a driver's grade."

"Now, on the morning in question, we have obtained copies of two delivery notes from the period before you left the dray and one from after," said Diane as she placed them in front of him. "The one from after you left was obviously signed by Robert. But the two from before you left were both signed by you. What do you think that tells me?"

"That I'm on a driver's grade. Mind you, so was Robert. Consequently, either of us could have signed them. I'm sure I could find examples where I was driving but Robert signed the delivery note."

310

"You see, it makes me wonder if it was, in fact, you who were driving the dray that day."

"Well, you can wonder all you like. I'm telling you that I wasn't."

"And there's no one to contradict your version of events, is there?"

"My client can't help that," added the solicitor.

"Let's talk about Alice Barlow for a minute. Her body was found at the bottom of a mine shaft on Hugh Stanton's land. Did you know about the existence of that old mine shaft?"

"No, I did not."

"That's strange, because you used to go camping on Hugh Stanton's field with your parents when you were a boy and you and your brothers used to throw stones down it."

"If you say so."

"It's not me who says so, it's your brother Piet who told us."

"He's got a good memory then. I'd forgotten all about that."

"Did Robert know about the old mine shaft?"

"I would imagine so. After all, he only lived a mile and a half away."

"Because we can't find anyone who says he did."

"That doesn't prove he didn't, though," added the solicitor.

"On the day Alice Barlow disappeared, she was last seen by a couple of German tourists. They had been staying in the same dormitory at the youth hostel as Alice and her friend. They bumped into her at the fork in the road as she was walking back to Bleckley. It was half past nine and, after chatting to her, they went off towards Foolow. Shortly afterwards, your brewery dray went past her."

"Inspector, I must object," interrupted the solicitor. "It was not my client's dray. It belonged to his employer. By phrasing it in that manner you are implying that my client was driving. He has already told you he wasn't even in the dray at that time."

Diane corrected herself.

"Shortly afterwards, a dray belonging to Sheffield Brewery went past them," she continued. "It then went past them twice more before they arrived in Foolow. How do you explain that?"

"I wouldn't know, I was in bed at the time. Perhaps Robert had forgotten his sandwiches."

"Perhaps indeed," Diane continued. "Shall I tell you what I think happened?"

"No, but I guess you're going to tell me anyway."

"On Tuesday, April 12th, you and Robert Hancock were extremely drunk after spending the day in the beer tent at Flagg races. And you didn't stop there as the two of you continued drinking in the Bulls Head after the races had finished. The next day you both still had a hangover, but you had to get up for work at 6am."

"Have you any proof that my client was extremely drunk, Inspector?" asked the solicitor.

"Yes, Reg Greatorex from the Bulls Head and Ellen Hancock have both confirmed that it was the case. Now back in those days, you both lived in Foolow, so there wasn't much point in taking two cars into work. As a result, Robert drove you both to work."

"So what does that have to do with anything?" asked Zes.

"I'm just painting a picture," Diane replied. "Once you arrived at the depot, the two of you set off in the dray and it was you who were driving now."

"My client has told you on numerous occasions that he wasn't driving, Inspector," added the solicitor.

"That's why you signed the first few delivery notes that morning, wasn't it?"

"No, I've already told you that either of us could sign the delivery note."

"It's the same reason why Robert wrote his initials on his gloves. He didn't have to. After all, there were only the two of you working out of Bakewell. You were hardly likely to pinch each other's gloves. It's just that the practice of writing your name on them had been drilled into you when you worked at Sheffield. So that was why you told Robert to do the same in Bakewell, even though it wasn't really necessary. Likewise, the two of you were both HGV drivers. Either of you could have signed the delivery note. It wasn't like in Sheffield or Staveley where the driver is more senior than his mate. However, the way you were trained was that it was the driver who always signed. So that was what you still did in Bakewell."

"If you say so. I say we were both drivers. Either of us could sign, no matter who was driving."

"Anyway, the first three deliveries went according to plan, and you arrived at the Bulls Head in Foolow at about a quarter to nine. You made your delivery and no doubt Reg, the licensee, teased you both about the state you were in the previous night. He offered you a hair of the dog, which the two of you accepted."

"That's correct. But it obviously didn't work, which is why Robert dropped me at my house."

"You left the pub at 9.25. We know this because the time is written on the delivery note. You then drove up the hill towards Bleckley. Five minutes later, you went past the German girls for the first time and, shortly after that, you knocked down and killed Alice Barlow. What should you do? Well, fortunately you were just by the old engine shed and you remembered that there was a disused mine shaft in front of it with the lock having been removed. Therefore, you decided to dump her body down the shaft. Robert wasn't at all certain about it. He wanted to do the right thing and reported the accident. But you reminded him that you had both been drinking. In fact, both of you were probably over the limit before you had the drink in the Bulls Head. But even if you hadn't been, you definitely would be now."

"As I've already told you, Robert dropped me off before he continued on towards Bleckley."

Diane just ignored Zes's interruption and continued.

"Sheffield Brewery, as it was called back then, had a dry site policy. None of their employees were allowed to drink whilst they were at work and that included people working on the drays. As a result, you both would have lost your jobs and you would have gone to prison for manslaughter. With this in mind, I bet you told Robert that if you were facing a prison sentence, you might as well come clean about the times when you covered for each other. All of a sudden, Robert was facing a far more serious charge than just drinking on duty. He had defrauded the company and falsified records. He could be looking at a prison sentence himself. At the very least, he would definitely be dismissed, and he'd certainly find it difficult to find another job where he lives that's as well paid as a drayman's job. He had got a mortgage to pay and a wife and family to support. What choice did he have but to go along with your plan?"

"This is all speculation, Inspector," added the solicitor. "Unless you can provide some concrete evidence against my client, I will have to call a halt to this interview."

"The two of you disposed of her body but, unfortunately Robert lost one of his gloves in the process. My bet is that it fell out of one of his pockets but that's unimportant as it somehow managed to disappear down the mine shaft. Robert then drove you home. I'm not really quite sure why he did that. Was it because you were in shock after what you'd just done? Anyway, Robert went back to Bleckley to make the delivery to the Three Tuns, which was why the lorry went past the German girls on three occasions in forty minutes. Of course, he'd missed the time window. But he had an excuse for that if anyone asked him about it. It was the same excuse he used to explain the dent in the front of the lorry. In other words, he said he hit a deer."

"Get up, we're going," said the solicitor as he got to his feet.

"I haven't finished yet," said Diane with such force that he immediately sat down again.

"Well, everything went according to plan, and nobody suspected you had anything to do with Alice's disappearance," she continued. "That is until December of this year when the four of us were stuck in the Three Tuns listening to Bung's ridiculous story about the Beast of Bleckley. I said I was going to open up the old mine shaft as soon as the snow melted and that made you panic. You knew we'd find Alice's body and Robert's glove at the bottom, which was why you decided to kill him. Without Robert around to give his side of the story, nobody was going to doubt what you said. After all, it was Robert's glove at the bottom of that shaft, and you knew Matt would remember that he was by himself when he delivered to him that morning. In fact, you even suggested that we speak to him about it. With all this evidence mounting up, logic would say that Alice's death was nothing to do with you. Am I not right, Zes?"

"It's a good story, Inspector," said Zes who hadn't lost his cool or shown much emotion whilst Diane was talking. "You've got a good future in crime fiction in front of you. The only thing is that I wasn't there as I keep on telling you. Robert dropped me off on his way between Foolow and Bleckley. It must have been because he killed Alice Barlow and knowing he was about to be discovered that made him commit suicide. He knew you were onto him and decided to kill himself rather than go to prison."

"That was precisely what I thought initially, apart from one small detail," Diane replied. "Robert didn't die when you hit him over the head and threw his unconscious body over Bleckley Edge. Although I can see why you thought he would be killed. After all, it has got to be a 300 foot drop onto solid rock. But what you didn't consider was the fact that there were three feet of snow on that day, and it was the snow that broke his fall. So there he is at the bottom of the cliff, his body's broken but he's not dead. He's unconscious, but then he comes around and what he did next tells me it was definitely you who threw him over that cliff."

Zes was starting to sweat now, and Diane had no intention of putting him out of his misery by telling him what Robert had done just yet.

"You're proud of your Dutch heritage, aren't you?" she said.

"Yes," he replied. "What's that got to do with anything?"

"You'll tell anybody who'll listen that your father is Dutch. You told me as much the very first time I met you."

"Where is this going, Inspector?" asked the solicitor.

"You know, when I was first introduced to you, I thought your name was Cec, short for Cecil. But it's not, as we now know. It sounds like Cec, but it's actually Zes, isn't it?"

"I've already told you that my correct name is Zes. I was my parents' sixth child. That's why I was called Zes."

"Because Zes is the Dutch for six," replied Diane. "And would you mind telling me what Stenen means in Dutch?"

"You obviously know what it means, otherwise why would you ask me?"

"You know, when you and I first met you said your father used to work at the Cannon brewery and you were betraying your family when you joined Northern United. At the time, I thought you meant you were betraying your father. But you didn't mean that, did you? What you actually meant was that you were betraying your family name. That's because the Cannon Brewery is run by William Stones and Company and that's what your surname means in Dutch, isn't it? It means stones."

"So what?" Zes replied.

"Well, it's because you told anybody and everybody that your name means six stones in Dutch, didn't you? You definitely told Robert Hancock. His wife told me when I phoned her last night after I'd had your name translated. Now, that fact is important because when Robert regained consciousness at the bottom of that cliff, he knew he was going to die. He had numerous fractures, it was below freezing and blowing a blizzard. He knew nobody would be able to come looking for him until the following day and, by the time they found him, he would have frozen to death. The only thing he wanted to do was to tell us who'd killed him, which is why, despite his injuries, he hauled himself up a bank under an overhanging rock where the snow couldn't get to him. He'd broken one arm and dislocated the wrist on his other side. He can't scratch the name of the person who's killed him onto the rock face. So he does the next best thing. He must have been in tremendous pain, but he still managed to pick up six stones and put them into his pocket. It was you who killed him and it's you who he wanted to implicate."

"Do not say anything," said the solicitor.

But Zes knew it wouldn't do any good.

"It wasn't because I was in shock that I had to go home. It was because I was covered in blood. When I ran her over, I tried to stop the bleeding, but she was too badly injured. We'd never have been implicated if I hadn't told Robert that he needed to write his name on his gloves. When you said you were going to look in the mine, he told me he was going to admit to his part in what we'd done. I couldn't let him do that. I told him to say he was always losing his gloves, leaving them in cellars and in pub yards. I told you you would never be able to prove our involvement, but he wouldn't have it. He said it had been on his conscience for more than seven years and now was the time to come clean. I'd known Robert for more than eight years and he was my best friend. But in many ways, he was too honest for his own good. A good little Catholic boy."

"And that's why you killed him?" said Diane. "Right, we are done here. Spencer, take him to the front desk and charge him."

Five minutes later, Zes Stenen was locked in one of the cells having been charged with one count of manslaughter, one count of pre-meditated murder, and one count of preventing the lawful burial of a body.

Chapter 44
Saturday evening, December 30th, 1978

Diane had offered to buy her team a drink in order to celebrate solving the case. Normally, they'd all have gone to the Spread Eagle, which was in Beetwell Street, close to the police station. But today she'd decided to take them to Frank McKinley's pub, the White Hart in Walton. It seemed appropriate really, as this was where she'd first heard about the closing time thief. In fact, it was when Frank introduced her to Bernie Sanders that the whole chain of events had started, resulting in five murders and six robberies being solved.

"You know, this year has turned out really well," said Diane as she sipped her pint of Great Northern Bitter. She was very grateful that Frank had decided to install it since she was last in. "I wasn't that keen when Jeff Barker told me he wanted to set up a specialist team to look at crimes involving the licensed trade. But it's been great fun, and I've really enjoyed working with you guys."

"Bloody hell, ma'am," replied Spencer. "You make it sound as if you're going to leave. It must be the drink talking."

"For fuck's sake, Spencer. You can call me by my Christian name, you know? After all, we have slept together."

"I think that's taking team bonding a step too far," said Superintendent Barker as he walked into the bar.

If she'd known he was there, Diane wouldn't have made such a comment. After all, she and Jeff Barker really had spent the night together after the LVA dinner back in April.

"Hello, sir," she said. "I didn't know you were going to join us tonight."

"What? And not go out for a celebratory drink with my most successful team? There's a lot of truth in the saying 'supporting another's success won't ever dampen yours'. Remember, Diane, a team that plays together stays together and, by the way, it's Jeff tonight, rather than sir."

"If you insist, Jeff," Diane replied but, at the same time, she felt a shudder go down her spine. It brought back memories of what had happened the last time he'd asked her to call him by his Christian name.

"So, Diane, what are you going to do on New Year's Eve?" Jeff asked her.

"Oh, I'll probably just spend it quietly at home," Diane replied.

"You can come out with us," said Alan. "We're going on a pub crawl around town dressed as convicts, all chained together."

"I think I'll pass if that's okay."

"In which case, you can always come with us," said Claire. "Some of the girls are going to the Aquarius Club to see The Rockin' Berries. It's only £25 per person and that includes chicken in a basket and Black Forest gateau."

"No, it's absolutely fine, honestly," Diane replied.

"You can't spend New Year's Eve by yourself, Diane," said Jeff. "I thought you were dating that vicar chap. Aren't you going to go out with him?"

"That's all over, I'm afraid, Jeff," Diane replied.

"Why don't you come here?" added Frank. "We are having a traditional Scottish Hogmanay. It'll be far better than staying at home watching Andy Stewart on the telly."

"Thanks for the invitation, Frank. But I don't really know anybody who drinks in this pub. I'd be like Billy no mates sitting in a corner by myself."

"No, you wouldn't," said Frank. "Actually, I had an ulterior motive for asking you. I'm finding it really difficult to find staff who are prepared to work on New Year's Eve. I wondered if you'd work behind the bar? You'll get time and a half, and I'll pay for a taxi home."

"But I've no experience. I've never worked behind a bar."

"You don't need experience," interrupted Spencer. "All you need is a low-cut top that reveals your cleavage."

Diane gave him one of her looks before remarking, "And fancy asking me in front of my boss. He'll think I'm moonlighting."

"Hey, as far as I'm concerned, it's undercover work in the licensed trade," added Jeff.

"And you can drink as much as you like," Frank continued. "My regulars are very generous when it comes to buying drinks for the staff, especially on New Year's Eve."

"You've convinced me. I'll do it," Diane announced before asking, "that twat in a dog collar won't be coming, will he?"

"Funny you should mention him," said Frank. "Haven't you heard? He's just been appointed as the new Bishop of Durham."

"Bloody hell," exclaimed Diane. "So Nick the Vic is now Bash the Bishop. Who'd have thought it? I always knew he was a wanker. What's his replacement called? Don't tell me? Is it Eric the Cleric, Kev the Rev or Hector the Rector?"

"Very funny, Diane," Frank replied. "I've no idea. He hasn't been appointed yet. Anyway, I wanted to ask if you're going to set up another licensee/police forum in the Derbyshire Dales?"

"Yes, I am," Diane replied. "But I'm not going to head this one up. I've decided to pass that honour over to Spencer."

"That's news to me," Spencer replied, choking on his pint.

"I have confidence that you'll do a really good job, Spencer," added Diane. "You'll get to visit some really great pubs and, don't worry, I'll come and hold your hand at the first meeting."

"That's very good of you, ma'am," he replied. "I can do the same for you when you next need help. Perhaps I can help you vet your next boyfriend?"

"That's not funny, Spencer," Diane replied.

The banter amongst the team continued for the next half an hour before Jeff Barker made his excuses.

"Anyway, I've got to go now," he announced after finishing his drink. "I just want to say that I am extremely proud of the way this team has operated since it was set up. A 100% clear-up rate is an outstanding achievement and I want to wish Diane and all the rest of you every success in 1979. I just want to leave you with one thought. A team is not a group of people who work together. A team is a group of people who trust each other."

"What a load of bollocks," added Spencer once Jeff Barker had left. "I suppose it would be inappropriate for me to mention that we haven't got a 100% clear-up rate. After all, we never solved the case of Grant Cartwright, the missing potholer."

"And I doubt we ever will," Diane replied. "And, may I just say? That's one of the most accurate things you've said in a long time, Spencer. A lot of the things you say are totally inappropriate. But on this occasion, you've hit the nail right on the head. Jeff Barker really does talk a load of bollocks."

Epilogue
Thursday evening, August 1st, 2019

It had been a hot day and Spencer Spooner had spent most of it in his garden, either sleeping or reading his book. At 6 o'clock, he came inside for his tea. He had to watch his cholesterol ever since having a heart attack three years ago. That was why Rachel had made him a chicken salad. If it were down to him, he would have preferred to have had a steak pie and chips with unhealthy gloopy gravy. But that was one of life's little pleasures that he could no longer indulge in. He also wasn't allowed any fried food, cake or chocolate biscuits and had to take statins every day. Sometimes, he wondered whether life was still worth living.

After finishing his meal, he settled down to watch the local evening news. To be honest, he didn't know why he bothered. There was never any news on it from around where he lived. Still, he switched on the TV just as the programme was starting and was amazed by what was on that night.

Good evening and welcome to tonight's Look North with Garry Hailsham and Emma Dale.

The camera panned onto a grinning Garry Hailsham who wore a powder blue suit with a white rose in his buttonhole.

We start tonight with the story that has had Derbyshire police baffled for the past 56 years, but which was recently solved by a pair of schoolchildren from Doncaster. We go live now to our reporter Keith Lee, who's in the village of Bleckley in the Peak District.

The scene moved to a bleak moor in North Derbyshire. Keith Lee was standing in front of the Three Tuns in the rain under an umbrella with the *Look North* logo printed on it.

Yes, Garry, it was 56 years ago that Sheffield potholer, Grant Cartwright vanished whilst trying to discover a new cavern system under Bleckley Moor. Despite a massive search, Derbyshire police were never able to discover his body and his disappearance has remained a mystery until now.

But two days ago, eight-year-old Jacob Richmond and his brother Larry, who's six, made a remarkable discovery. It was whilst they were camping with their parents here in Bleckley that they went to play in nearby woods with Tyke, their Yorkshire terrier. Well, Tyke is an inquisitive little fellow and when he disappeared into a hole in the ground, the two children thought they'd lost him for good. Many children would just have given up, but brave little Jacob decided to crawl into the hole in search of their dog, and it was there that he made his grim discovery. For the small hole opened up into a large cavern. Not as large as the ones we have up in Yorkshire, but large by Derbyshire standards. And inside the cavern were the skeletal remains of a man and what appeared to be a large dog.

The police were called, and they have now identified the body as being that of Grant Cartwright, the missing potholer. Furthermore, the skeleton of what was thought to be a dog has been identified as a wolf. Subsequent tests on its remains have revealed it died from strychnine poisoning.

It is thought that the wolf is the one that escaped whilst being transported to a zoo in Matlock two months before Grant Cartwright went missing. A police spokesman said they think the wolf was hiding in the cave when Mr Cartwright disturbed it. Cornered, it attacked and killed him. Shortly afterwards the wolf itself died after taking some meat back to its lair that had been laced with strychnine by a local farmer. It seems he had laid a trap for the wolf after blaming it for killing his sheep.

For years, it was believed that the cavern system Mr Cartwright was looking for when he disappeared was under Bleckley Moor. But, in fact, the entrance was hidden under Bleckley Clough about half a mile away. According to Derbyshire police, that is the reason why their search for Mr Cartwright proved fruitless all those years ago. Put simply, they were looking in the wrong place.

Sheffield Caving Club plans to explore the whole system in the near future and a spokesman told me that they intend to name the new cavern after Grant Cartwright.

Meanwhile, Jacob and Larry are just pleased that they've got little Tyke back again safe and sound.

This is Keith Lee, reporting for Look North from Bleckley near Sheffield.

The camera panned out and a couple of seconds later the shot was now back in the studio again with Garry Hailsham.

Thank you, Keith, and thank goodness for Tyke and those two schoolchildren from Doncaster.

Now on to other news. I'm sure I don't need to tell you what day it is today. Yes, it's the best day of the entire year. For today is Yorkshire Day and people from all over God's Own Country have been out celebrating. Our reporters have been out and about to witness the celebrations. Later we are going to hear from the people of Barnsley, Halifax and Scarborough. But first, we are off to South Yorkshire to see how the people of Chesterfield have been marking Yorkshire Day.

"Bloody hell," said Spencer as he switched the TV off in disgust. "Won't the BBC ever learn? Chesterfield's not in bloody Yorkshire. It's in Derbyshire"

The End

Author's Notes

When I was a teenager, my parents used to keep their caravan in a farmer's field outside Birchover in the Peak District. It was only twenty minutes' drive away from Chesterfield, but it was a different world.

About a mile from the village were the remains of Mill Close Mine, which at one time was the largest lead mine in the world. In 1939, it was the last lead mine to close in Derbyshire. Nature has subsequently reclaimed the land on which the mine buildings once stood. Nowadays, the only hint that it ever existed are the remains of the old engine shed and traces of the old mine shaft, which can still be seen in front of it. These include a large concrete cap, which was placed over the shaft when the mine closed. Over the years, pieces of this concrete cap had broken off, partially revealing the old mine shaft underneath. My brother and I used to drop stones down the shaft and count the number of seconds until they hit the bottom. It took a long time, which both thrilled and terrified us in equal measure.

During the 1960s and '70s, my father worked for Whitbread's, which provided the beer tent for Flagg races. My father would go and check that everything had been set up correctly and sometimes, if I was lucky, he'd ask me to go with him. It was fascinating and, of course, it always snowed. Horizontally.

Flagg races had been run every Easter Tuesday since 1892. It was the only meeting in the country that still had a traditional point-to-point race with the riders starting in the village and finishing on the racecourse. Furthermore, Edward VIII once took part when he was the Prince of Wales. But the meeting in 2013 was the third in succession that had to be cancelled because of the weather. Flagg races have not been run since.

The Three Tuns is a fictitious pub, although anyone who knows the Peak District will be able to work out which pub it is based on. However, all the other pubs and hotels in the story are real. Here is a list of the licensed premises that are mentioned along with details of what has happened to them. Details are correct at the time of writing. For the sake of sanity, a pub name is preceded by 'the' in the book even though its official name might begin with 'The'.

- The Miners Arms, Eyam: still a pub
- Terminus Hotel, Chesterfield: demolished and flats built on the site
- White Hart, Walton: demolished and a house built on the site
- Ye Olde Bulls Head, Little Hucklow: the sixth oldest pub in the UK; when I began writing this story it had been derelict for several years but has since reopened as the Blind Bull; for simplicity sake called the Old Bulls Head in the book
- Crown Inn, Wensley: now a house
- The Plough Inn, Flagg: closed
- Bulls Head, Wardlow: closed
- The Nettle, Fallgate: like our pub in North Yorkshire, one of the top fifty country pubs in England according to *The Times*; now housing
- Three Horseshoes, Spitewinter: now a house
- Bull i'Thorn (or Bull i'th Thorn Inn), near Flagg: was closed; reopened as The Bull Yard pub and campsite but only open in summer

- Anchor Inn, Bakewell: now part of the Wheatsheaf Hotel next door
- Bulls Head, Eyam: closed in 2000; converted into flats
- Rutland Arms, Baslow: now a Co-op
- Tan Hill Inn, Richmond: still a pub
- Lion Inn, Blakey Ridge: still a pub
- Castle Inn, Bakewell: still a pub
- Peacock Inn, Bakewell: still a pub
- Bakewell Workingmen's Club: still a club
- Monsal Head Hotel, Bakewell: still a hotel
- The Bulls Head, Foolow: still a pub
- The Bulls Head, Monyash: still a pub
- Rose & Crown, Eyam: now a guesthouse
- The Spread Eagle, Chesterfield: just re-opened after being closed for three years

William Stones's Cannon Brewery was founded in Sheffield in 1865. In 1968 the brewery was acquired by Bass Charrington, which closed it in 1999.

I'd like to thank three people for helping to inspire this book. The first is Jacob Rees-Mogg who, when he named his sixth child Sixtus, gave me the idea for the name Zes. The second is Jan Steen (1626 -1679), the Dutch artist, whose surname means stone in English. I eventually decided to change this to Stenen, the plural of stone, as this fitted the storyline better and also matched the name of the brewery in Sheffield. Finally, there is the drayman who left one of his work gloves in the cellar of our pub in North Yorkshire. The glove had his Christian name written on it in biro.

About the Author

Ian Walker was born in Chesterfield in 1956. His father was the chief clerk of a brewery in town and his mother was a ballet teacher.

He went to Chesterfield School before gaining a place at Leicester University where he studied Chemistry and Maths.

After graduating, he got a job working in the laboratory at Truman's Brewery in Brick Lane, London. The following year, he transferred to Watney's Brewery in Mortlake, where he moved into the sales department eighteen months later.

Several sales roles followed until he became Regional Sales Director for Scottish and Newcastle in the West Country.

All this came to an end in 2006 when, aged just fifty, he suffered a stroke and had to give up work. After twelve months of physiotherapy, he felt sufficiently recovered to buy a pub in the North York Moors along with his wife Eunice.

In the eight years that they owned the pub, they achieved listings in both the *Good Beer Guide* and the *Good Pub Guide*. They were also included in *The Times* list of the top fifty places to eat in the British countryside.

In 2016, he decided to retire and move back to Chesterfield after forty years. He and his wife live just around the corner from the house where he grew up and where his mother still lives. He has two grown-up sons from a previous marriage.

Hair of the Dog is his fourth novel and the second in the DI Diane Rothwell series.

Printed in Great Britain
by Amazon

12480808R00190